LOVE AND TRUST

A Beach Reads Billionaire Bachelor Contemporary Romance

~ Book III ~
The Summer Sisters Tame the Billionaires
Book Club Edition

Jean Oram

Oram Productions Alberta, Canada

Printed in the United States of America unless otherwise stated on the last page of this book. Published by Oram Productions Alberta, Canada.

LIBRARY OF CONGRESS CATALOGING-IN-PUBLICATION DATA

Oram, Jean.
    Love and Trust: A Beach Reads Billionaire Bachelor Contemporary Romance / Jean Oram.—1st. ed.
        p. cm.
    ISBN 978-1-928198-02-4 (paperback)
    Ebook ISBN 978-1-928198-03-1
1. Romance fiction. 2. Sisters—Fiction. 3. Lawyers—Fiction. 4. Romance fiction—Small towns. 5. Love stories, Canadian. 6. Small towns—Fiction. 7. Muskoka (Ont.)—Fiction. 8. Interpersonal relations—Fiction. I. Title.

Summary: Lawyer Melanie Summer must convince ex-developer Tristen Bell to help her fight against a development in Muskoka, Ontario. Unfortunately the single dad has no plans to slip into his old suit...until things get personal.

First Oram Productions Edition: April 2015

Cover design by Jean Oram

Dedication

To my grandmothers. For helping me rediscover Muskoka each summer.

A Note on Muskoka

Muskoka is a real place in Ontario, Canada, however, I have taken artistic license with the area. While the issues presented in this book (such as water shed, endangered animals, heritage preservation, shoreline erosion, taxation, etc.) as well as the towns are real, to my knowledge, there is no Baby Horseshoe Island nor is there a Nymph Island, or even a company called Rubicore Developments. The people and businesses are fictional, with the exception of The Kee to Bala and Jenni Walker—you can read about how she ended up visiting Muskoka in the acknowledgements.

Muskoka is a wonderful area where movie stars and other celebrities do vacation. Yet, having spent many summers in the area during my youth and adulthood, I have yet to see a single celebrity—though a man I presume to be Kurt Browning's (a famous Canadian figure skating Olympian) father did offer to help me when the outboard fritzed out on me once. Damn outboard.

You can discover more about Muskoka online at www.discovermuskoka.ca/

LOVE AND TRUST

Aug 2017

To the Sylvan Lake Library,

I've spent many summers both in Muskoka & Sylvan—top 2 Canadian destinations in my mind!

XO

Jan Cram

Chapter One

Melanie slammed the door to the Super Duty Ford pickup and swore under her breath as the machine sent gravel flying across the Steel Barrel's parking lot. She waved away the dust, the sun's heat prickling her bare arms. Not only was she was stuck outside a biker bar in the middle of nowhere, but she was wearing a 1950s-style halter dress that placed her cleavage on display, and she'd left her purse on the passenger seat of her date's truck.

Easy pickings.

She turned to the retreating truck, giving her now former date, Stedman, the finger.

This was the last time she would allow her sister Maya to badger her into getting out of her comfy oversized T-shirts and into the dating world. Not that she'd put up much of a fight, seeing as the two eldest Summer sisters had fallen in love last month, and everyone had agreed that it was now Melanie's turn to do the same.

She trudged across the gravel lot in her kitten mules. Were they kittens *and* mules? How did that work? Oh, who cared? She was never wearing the shoes again, seeing as the experiment of reinventing herself had failed miserably. Stedman had made assumptions based on her appearance. Namely, that she wouldn't argue with him—even though he knew she was a lawyer. Fat chance on that one, buddy. That, and have sex with him behind the abandoned roadside motel next door. As soon as she got home she was tossing off this getup and climbing straight into her old wardrobe of jeans and big, comfy T-shirts.

Her sisters could call it hiding, but it didn't attract jerks who left her outside biker bars with no way home. If she wanted passion she could find it in a sex shop, along with a package of AA batteries.

The Steel Barrel, like many places along Ontario's backwoods highways, was a fading, falling down establishment, although this one was rumored to be a gathering spot for the local chapter of the Hells Angels. A closed gas station stood on the far side of the bar, growing weeds, with scrap metal piled high behind it.

No phone booth. No purse or cell phone, because Stedman had spun off so fast Melanie hadn't fully realized what was happening.

She was a lawyer. Supposed to be intelligent and savvy. But apparently she wasn't that street smart when it came to men. If she'd had more than five dates in the past...oh goodness, she didn't want to try and count how many years it might be...she probably would have seen this coming.

It was the last time she'd try online dating.

Why was she spending time chasing men, anyway? She should be at the office, trying to catch up on the mounds of paperwork avalanching off her desk. Besides, if destiny actually existed and did have her, the third Summer sister, in its sights to take the next fall, then destiny could get off its butt and come find her. Preferably, with a man in tow.

Melanie glanced at the bar one last time, then scooted by an ancient, sun-bleached Ford with a flat tire. Only two hogs in the parking lot. That should make it less scary inside, right? She carefully crept up the rotting wood steps and braced herself to peek into the suspiciously quiet tavern. Shouldn't there be music blaring and people being tossed through the grimy windows? She checked the sun, which was still fairly high in the sky. Maybe it was too early?

Hoping for air-conditioning, she daintily pushed through the saloon-style door. Nope, not a chance. The only coolish breeze to touch her skin was from the door swinging back to slap her on the rear.

To the right was a pool table with green felt worn down to its backing. Small tables crowded the rest of the room. Melanie tried to walk naturally, even though all eyes had turned to her, watching her every move. One bartender, two scary bikers, and a guy in a ball cap who appeared to be none of the above.

Keeping her eyes straight ahead, she took a seat equidistant between the bikers and Ball Cap. Her bare elbows stuck to the bar's surface and she peeled them off, giving the man to her right a weak smile. He not only seemed to be the best bet out of this place—although he was likely the guy with the flat tire—he also looked vaguely familiar. He was about a decade older than she was and definitely cute. Judging from the way the sleeves of his button-up shirt were rolled to reveal his strong forearms, she'd bet her last dollar, which was riding in Stedman's truck, that he'd been a businessman at one point.

The bartender stepped closer, the chains hooked on his stained jeans clanging ominously. He stroked his long beard in a leisurely fashion as he took her in, his demeanor meant to be intimidating. And totally working. He knew she didn't belong here—she didn't belong anywhere. Not even in her tight-knit family of four sisters.

The bartender was across from her now, fist nestled in his open palm. Fearing that she was about to get kicked out for not buying anything, Melanie spun on her stool to face the quiet man beside her. "Excuse me, do you have a phone?"

He nudged up the brim of his cap, then, as if realizing he was wearing it indoors, took it off and placed it over his right knee, perhaps so it wouldn't get sticky on the bar. His gentle gaze took her in. All the way from her silly shoes to the mess of curls hanging limply over her shoulders. "Yeah," he said slowly.

"Could I borrow it to make a call, please?"

The man patted his jeans pockets. "How do I know you aren't going to run off with it?"

"How fast can a woman run in heels?" she replied, as sweetly as her panic would allow. The bartender was pushing his fisted knuckles into his other palm now, biceps flexing. Really big biceps. Biceps that probably could lift her up and chuck her out the door from where he stood.

The quiet man gave her a crooked smile that caused her heart to stagger as he handed over his phone. "I'm sure I could outrun you."

"Thanks." Melanie tapped in Hailey's number with shaking hands. No answer. She tried her other two sisters, as well as their family friend, Simone, leaving messages with all of them. Sighing, Melanie handed the phone back, her eyes darting to the bartender, who had moved back to chat with the bikers, even though he kept one eye on her.

"Car break down?" the man asked, pocketing the device.

"Something like that."

He took a slow sip of his drink and watched her.

"Okay, fine. My date dumped me here when I wouldn't have sex with him behind the motel next door. I didn't get a chance to grab my purse and phone out of his truck."

The man's eyebrows rose ever so slightly and he quietly set down his drink, blinking once. "Well. That wasn't very gentlemanly."

"Last time I try online dating. 'Down-to-earth, back-to-the-basics' apparently means 'entitled prick who demands sex on the first date.'"

The corner of the man's lips twitched and his fingers grew tight around his pint of beer. He cast a glance around the room, sitting taller as though on the lookout for trouble. "I apologize on behalf of mankind," he said finally, resting his gaze back on her.

"No need. That was officially my last date. I'm turning in my dance card. Tomorrow I will be going to the SPCA to pick up my ten cats. They come free when you take the vow of spinsterhood. For each year you keep the vow you get an extra cat. It's a pretty good deal when you think about it."

The man let out a surprised bark of laughter.

She turned to him, putting on a prim act. "What? I will make a fine cat lady."

His lips twitched again and his eyes glimmered with humor.

Melanie relaxed, propping an elbow on the sticky bar. "You look familiar."

He focused on his beer, the quiet, closed look returning. She tapped the bar with a fingernail as she ran through the list of possibilities of where she might have seen his cute chin and slightly shaggy haircut. "It was a photo! Did Hailey—she's my sister—photograph you? No, newspaper. That's it. I've seen you in the paper. *Bracebridge Examiner.*"

The man adjusted his position, angling his shoulders away from her. "I'd offer you a ride, but I'm waiting for a tow truck."

"Flat tire?"

He gave a short nod.

"You're sure that's the only thing wrong with that old beast? It looks like something Henry Ford may have personally christened."

Her companion gave her a half smile of acknowledgment, his shoulders slowly relaxing.

"I like it," she said. "The truck."

He shifted back her way. Progress. She'd win a ride from him yet. She was good with people, and as like everything else in her life at the moment, she just needed a little more time.

"I like things that have a bit of character as well as a story," she said, edging closer. Not into his space, but enough to let him know she was comfortable around him. "Older stuff that's not all perfect and glossed up. You can tell it's had a life. Adventure. Character. Embraced, not hidden." She leaned her head toward his, as though confiding a secret, pleased when he echoed her posture. "And that truck has character in spades." Melanie straightened and slapped the bar with her right hand. "Tristen Bell! That's who you are."

"Bingo. You won the toaster." Tristen hunched over his beer, something she couldn't identify masking his earlier interest. He was cute, if slightly distant. He had a certain something that intrigued her, and a way of looking at her that made her feel *seen*. It was silly, but if he kept playing his cards right and he wasn't careful, she just might develop a little bit of a crush on him.

"You retired or something," she continued. "Although you look pretty young for that." He couldn't be an hour over forty. Although the well-washed shirt, casually rumpled hair and strong cords of muscles lining his forearms could make the former real estate mogul appear younger than he was. But still, nowhere near retirement age. Even his truck had to have a few decades on him.

Yep. Definitely crush-worthy.

According to Maya's fiancé, Connor, his friend Tristen Bell had made billions with his land development company and was one of Muskoka's most eligible bachelors, even though he had practically turned anti-social after his divorce. No arm candy. No long string of babes trailing in his wake.

Melanie held in a sigh. Yep. She could feel a crush coming on like a big ol' head cold—despite her vow to stay away from men and the world of dating.

"Not truly retired. I still sell a bit of real estate," Tristen said, his shoulders hunched defensively.

"My sisters and I are wondering how to stop a major development."

Tristen stood before she could say more. "I think I'd better wait outside for the tow truck."

The bartender, who had been chatting with the bikers, shot a glance Melanie's way, head tipped back in scrutiny. Was he checking to see if she was okay, or was he making sure she wasn't stealing his ratty cardboard coasters? She spun off her stool and followed Tristen outside.

Earlier, it had been difficult to imagine him sitting at home, alone, with those sexy forearms and broad shoulders. But the way he played hot and cold could definitely explain why he was single. Then again, that kind of behaviour in men wasn't exactly atypical. Guys drooled over her sister Maya, but Melanie? Not so much. They usually got that distant, slightly constipated look and pulled back if she tried turning on the charm.

Nothing new, so why take it personally?

The sun struck her with its heat as she stumbled onto the wooden porch.

A hand steadied her with reassuring strength.

Swoon. Earlier, she'd had to resist the urge to touch the bare skin that stretched over the muscles flexing below Tristen's rolled-up cuffs. She'd always been a sucker for strong arms. Something about a man being able to lift her without grunting and straining had always been a turn-on. And now him steadying her? Goodness, she was crushing. Big time. And totally struggling to keep from stroking his arms.

"Thanks."

He gave her a small nod of acknowledgment.

She pointed to the old truck. "Shall we fix it?" Anything to get out of here and avoid walking home along the highway in her heels.

"The lug nuts are rusted up. Can't turn them."

Melanie stared at the old truck's wheels, then at Tristen's strong, yummy build. "I have an idea."

He glanced at her dress and winced. "I'm not sure I like ideas."

What was that supposed to mean?

"You'll like this one. Trust me." She climbed up the bar's steps again, Guns and Roses now blasting. The bartender was absent and Melanie glanced around before making her way back to her vacated seat, where she leaned over the bar and swept up a handful of lemon wedges. She could be debarred for stealing. Did this count as theft? She certainly hadn't paid for them. Turning to go with her pilfered fruit, she paused for a half second. The biker with the massive beard was staring at her as though he knew her. She gave him a weak smile and hurried back outside.

"You're going to turn lemons into lemonade?" Tristen asked.

"Something like that. First, here's the deal."

He crossed his arms and leaned against the truck's back fender. "I'm not interested in marriage."

She choked on her laughter.

"What?" His brow furrowed in displeasure.

"Do I look like I'm trolling for a husband?" She fluffed out her skirt. "Okay, yeah, maybe a bit, but I don't usually dress like this. I'm more of a T-shirt and jeans kind of girl."

"That's too bad. The look suits you. You have nice legs."

Melanie struggled to accept the compliment, but found she couldn't, given the lump in her throat. She was a Sasquatch. Always had been, since the puberty fairy had sprinkled her with that evil, magical dust. Tristen didn't seem to be walking with the aid of a white cane, so why the false compliments?

"I already turned down one offer of sex this afternoon, I'll turn down another." She widened her stance. "Forcibly if need be."

A hint of color tinged Tristen's cheeks. "That was a compliment. Ever get any of those, or does your quick offense usually cut them off?"

She narrowed her eyes.

"You are beautiful, you know. And just for the record, women are supposed to lap up compliments."

"I'm not a kitten at the milk bowl." Melanie turned away. "All I want is a ride after I fix your truck."

"Deal."

She stole another quick glance at him. He was still in that sexy pose, arms crossed, one ankle hooked over the other, and watching her as though trying to figure her out.

Desperate to put them on friendly terms again, she took the hand that wasn't cupping the lemons and ran it over the truck's curved hood. It was a classic 1960s Ford, with an almost vertical windshield. Not something she'd expect a man with supposed billions in his bank account to be driving. "How did you end up with a vehicle like this?"

"I needed a truck during renovations and my neighbor had one for sale."

"I thought you had someone else do those for you?" That's what the article had said.

His shoulders tightened as he straightened up again, and his voice became formal, businesslike. "I'm at a disadvantage." He met her eyes, slow and sure as he shook her hand. "I have the honor of meeting…?"

"Melanie Summer." She straightened her spine, tugging her hand from his grip. The way he'd held it, focusing all his attention on her after complimenting her, was doing strange things to her mind and body. If she didn't know better, she'd think she'd sped straight from a developing crush to full on, unabridged lust.

She obviously needed to get out more.

"No relation to Daphne Summer, by chance?"

Melanie held in her smile. Damn. He was a real estate developer. Of course he knew her youngest sister. He'd probably met her head-on, seeing as she was responsible for almost every protest against local land developments over the past few years. And there had been plenty.

Melanie tipped up her chin. "She's my kid sister."

"I have one of her paintings in my living room."

Melanie forced her gaping jaw shut. "Her paintings?" Lately, Daphne had started selling her artwork at local farmers markets to help foot her portion of the family's overdue tax bill on their century-old cottage. First Maya's fiancé had ended up with one of Daphne's paintings, and now Tristen, too? This was getting weird. Although the two men *were* friends. Maybe it was a guy thing to shop for artwork together.

"What?" Tristen gave her a puzzled smile, his eyebrows wrinkling in an endearing way that made Melanie want to run a finger over them to see if they'd smooth out. "It caught my eye. A man can buy things without it becoming a big deal, you know."

Wow. Defensive. The ex-wife had obviously helped provide him with a little touch-and-go baggage before they split up.

He apologized under his breath.

"Well, how about that?" Melanie teased. "You have taste."

"Mentioning your beauty earlier doesn't prove that?" A hint of mischief flickered in his gaze and she crossed her arms over her chest, then remembered the lemons still in her left hand. All right, no more flirty games. She needed to get them out of here.

"Okay. The deal is, if I fix your tire you'll give me a ride to Port Carling. Will you do that?"

"How terribly convenient." Tristen resumed his casual stance, sizing her up in a way that she figured she wasn't supposed to notice. "I'm heading that way myself."

"Don't you live there?" she asked, tired of the games.

"Stalking me, Ms. Summer?"

"Newspapers." She bit back a dig about keeping track of the billionaire jerks who might be in her neighborhood.

"Don't believe everything they tell you."

"So then you're not divorced and hiding out in a cottage that you made into a year-rounder?" So much for keeping her digs to herself.

Tristen's face lost its playful expression. "Are you going to fix my truck or do I need to send you back into that bar, where the bikers can continue to undress you with their eyes? Because as much as you get under my skin, Melanie Summer, I'd like to think I'm gentleman enough to help a woman in distress. However, you are making that rather difficult."

Melanie sucked on one of the lemon wedges. "You don't believe I can do this."

Tristen waved a hand at the flat tire. "Be my guest, lemon girl."

"Watch and learn." She held the lemons over the lug nuts and squeezed, letting the juice run between them and the rim, hoping the acidic liquid would break the rust's bond. Moments later she licked her fingers and placed the lemon rinds in Tristen's hand. With a smile, she turned and walked over to the pile of scrap metal in the weedy yard next door, hoping she'd find what she needed and wouldn't end up looking like a fool.

She could feel Tristen watching as she poked through the scrap until she came across what she was looking for. She hefted the two-and-a-half-foot-long pipe and walked back to the truck.

"You're not going to whack me with that, are you?" he asked, pretending to cower. "I swear I'll never compliment you again."

She rolled her eyes. "Hand me the wrench, please."

After whacking the lug nuts with the pipe to loosen anything she could, she fitted the X-shaped wrench over the first nut, then slipped the pipe over the wrench's handle to give her more leverage. Praying the lemon juice had loosened the rust, she carefully applied her weight to the wrench and pipe extension, shifting her feet to add more pressure. Son of a gun. That really was stuck fast.

"Troubles?" Tristen asked, his lips curving into a perfect grin, exposing a fine line of white teeth.

Without a word, Melanie smiled back and turned to sit on the pipe, holding tight while she bounced up and down, hoping to budge the nut. There was one thing a gal learned growing up in a household of women, and that was how to get creative in solving problems when there wasn't a lot of cash around. Not that she was stellar at it, but still. She could hold her own. Usually.

Sweat gathered on her brow when the bikers came out onto the sloped porch to have a cigarette while leaning over the railing to enjoy the show she was putting on. Another unsuccessful bounce. Tristen glanced toward the road as if hoping for the tow truck.

Melanie bounced harder, giving the pipe and wrench a sudden jolt. The rust cracked and the nut turned, dumping her in a heap on the gravel.

Tristen was at her side in a flash, cupping her elbow as he helped her up. "You okay?"

"Fine." She brushed off her skirt and smiled brightly. "One down. Four more to go."

The bikers chuckled, taking leisurely drags on their cigarettes. Melanie refrained from mentioning that they needed to maintain a nine meter radius from the building's entrance to be compliant with the Smoke Free Ontario Act, and set about fitting the wrench over the next nut. Tristen handed her the pipe, which had slid off during her spill, but he refused to let go. She pressed her body close to his to show she wasn't intimidated. "What?"

"Need help?"

"I'll finish the job, thanks."

She repeated her earlier actions—without being dumped on the ground—and the bikers cheered with each freed nut. Melanie curtsied for her audience when the new tire was finally in place, and thanked her lucky stars that her idea had worked. She was hot and dusty, but pleased.

"A round of whiskey for the pretty lady," one biker hollered.

"I think you're one of them now," Tristen whispered. Melanie watched as he put the wrench and jack away. "You want to go in," he noted in surprise.

She shrugged. She kind of did, and not just because she was thirsty.

"I can wait to drive you home, if you want." His voice was gentle, caring. Almost big-brotherly. But it wasn't fully platonic; there was a certain possessiveness in the way he held himself. Closer than a brother would stand. He watched her for a moment, maintaining eye contact long enough that she thought he might actually be interested. And not just in her safety.

"Better cancel that tow truck." Melanie slipped past him, hoping the free drinks would cure her hands of their Tristen-induced palsy.

WOW. THE BIKER HAD been serious about providing a whiskey for her troubles. She finished the drink quickly, happy to see it was curing her trembling hands. But just as she pried her elbows off the sticky bar to excuse herself, the second biker, the man with the long, tangled beard, stepped up with another. He took the free spot beside her, which had been vacated by his buddy, Kane.

Seated on her other side, Tristen bristled. So far he had remained silent, avoiding the revelry, but now he laid a gentle hand on her arm. "Are you ready to go?"

Of course she wasn't. She had male attention, and the bikers were buying her drinks. She was the only game in town and she'd judged these men wrongly. She had to make it up to them by absorbing their surprisingly kind, almost fatherly tributes. It was a sensation she hadn't felt in over a decade, and it was good. Really good.

"To think. With a few wedges of lemon she could do what that man with the big arms couldn't," laughed Kane, nodding at Tristen, who inhaled slowly, his grip tightening around his truck keys.

The bartender leaned over the bar, palm outstretched to Melanie. "I think you owe me some lemon wedges, miss."

All eyes turned to her. She had relayed her story of her date abandoning her, drawing a suitably aghast response from her audience. Everyone knew she had no money on her.

Tristen shifted, leaning to one side to get the wallet out of his back pocket.

"He's kidding," she said lightly, hoping she was correct. Tristen smoothed a five dollar bill on the bar as the others broke into guffaws.

"Just trying to help," he muttered. "Can we go now?"

Melanie bumped her shoulder against his, the two shots warming her gut. "Aw, it's okay. They're just giving me a hard time. Thanks, though. I appreciate it." She met his eyes and smiled, reaching over to give his chin a gentle squeeze.

The bikers began discussing engine repairs, and Melanie

hoped they wouldn't ask her to fix something. While she'd been driving a motorcycle for the past few months as a way to save money, it would be a stretch to say she knew much about them.

"Sure can hold a drink," Ezra, the bearded biker, remarked as he purchased another round. His silver skull rings shone in the light as he slid a glass her way.

"Don't ask me to walk a line!" Melanie said, raising her third whiskey in the air. The men lifted theirs in turn, with crooked grins. "I hope nobody is driving." She let out a giggle. They were in the middle of nowhere on an old Ontario backwoods highway. Of course they were driving.

"Order of rings, Scar," Ezra said, and the bartender disappeared into the back room.

"Why do you call him Scar?" She hadn't noticed any marks on the man's smooth olive skin.

"*The Lion King* is his favorite movie. He likes to think he's tough, so we call him Scar, after Simba's evil uncle."

"No scars?"

"Only of the emotional variety," snorted Kane, his eyes slitted in a glare that didn't match his tone. Bikers were a strange lot. All kittens on the inside.

Melanie placed her empty glass on the bar.

"Ready?" asked Tristen.

She wanted to tell him to take a chill pill. But seeing as he was the only one in the bar not drunk, since he'd declined every offered shot, and the only one who had offered her a ride—not that she didn't think she could snag a weaving, incredibly fast and blurry lift back to town on the back of a Harley—he was her safest bet at the moment.

And safety was her middle name. Melanie Safety Summer. Had a certain ring to it, didn't it?

"This was a wonderful way to top off my afternoon, boys,"

Melanie said, wondering if it was wise to call bikers "boys". If she wasn't careful she might hit a hot button and break the little bubble of harmony that made her feel she was one of them, and end up with an angry duo on her tail. And she really didn't think Tristen's old truck could outrace or outlast these bikers and their hogs. "I enjoyed talking to you."

"What do you do for a living, Melanie?" asked Ezra, turning to face her. His eyebrows were as out of control as his beard, practically hiding his eyes as he lowered them to peer at her.

Ezra wasn't fierce—he was shy! That was so incredibly sweet.

"I'm a lawyer," she said, trying to own the fact, but knowing that it likely wasn't a favored occupation here in the Steel Barrel. Or anywhere on planet earth.

"I knew you were a smart one!" called Kane, slapping his buddy on the back so hard that Ezra turned to glare at him, fist raised. "Didn't I say she was smart?"

"Anyone who uses lemons to save a man like Mr. City here is smart, you dumb-ass," Ezra growled.

There was a muscle flickering in Tristen's jaw.

"Aw, come on, guys," Melanie said with a laugh. "He's lived out here for a few years. He barely even looks like a city slicker now."

They all stared at Tristen, who sat up taller, straighter. Okay, so maybe the neatly rolled up sleeves of his shirt kind of said "city." That and his current posture.

"Okay then? So? Anyone have a good story to share?" Melanie asked, breaking the silence. They couldn't leave on that note.

Ezra turned his crystalline eyes to her, his bushy brows low again, his voice quiet. "You a divorce lawyer?"

"Aw." She gave him a light nudge with her elbow. "Hung out with me for less than an hour and already looking to ditch the old lady?" The whiskey was loosening her tongue.

Tristen's fingers tightened around her elbow. Time to go, yeah.

Not a bad idea. Melanie glanced at Ezra, but instead of murdering her and tossing her body in the bush out back, he let out a good-natured laugh, then gave her chin a none-too-gentle chuck with his fist.

Okay, he needed to stop wearing so many funky rings if he planned to do that to townies.

Tristen edged closer.

"Ezra here's an accountant," Kane said. Melanie tried to mask her surprise. "But he can't figure a way to leave the marriage with his nuts intact."

Tristen muttered, "Good luck, pal."

"What was that?" Ezra leaned across Melanie, his odor surprisingly fresh and clean, which was nice after all that whiskey and the heat. She wasn't sure she'd be able to handle the smell of greasy hair and BO. He dropped his cocktail napkin, which he'd neatly folded into a square.

"The woman always wins, so why waste your time and energy fighting her?" Tristen muttered. "Just roll over and play dead."

"Not my style." Ezra gave him a hard look, but Tristen surprised Melanie by holding his ground and making the biker break eye contact first. Tristen's fingers closed into a fist and she feared he must be battling something big inside, and for her sake, holding on to a very short and slippery rein.

She turned back to Ezra, blocking his view of Mr. About to Blow His Top. "Come by the office and we'll get you sorted out. Main Street, Bracebridge." Melanie slid off her stool, the floor seeming incredibly far away from her feet. They hit after at least a foot or two of free fall she hadn't expected, and she stumbled slightly, Ezra and Tristen steadying her at the same moment. A possessive charge crackled between the two and Melanie finally got why women went to the bother of getting dressed up.

She might just become a dress gal, after all.

"Thank you. It was fun meeting you," she said to the bikers. "Say goodbye to Scar for me."

"Come back again, Lemonade." Kane winked.

"You ride?" Ezra called to her as she headed out.

"I have a bike, but it's not… I'm not…"

"What kind?"

"A Suzuki."

"What model?"

"Inazuma 250." It wasn't the fanciest bike on the market, but it was affordable and economical.

Ezra nodded, his fingers tangling in his long beard as he assessed her—mostly her legs, she noted. "A gal like you wouldn't have issues with the seat height, and it's nice and light. Good fit."

"I like it."

"Come ride with us sometime."

"Right. That would be nice."

She swallowed her apprehension as Tristen gripped her elbow and steered her out of the bar.

"They are so sweet!" she said as they trundled down the steps. The heat of the day was oppressing as ever, but the intensity of the sun had dropped a notch. They must have been in there longer than she'd thought. "Unexpected fun. My favorite."

"You're drunk. That was not fun," he grumbled, strong-arming her forward.

"Think he'll stop by for divorce help?" she asked as she missed the last step, doing a funny leg bend that would have deposited her on her butt if Tristen hadn't been there to catch her. Sweet, sweet-smelling Tristen.

"You smell good. So did Ezra, actually. I didn't expect that. What kind of shampoo do you use? Does it have ylang-ylang in it? I like saying that. It's a fun word. At first I thought it was a joke, you know? But it's real. A tree with pretty flowers."

Tristen gazed at her steadily, still holding her shoulders as though he wasn't sure she'd remain standing if he let go. "I can't believe you drank that much whiskey. Straight."

"I made it through law school, didn't I?" She let out a giggle. "Can we sit down now? My legs feel funny. And I'm hungry. We should have waited for the onion wings—rings. Wings would be something. Flying onions. Isn't that the name of a restaurant?"

Tristen gave her a look she couldn't decipher, and shook his head, helping her into his truck like a perfect, sweet-smelling, gentlemanly hero.

He was already her favorite.

Chapter Two

Tristen had never met a woman quite like the one sitting in the passenger seat of his beater, and he'd met plenty of interesting and unpredictable women in his thirty-seven years of life. However, it seemed as though he still had plenty to learn about the fairer sex. And Melanie Summer, in her unassumingly sexy dress, who had figured out how to defeat an ancient, rusted-up lug nut with nothing more than lemons and a decent knowledge of physics, was sure to be another puzzle he'd never sort out.

Add in the way she'd won over the bikers? Unprecedented. If they'd both broken out into song and asked her to give them a makeover, he swore he wouldn't have blinked in surprise.

There was something magical about Melanie. At first he'd felt the need to protect her—she was an abandoned woman in a rough area and he'd been raised right. But the more he got to know her, the more his need to protect had morphed into something more innate and primal. For the life of him, he couldn't figure out what had changed, or why he feared if he let her out of his sight something would happen to her. Or that he would miss one of her unexpected quirks that would make him smile.

The woman in question shifted in her seat as they rolled into the village of Port Carling. "Can I buy you a drink to thank you for your rescue services?" She asked the question so casually it was as though she was already expecting the rejection he had begun to plot.

"I think you rescued me," he replied, trying to figure out her sudden lack of bravado.

Melanie's voice quivered slightly, her hands a tangle in her lap. "I was so sure Scar was going to throw me to the hordes, and my family would never see me again." She gave a laugh that was too tight to hide the fact she wasn't joking. When she'd waltzed into the bar as though she owned it, he'd been dazzled by her confidence. She'd struck him as a woman who knew what she wanted. And yet here she was, acting scared.

Her hands relaxed as her dark, worried expression gave way to a sunny laugh. "Who knew they were such a nice bunch of guys? I feel so silly."

Tristen didn't think they were nice. The way the bearded one had kept eyeing her pale neck, well, he could have sworn the guy had been measuring it to see if his hands would fit around it. "Maybe stay away from them, just in case."

She laughed again, brushing him off. "You're so funny."

No, he wasn't. Not at all. "He was eyeing your neck, Melanie."

Tristen's hands shook on the steering wheel. Didn't she understand the way the world worked? The way bikers operated?

"He makes necklaces, Tristen. While you were canceling the tow truck he told me I inspired him. If I go to the farmers market in Bala next week he'll have a hematite and chain maille choker for me."

Choker. Man, she did not *get* it, did she? "Make sure you don't go off with those men alone."

"Yeah, sure. Of course." She waved a hand, dismissing his concerns as she mowed her way through his offered bag of beef jerky. The girl could eat, he'd give her that. But she was acting as though these men were just regular white-collar workers dressing up tough on weekends, not members of the Hells Angels. Not that he knew if they were gang members or not, but they probably were. Accountants did not look gnarly, and Ezra looked incredibly gnarly.

Tristen rubbed his forehead and focused on keeping his truck between the narrow painted lines as they wound through the hilly town. The tires hit a bump and the fieldstones he'd picked up earlier clattered and banged in the truck's box.

What was it about this woman that made him want to hide her away? Part of him said it was to keep her safe. The other part said he was afraid others would see just how delicate and wonderful she was, and take her away.

Hadn't he learned anything from his ex? He needed to stay as far from women as possible. At least until he figured out his crap.

"Where am I dropping you off?" he asked, his voice gruff.

There was a familiar look of disappointment in Melanie's eyes and he tried not to feel guilty for being relieved. Disappointed women didn't expect anything from him long-term, and didn't go looking to change his bachelor status and mend his heart, or whatever else seemed to crank their engines. Not that Melanie was the type to do that, especially since he hadn't exactly strutted his manly side so far today. She probably thought he was a joke.

In fact, he was a joke. She had been right about him hiding out in Muskoka for the past two years. Since his wife filed for divorce, to be precise. He'd run from Toronto like a dog with its tail between its legs, confused and wondering what the hell planet he'd ended up on.

But he knew that an innocent thank-you supper with Melanie would turn into something bigger. She'd wowed and wooed the hardened hearts of bikers, so what chance did a man like him have? She was fatally tempting. Sexy. Demure.

"At the boutique up the hill past the locks," Melanie said. "I left my motorcycle there."

Tristen glanced at her bare legs. Motorcycle in a dress? Who in tarnation was this woman?

Who cared? He needed to ditch her. And fast. Being intrigued meant trouble. And where women were concerned, he'd had enough trouble to last him at least another decade.

"Yeah, I know," she said, catching his look. "Practicality is my latest middle name. It used to be Safety. I really can't decide between the two. I guess I should have introduced myself properly. I'm Melanie Practicality Summer." She put out her hand to shake his.

He gave her a look, keeping his hands on the wheel. She heaved a heavy sigh and fingered the hem of her skirt with slim, delicate fingers, inadvertently revealing more thigh. Then she leaned forward, her palm resting on the door handle, ready to exit even though he was still a ways from her stop. She was taking his lack of enthusiasm over a drink as a personal rejection.

Women. Damned if you do. Definitely damned if you shut them down.

He stopped outside a house that had been converted into a two-story clothing shop. "Thanks again," he said. "Appreciate it." He stared at the motorcycle. "Are you okay to drive?"

Who was he kidding? Of course she wasn't.

"The beef jerky helped. Thanks."

"You sure?"

"Yeah, it's not far."

"The greatest percentage of accidents occur less than five miles from home."

"A misleading statistic. Most of your driving happens there."

"I'll give you that one, but I still think I should give you a ride the rest of the way home."

Melanie swung the squeaking door open and paused, half in the truck, half out, the skirt of her dress bunching up behind her butt. "A friend thought maybe you could help me and my sisters with some development stuff in relation to our family cottage. Could I call you sometime?"

Aha. A rich chick with a cottage. That's what the bit of intrigue had been about, the missing piece of the Melanie puzzle: she was a rich chick trying to be some girl without a trust fund for the afternoon.

Funny, but he'd pegged her as a local. Granted, there were a few locals with cottages, but really, it didn't matter, did it? He didn't need to get wrapped up in a high maintenance and dressed-to-kill babe like her. And it was a sure bet she was all of the above. In other words, danger with a capital *D*.

And developments? An emphatic, resounding no. Toronto would get the winter Olympics before he ever dug back into that mess and allowed it to take over his life, turning him into the monster he'd once been. Anything to win the deal. The side of himself he'd carefully and purposefully locked away. The beast would remain shackled until he was certain it had been slaughtered and couldn't achieve reincarnation. That meant Melanie Summer was not allowed anywhere near his life.

"So?" She gave him an expectant look. "Could you? Please? I could make you supper or walk your dog in return."

First Alice Estaire hadn't got the hint that he didn't need a woman in his life, and now this one. It had taken eight months of peeling Alice off his arm to discourage her. Sadly, she knew where he lived and had "popped in" at strange times, hence him getting his early warning system installed. AKA Max.

But now Tristen had Melanie offering to walk his dog? Did it ever stop? What was with Muskoka women?

"The seat is covered in dog hair," she said. "It was a joke. Quit freaking out."

"I'm not freaking out."

"I'm trying to say that I don't expect you to give your time freely. I know you're a busy man." Her gaze ran down his worn shirt and jeans.

Ouch. That was a dig.

"What do you need, Melanie?" He winced. That sounded like a yes, didn't it? His cell phone vibrated on the seat next to him and he flipped it over to check who was calling. His ex-wife, Cindy, a woman who had been purposefully and successfully avoiding him for five months.

"I need help with figuring out how to stop a development," Melanie said.

"Not my thing." He picked up the phone, waiting for her to be polite and excuse herself so he could take the call.

"I only have a few quick questions," she blurted, sensing he was in the process of shutting her down. "Surely you know—"

"Sorry, I really have to take this. If I think of anyone who can help, I'll get in touch." He reached across the seat and closed her door, leaving Melanie standing on the sidewalk, looking crushed.

Get over it, woman. I'm not your type. I'm old, jaded, and dealing with an ex-wife. You are young, smart, beautiful, and completely out of my league. Move along and, for the sake of mankind, don't sway those gorgeously round hips of yours as you go.

He answered his phone, the corners of his lips turning up in a smile as Melanie unceremoniously shoved a helmet over her curly hair. All dolled up and ruining the look with headgear.

What was the expression? Brains before beauty? Seemed like a good idea when riding a crotch rocket. And though she was walking straight, he still didn't think she should be driving. He rolled down the window to call out to her while his ex-wife ranted in his ear. Holding his thumb over the phone's speaker, he leaned out the truck window. "Shouldn't you be wearing leathers with that dress? A dragonfly smacking into your arm will give you a bruise the size of a grapefruit."

"Are you listening to me?" asked his ex.

"Yeah, yeah, of course," he said into the phone.

Melanie whirled, sticking out her tongue before flipping down the helmet's visor. He laughed, feeling more alive than he had in ages.

Not good.

He popped his door, prepared to make her accept a ride the rest of the way home. Melanie pushed her bike onto the road, but began walking alongside it, the engine off.

"Let me give you a ride," he called from his seat. "Or push your bike. It looks heavy."

"I'm fine," she snapped back.

He found himself laughing again. Had he managed to get under her skin the way she'd gotten under his? And why did that feel so satisfying? So full of promise?

Meanwhile, his ex continued on about how she needed to get Dot, their seventeen-year-old daughter, out of the house for the next two weeks. Both he and Cindy had been pretty determined at that age, and had defied their parents by eloping on their shared birthday—the day they'd turned eighteen. While that hadn't worked out so well in the long run, with the exception of having their daughter, they'd had fun and lived life the way they'd wanted to. It didn't surprise Tristen that Dot seemed to have a similar streak burning through her veins.

"And you expect...what was it, Cindy?" He paused as though thinking, before delivering the dig he knew would drive her around the ex-wife bend. "An absent, emotionally constipated man who is incapable of expressing love to somehow straighten out the daughter who knows me so little she bought me a tie for Father's Day?"

"At least she thought of you."

"I remembered her birthday this year, thank you very much."

Melanie gave him one last glance over her shoulder, through the visor, then tucked her skirt under her backside and plunked herself on her bike—a move he interpreted as the equivalent to "kiss my butt."

His heart caught in his throat, but she merely coasted down a driveway. Home.

He relaxed, smiling at the image of a gal in an old-fashioned dress on a bike giving him 'tude. How could she have possibly felt intimidated in the biker bar, especially when they'd all crowded around her like birds to a feeder? And why did Tristen want to get to know her better? His raving ex had taken him to the cleaners and he'd all but rolled over and told her to give it to him with steel-toed boots. And here he was...

Stupid.

He'd promised he'd straighten himself out before dating again. Ruining one woman's life was one thing, but to knowingly do so to another was not something he could do and keep his head held high.

"Cindy, enough," he said, stopping his ex-wife mid-rant. He knew girls needed their fathers or at least a male role model, but he didn't figure his ex actually believed he should take Dot for that reason. Something else was up, and honestly, he didn't care what it was. "Send Dot. I'll straighten her out."

He'd figured out how to fix and build stone fireplaces and patios. Surely he could fix his little girl's world. And if he did manage to straighten out a teen he barely knew, then maybe he could start down that lonely, dark path of finally becoming a decent man who didn't ruin the lives of others.

TRISTEN PULLED INTO HIS driveway just outside town, staring unseeing at the cottage he'd converted into a year-round home. He wrung the steering wheel of his old truck and sighed. Sunshine fell through the maples overhead, leaving dappled shadows on the faded hood. He'd set something in motion, answering his ex's call. Something he wasn't sure he was prepared for. But he'd been hiding out for two years and he supposed it was time to face snapshots of the man he used to be, and the consequences that had ensued. Including a daughter who failed to have a father figure in her life.

Tristen watched the shadows dance across the windshield, and sighing, slipped out of the truck, then made his way across the gravel driveway. He had a guest room to prepare and a stone wall project to put the finishing touches on over in Gravenhurst before Dot came in the morning. Neither tasks were huge, but he didn't have time to dawdle if he planned to download a book on how to parent a teen. Why did Cindy, who had been perfectly content to allow him visitation rights for only a handful of hours a year, suddenly want him to take Dot for two full weeks? Was she trying to get even for the times he'd left her to take care of their daughter while he worked twenty-hour days on an unexpected project?

He turned back to his truck, remembering to check on his spare. He smiled and shook his head. Melanie. What a gal. The tire was still holding air, which meant one less urgent thing to worry about. Bounding up the two steps, he opened the door and headed straight to his tablet.

As he searched for a book by that Dr. Spock guy he'd heard

about, he let his massive Bernese mountain dog, Maxwell Richard III, out the back door. Discovering Dr. Spock seemed to think childhood ended years before Dot's current age, Tristen began browsing online stores for Max-sized dog doors that would let the dog come and go from the house as he wished.

No. No distractions. He had to face this. No resisting. This was important. Scary, but important. Sixteen hours, minus eating, sleeping and working, didn't give him a whole lot of time to bring himself up to speed on teen rearing. He checked for a "What to Expect" for parents of teens.

Nope. Apparently the first two years of parenting were *The Years*. If you didn't have the skills by the time your kid was two, you were, essentially, hooped.

He placed the tablet on the coffee table and rested his head in his hands, his fingers finding plenty of hair to dig through. He needed a haircut. Sliding the tablet closer, he opened a browser and typed "How to Raise a Teen."

Now he was getting somewhere. Plenty of results.

How to Cope When Your Teenager Suddenly Becomes the Scariest Person You've Ever Met: Puberty and the Teenaged Girl.

Yep. Screwed. How was he, a man who had left parenting to Cindy, going to father a hormonal, strong-willed girl he didn't even begin to understand? He knew nothing about her. Nothing.

He moved to the kitchen and cracked open a beer, pouring it into a chilled glass.

In his mind, Dot was still the tiny baby who fit in his arms and had been named after his grandmother Dorothy. But Dot wasn't an infant any longer. She was a young woman struggling to discover her sexuality. He hoped Cindy had all that stuff under control, because there was no way he was equipped to deal with it.

If not, maybe seventeen wasn't too old for summer camp.

Or a job. Perhaps he could find her a job. Possibly two or three, so he didn't have to worry about mood swings, boyfriends, curfews, or figuring out how ask her not to flush tampons into the septic system.

Tristen dropped his head into his hands again. How was he going to deal with this? How was he going to contain and care for a young woman who was on the brink of adulthood and independence? He hadn't even been able to keep Cindy happy, and she'd been a fairly stable adult. He'd screwed up so badly the woman had thought he'd been avoiding her, while he'd spent years striving to build up their business—which was now all hers—so he could set them up for a fantastic early retirement. He'd worked long and hard to provide all the things he'd thought she wanted. And what did she do? Freak out and tell him he wasn't there for her, and that he was an awful human being.

His front door swung open, and relieved for any kind of distraction, Tristen waved his friend Connor MacKenzie in.

"Still engaged?" he asked.

"Still looking, but not seeking beautiful ladies?" his pal retorted, grinning like a fool as he sat down.

"Always looking. Gave a pretty one a ride home today."

"Did you now? I thought you looked more exhausted than usual." Connor peered about as if searching for a hidden woman.

Tristen frowned and idly flicked a fly away from his beer. Something about Connor and today was trying to connect in his mind.

"You look like you're trying to push out a porcupine. What's up?" his friend asked.

Tristen scowled and took a sip of his brew, then paused. "Sorry, did you want one?"

"Nope, still trying not to die. And now that I have a reason to live and a wedding coming at Christmas, I need to stay trim and in good shape." He patted his stomach. "Plus, I'm kind of enjoying this not-burned-out feeling."

"Told you you should try leaving the city," Tristen said with a wink. His friend had been out of the city for only two weeks and he already looked like a brand-new man. Tristen walked to the fridge and tossed Connor a bottle of water, the plastic misting with condensation almost immediately.

"Thanks. And if I remember correctly you did not tell me to leave the city."

Tristen leaned against the granite kitchen island. "So?" He waited for Connor to cut to the chase. His friend wanted something, but whether it was how to build a stone fireplace—a skill Tristen had acquired since moving here two years ago—or to borrow a million dollars, he didn't know.

Max nudged the patio door open and threw himself on the floor by the door where the breeze was the best, ignoring Connor. The next time Tristen got a dog, he was doing his research and getting a real guard dog. Something with fangs, or that barked when people popped by.

"I told you about how Maya and her sisters might lose their cottage?"

"Really?" Tristen straightened. "Why?"

"Back taxes."

"You're joking!" He'd met his buddy's fiancée only a couple times, but she didn't strike him as the kind of gal who would let something like paying her taxes slip for a few years.

"Nope. Some sort of thing about her older sister being in charge of the trust and not being able to take care of everything." Connor pushed a hand through his hair, then patted it flat. "I want to bail them out, but they're pretty intent on doing it themselves. You know how women can be. But the tax sale is at the end of the month."

Tristen nodded, keeping his attention on his beer glass. "Going to buy it back for them?"

"Maya would kill me."

"Why not do it secretly?"

"Nothing ever stays a secret."

"True. Early wedding gift?" Things were clicking in Tristen's mind. "Maya has a couple of sisters, right?"

"Three. Hailey, Melanie, and Daphne."

"Son of a…" Tristen's Friend-About-to-Ask-a-Big-Favor radar began blinking a warning. "You're here to try and drag me into that mess, aren't you?" He set down his drink. "You know I don't do development stuff any longer."

"Maya's already asked you?"

"Melanie." Tristen locked his jaw so he wouldn't say something that would make Connor kick his ass.

"I didn't think you'd met," his friend said, leaning forward.

"We did. She asked me. I said no," he replied, trying not to snap.

"Oh." Connor took a long pull on the bottle of water, his eyes on Tristen. "Why?"

"I'm not asking you why you're not drinking the beer in my fridge, now am I?"

"That's different. I'm choosing a healthier lifestyle and am pretty up front about it." Connor stood. "You're hiding out."

Tristen dumped the rest of his beer, plunked the empty glass in the dishwasher, slamming it shut. It was one thing for him to know he was hiding out, quite another if others could see it. "It was nice visiting, but my daughter is coming tomorrow. I'm not interested in babysitting some girls who don't pay their taxes."

"Whoa! Whoa!" Connor put out his hands out as though calming a spooked horse. "The taxes have nothing to do with this. They just need to pick someone's brain on how to stop a development that's infringing on the rights of others, that's all."

"All developments do that, and I don't have the time," Tristen said a little too tightly.

"It would mean a lot to me if you could point them in the right direction." Connor's voice was low, and Tristen could see the anger fizzling below his friend's calm surface. "This area is important to them, and with you living on the river you should care, too. The developers are going to be using this waterway to get to their fancy island resort. From construction through to the end of time. There's going to be an increase in river traffic. Right outside your door. You'd be wise to express interest in what they're trying to accomplish."

Tristen rolled his shoulders and pushed the heel of his hand against his chin, adjusting his neck. Connor was pushing his buttons, and he was certain his friend meant to. They'd done business back in Toronto and he knew Connor's game face. All Tristen had to do was allow Connor's arguments to spill off him and it would all go away. Shut up and stay out.

"The developer is going to destroy Muskoka's Heritage Row and quite possibly, the surrounding environment."

Heritage Row, a strip of four old cottages, was picturesque, quintessential cottage country. In other words, this battle was likely to get messy. Definitely be wise to stay far away from it.

"Sorry, man, my daughter needs me." Tristen's eyes caught the large sunflower painting across the room. Daphne Summer. Melanie's sister. He was going to have to move the painting to somewhere he rarely saw it, judging from the amount of emotions whirling through him right now.

Melanie was in trouble. She needed his help.

"You sure your kid needs you 24-7? Isn't she out chasing boys by now?"

Tristen guided his friend to the door. "Don't poke at me,

Connor. This is my chance to make things right with Dot." He lightened his tone, struggling not to be a complete and utter jerk. "Maybe she'll get me a rock identification guide for Christmas instead of cuff links. I don't want to wreck my chances of that."

"I'll buy you the damned guide, man. They need you. The developer is Rubicore."

Tristen clenched his fist. Aaron Bloomwood was part owner and their front man. The two of them had gone head to head in many fights back in the day. Each time, Tristen had won—by the skin of his teeth—and only because he'd had a reputation, and a large corporation backing him. Now? He had nothing. He was a nobody. He didn't even have the determined beast that used to run the show, because that side of him was not coming out to play. Ever. Again.

"Aaron Bloomwood still trying to make a name for himself?" he asked despite himself.

Connor nodded.

Tristen slowly shook his head. Definitely no way he could help out. Aaron brought out the beast in no time flat. With a fight like the one the Summers were gearing up for, you had to be all in. And the one thing Tristen had promised himself when he'd fled Toronto was that he would never do that again. Not for anything.

"You're out, aren't you?" Connor asked.

Tristen thought of the beautiful woman on a motorcycle and how she was in over her head. She needed his help. She wasn't a trust fund baby as he'd thought. She was just some gal trying to keep something in the family. Trying to keep it together—something he understood all too well.

"I'll think about it, but my answer, for the record, is still no."

Chapter Three

Melanie bunched the handmade dress into a ball and whipped it into the corner of her basement bedroom, thankful Daphne and her daughter weren't home to witness her mini freak-out. Sucking in a deep breath, she smoothed the worn XXL T-shirt over her ribs, wishing, not for the first time, that she had a willowy frame like her older sister Hailey. But no, puberty had decided to give her melon-sized breasts and a massive growth spurt that had earned her the nickname Sasquatch from her first boyfriend, Lix Levenson.

For what it was worth, she'd tried putting herself out there in hopes of discovering what was missing in her life, but she'd failed. There had been no sudden finding her place in the world, no sudden sprouting of confidence, no sudden sensation of feeling comfortable in her body. She kicked the dress farther into the corner for good measure and yanked her hair into a sloppy bun. What a goof she'd been to believe it was possible. And to think, after leaving the Steel Barrel, she'd been ready to ask Simone, the dress's designer, to make her a closetful of them. But now, no way.

Melanie hadn't been seeking humiliation but that's what been served up cold. Today she had been nothing more than a dressed-up version of the self she was trying to avoid. Evidence for the jury: Stedman had left her by the road; Tristen wouldn't accept a drink or meal or let her pick his brain, and had practically run away from her. She'd always prided herself on her connection skills when it came to people, but when it came to men...

Sure, the bikers seemed to have been smitten by her and her dress, and as kind as they were, they weren't the type of men looking to do marriage and kids with a lawyer.

Her life was in free fall. Not only had her landlord kicked her out of the rental she'd shared with her friend Nora so he could sell it, but Melanie was now depending on her baby sister to keep a roof over her head. At least she and Daphne could split the rent, and maybe somehow save up enough money for their portion of the cottage's overdue tax bill—even if it meant living in the unfinished basement and keeping her antique teacups in a cardboard box. Eventually, Melanie would have her student loans paid off and would be making more than the pittance that trickled into her bank account. As a first-year lawyer she was optimistic about having her financial life pull together, but that day had yet to dawn. Kind of like the one where her love life began to emulate something other than a horror flick.

She stomped up the stairs to the main floor of the tiny Cape Cod style home and just about bowled Daphne over.

"You're home!" she said to her sister.

"How was your date?"

"Where's Tigger?"

"Wow." Daphne waved a hand in front of her nose. "What were you drinking?"

"Whiskey."

Melanie ducked so she didn't have to catch Daphne's chiding look, and grabbed her five-year-old niece, who had bounded over, her ever-present party dress flouncing against her scab-covered knees.

"How's riding a two-wheeler?" Melanie asked, setting her down after a ginormous hug.

Tigger scrunched her nose. "It's hard." She tugged on her mother's hand, dragging her shoulder down. "Can I have ice cream? *Please?*"

"No sugar until after supper. If you're hungry, have an apple."

"I don't want an apple."

"Then you're not that hungry. Go play."

"It's hot out."

"Then play inside." Daphne turned to Melanie. "How was the date?"

Someone banged on the front door and Melanie took the opportunity to escape her sister's questions. She glowered out the peephole and swung the door open. "Go away!" she snapped at Stedman.

"I wanted to apologize." He offered her red clutch as though it was a bouquet of flowers.

Melanie snatched the bag. "Apologize for leaving me on the side of the road outside a biker bar? Or for lacking the ability to comprehend that no means no?"

She could hear Daphne shuffling in the room behind her, likely unable to avoid eavesdropping due to the house's small size. And while Melanie enjoyed being able to hear her sister read Tigger bedtime stories each evening, from her spot in the basement, this wasn't a conversation she particularly wanted to broadcast—especially since she might say something Tigger would end up repeating at an inopportune time.

Stedman tossed his head, sandy curls sweeping off his forehead. "Yeah, that."

"Which thing are you apologizing for, exactly?"

"Um, both?"

"Thank you for bringing back my purse." She began closing the door on him. "Wait. How did you know where I live?" She'd intentionally met him outside Simone's boutique instead of having him pick her up. Online dating and all that. Although getting into his truck likely hadn't earned a high score on the "how to be careful on your first date" rating scale.

Stedman shot her an impish smile and she slammed the door, flicking the dead bolt into place. Men.

Where was that ice cream Tigger was asking for? Would Melanie be a bad aunt if she sat down at the kitchen table and ate it all? Out of sight, out of temptation?

Her purse began ringing and she dug through it for her phone.

It was her sister Maya.

"Hey," Melanie said. "What's up?"

"Connor just talked to Tristen Bell."

Had Connor been able to sweet-talk Tristen? It wouldn't be a hardship to spend more time around that man and his beefy biceps despite his hot-and-cold persona. Plus, the sisters could definitely use his expertise.

"He's out."

Melanie sighed, feeling let down all over again. "I figured as much."

"I thought he'd say yes to Connor. Being old pals and all."

What a buttcake. That was the problem with billionaires. They always stuck to themselves and never felt the need to help the little guy. Heck, he might even own shares in Rubicore for all she knew.

"We'll find someone," Maya said. "You're good at talking to people and connecting and all that. Connor says to watch Rubicore carefully in case they take shortcuts."

Melanie made a noncommittal sound.

"Dang." Her sister laughed. "From what Connor's said about Tristen I figured the two of you would make a great pair."

In bed.

Wow, where did that thought come from?

"Mel? Still there?"

"Yeah. Right, um, I'll think on it, okay?"

"Do you have your cottage money yet?"

"Almost." Almost being pretty darn far from pulling her share out of the sky. One month until the century-old cottage was whisked from their possession if things didn't change. "Have you got yours?"

"I'm trying to convince Connor to give me a finder's fee for that dental device we're investing in, but he's so friggin' difficult."

"Tell him it's for the cottage and I'm sure he'll agree to give it to you."

"I want him to give it to me because he feels I deserve it, you know?"

"Then set up a finder's fee for the next investment. You have a month. Not a lot of time, but how long did the last one take you? A few weeks at best."

"Hmm. I wonder."

Melanie could practically hear Maya pondering an idea, weighing it for potential.

"All right. I'm on it. Thanks, Smelly Mellie."

"Pushy broad."

Maya laughed and hung up on her. Shaking her head, Melanie dug through the kitchen freezer. She jumped when Daphne appeared at her side, all petite and pretty in her flowing cotton dress. A mere woodland nymph compared to her. It made Melanie want to sit down so she didn't feel like Gigantor.

"Was that your date? Stedman?"

"Maya." Melanie closed the freezer, deciding against the ice cream. No need to add to the massive boobage. Maybe Maya would be up for meeting for drinks somewhere instead. That always seemed to go to her waist, which was easier to disguise due to said boobage. Comfort food of the liquid variety. Plus, hanging out with Maya, the lucky duck, might allow some of her fabulous dating and career luck to rub off on Melanie.

In her dreams.

"I mean at the door," Daphne clarified.

"Yeah. Forgot my purse in his truck."

"The date was that good?" The hope in Daphne's eyes was disgusting. Disgusting because Melanie had wanted it, too.

"No. It sucked. How was your day?"

"Great." Her sister's face lost its usual sunniness. "Well, except we got another notice about the tax sale. Registered letter." She grabbed an envelope from a large bowl and handed it over.

Melanie scanned it, then said, "Nothing we didn't already know. Just another warning. It's procedural. Covering their butts and all that."

Daphne sat, her elbow anchored on the kitchen table in order to hold up her head of crazy, light brown curls. "Maybe we should stay out at Nymph Island to allow destiny to give us a real shot."

Tempting. The family lore said the island was enchanted. Or at least it was good at hooking up female members of the Summer family. Their great-grandmother, grandmother, mother, and now Hailey and Maya had all fallen in love while spending time out at the ancient cottage. Plus, the two eldest sisters had had their careers take off in the last month. Even for a logical-minded lawyer, those facts were hard to discount.

But if the two youngest Summers—Melanie and Daphne— couldn't cover their portions of the cottage's back taxes, their family was going to lose the place.

"So? Nymph Island?" Daphne asked, pulling Melanie from her thoughts.

"Yay! Let's go to the cottage!" Tigger crawled out from the

cupboard under the sink, where, evidently, she had been playing hide-and-seek alone. "Wait!" She held out her hands, feet planted far apart. "I have to get my fairy box."

"I don't think we're going right now," Melanie said slowly.

"Well, I think we should," Daphne said decisively. "Use it while we have it. Do you have any dinner plans?"

Melanie shook her head.

"Then let's go. We can pick up a lumberjack sandwich on our way out. Instant picnic for six dollars. What do you say?"

Six dollars wasn't going to make or break them.

Tigger clasped her fingers together under her chin and batted her eyes at her aunt. Melanie laughed and threw up her hands. She could never resist her niece, who was a bright ray in her days. Every emotion that ran through that child was pure and real. She was the one true thing in Melanie's life. "Fine," she declared.

The girl was out of the room, nothing more than a flash of party dress, eager to collect her box of small treasures intended for the fairy houses she built on Nymph Island.

Melanie picked up her purse. "I met Tristen Bell today." Her body had a mini battle with itself over Tristen's confusing appeal and sudden, sharp rejection.

Daphne's face brightened expectantly as she waited at the door for Tigger to catch up with them.

"Maya says he won't help with Rubicore—and he said the same to me."

"Oh, well." Daphne didn't seem particularly perturbed. She jiggled her van keys as Tigger raced by, fairy box cradled against her chest.

Melanie paused to watch Daphne climb into the unlocked Dodge Caravan. She couldn't quite put her finger on her sister's cavalier mood. Usually she was all over developers.

"Don't you lock your van?" she asked as she got in beside her, noting that all the windows were down.

"Nah. It gives me a sense of adventure, never knowing whether there is an ax murderer hiding in the backseat." Daphne let out a burst of laughter, shaking the vehicle with the sound.

"I'm not an ax murderer," Tigger stated darkly, and her mom laughed again.

"Right you are!" Backing into the street, she said to Melanie, "Did you hear? A few local environmental agencies are swinging their weight to protect the spotted turtle habitat Finian found near Bala and not only is there a private firm acting like they want to hire me, but Environment Canada is, too."

"That would be amazing." Maybe that was why Daphne was in a strange mood. Her sister had always shunned the idea of a something as rigid as a nine-to-five desk job—and especially for the government—but as a single mom, the prospect of decent pay, benefits, a pension as well as paid holidays might be just too darn tempting. Something like that would be a far cry from the odd jobs she took now to pay the bills so she could volunteer as an environmental spokesperson.

"Yeah, maybe." Daphne shot a wistful glance into the backseat, where her daughter was kicking out her legs, eager to go.

"Oh! I can't believe I forgot." Melanie bounced in her seat. "Guess who has a Daphne Summer original?"

"Connor MacKenzie. He already told me."

"Nope. Someone else. Tristen Bell."

Daphne cast her a sidelong look and Melanie quickly glanced away, certain she was blushing.

"Cool. I appeal to the early retired business tycoon. I wonder where you advertise to reach them?"

Melanie snorted a laugh. "Oh, and I found something in a flea market for Tigger," she added, digging through her small purse for the trinket she'd picked up before her date. Swiveling, she handed a tissue-paper-wrapped object to her niece.

"For me?" she squealed. "It's not even my birthday, Auntie Mellie-Melon."

Melanie laughed at the nickname, pleased to see her sister smiling, too. "Careful. It's an antique."

Daphne shot her a worried look.

"It was only $1.75," she whispered.

"A fairy! Thank you." The girl clutched the small figurine, its wings peeking out from between her fingers.

"Remember: you can sell them when you want to go to school or buy a house or—"

"I want a Barbie house. Will this buy a Barbie house?"

"Um..."

"Honey," Daphne interrupted, as she steered the van into the grocery store parking lot, "your aunt means when you're a grown-up. A house for you to live in."

"Oh. Okay." Tigger turned the figurine over, assessing it. "When I'm married?"

"Or before then," Melanie said, having visions of her niece in her own position—with no money, no man prospects, no home, just a bunch of antiques she felt she couldn't sell because she'd become attached to them and the stories they held from the past.

"Well, if you can't make a go of online dating," Daphne said, changing the conversation, "there's no way I'm diving in. I'll take my chances with Nymph Island."

"You don't really think destiny's going to match us up with our mates if we hang out on the island?"

Daphne lifted a shoulder and looked away.

"Oh, my word. You do!" Melanie shouldn't be surprised. Her sister was the most likely of the four of them to fall for gooshy stuff.

"It happened to Hailey and Maya already this summer. And our mother, grandma and great-grandma in years past."

"Too bad that's not something I could put on the application for heritage status. I keep thinking there's something I'm missing. Some clue that will help us save Trixie Hollow. All those years. All that history. All those stories. And then Rubicore coming in to ruin everything…"

Daphne said with a sigh, "We need a miracle, Mel."

Rubicore didn't care about anything the sisters did. Peace, quiet, history, heritage, the environment… Rubicore's resort would be like having a buzzing shopping mall plunked in the middle of an idyllic farm. Not only that, there would be rich people laughing and playing next door in fancy digs, while they themselves wondered if they'd be able to keep their own dilapidated cottage standing.

Her sister's cheeks flushed and she gripped her keys hard enough that Melanie worried she'd hurt herself. Just as she reached across to touch her hand, hoping to get her to relax a bit, Daphne sighed and muttered, "Nuts."

"Josh is allergic to peanuts. So is Kyra," piped up Tigger. "They get chipmunk cheeks and a rash."

Daphne turned sunny again. "Okay. Inside to collect our picnic."

A few minutes later they were all back in the van and on their way to the marina where they kept the family's boat.

As they pulled up, Melanie leaned forward, staring out the window. Someone was checking out their Boston Whaler, tied to a dock. And not in an "interesting old boat; miracle it still floats" sort of way.

"Who is that man standing beside our boat?" she asked.

Daphne sat straighter in her seat. "Is he getting in?"

He definitely was. And just because he was wearing a suit didn't mean he wasn't capable of stealing it.

Melanie cast a glance in the backseat, where Tigger was gathering up her fairy box to climb out of the van. "Stay here with your mom, okay, Tigger? I need to talk to someone before we go to the island."

"Who?"

Daphne opened her door. "I'm coming with you. No, wait. On second thought, I'm calling the police." She lifted her phone to her ear, holding Melanie back with a gentle hand.

Melanie slipped free of her grip and got out as the man left their boat. Hurrying along the pier, she caught up with him before he turned down a side dock, away from her.

"Hi," she chirped. He gave her a quick nod and continued. "I see you were in my boat just now. Is there anything I can help you with?"

He paused. "I'm sorry?"

"My boat. What were you doing in it?" Melanie drew herself taller, folding her arms across her chest.

"I was leaving a message in Maya Summer's boat."

Oh, that was rich. Maya was calling it her boat now? The Whaler belonged to all of them. Sure, Hailey made certain it was always taken care of, but still. It belonged to the whole family. Just like the cottage.

"I'll be sure she gets it," Melanie said, striding toward the aluminum vessel.

His steps quick, the man followed her, as though playing shadow tag. It was creepy. Plus, who wore a suit in Muskoka?

Melanie whirled. "Do you have a problem?"

He nearly rammed into her. "I want to be sure the message gets to Maya."

"She has a boyfriend. A very large boyfriend."

A cool expression masked whatever the man might be thinking. "I will gladly retrieve it and deliver it myself." His voice was polite and businesslike in a way that raised Melanie's hackles. He gave her a small, false smile, as though that would warm her. "I was under the impression that was her boat."

"I'm her sister and we share the boat. I can give it to her."

Melanie could almost hear him thinking. He must have already met the well-put-together Maya and maybe pretty, willowy Hailey. Just wait until he saw Daphne, cute as a button, lively and vibrant. Able to wrap whole crowds around her pinky like some sort of snake charmer. Melanie could feel it coming, the up-and-down look, followed by the stale joke, "No wonder you're a tomboy. You probably didn't get much time in the washroom to get ready in the mornings, with three other sisters. Five women in the house! Ha, ha, ha."

Mirror time was not the specific reason for her lack of va-va-voom in the girlie dress-up department.

"Yeah. Four of us sisters," Melanie said. He went to open his mouth. "And yeah, it was difficult getting mirror space in the mornings, but you know, you learn to adapt, and Mom put up extra mirrors in the hall, with small shelves underneath for those who were waiting."

The man gave her a blank look.

Melanie climbed into the open-decked boat, ignoring the way it rocked as she scrambled to find the note before the man could join her and snag it. Her fingers closed over an envelope tucked on the dashboard and she slid it into her pocket, keeping her back to the man.

He was still on the dock. "I haven't introduced myself."

"Right. You have not."

He held out his hand with a jerk.

Slowly, Melanie moved to the side of the boat, then climbed

onto the pier, reaching out to shake his hand once she had a firm footing. "Melanie Summer."

"Aaron Bloomwood."

Aaron from Rubicore Developments. Well, well, well. What was he up to? And what was Maya keeping from the rest of the family?

It wasn't that Melanie didn't trust her sister, per se. Okay, she didn't. Melanie didn't kid herself that Maya might try and wrangle them a better deal, then tell them at the last minute, hijacking things to go the direction she wanted—which probably wouldn't be a bad thing. But Melanie didn't like surprises, and this reeked of one.

Staring into Aaron's stony eyes, she felt like a fool. He knew more than she did, didn't he?

"And Maya will know who you are?" she asked, hoping her cheeks didn't flush as she pretended ignorance.

"Yes. I'm with Rubicore Developments. We made an offer to purchase your family's island that your sister found deficient."

That sounded about right.

"This note is additional to the offer. A proposal of sorts. Can you please ensure she gets it? It is time sensitive."

Now *that* was intriguing. The envelope was definitely going to get steamed open as soon as Melanie got a chance.

MELANIE AND DAPHNE sat on the veranda of the old cottage, Tigger having devoured her portion of the picnic so she could hurry off with her latest treasures—a nickel, an acorn, a leaf shaped like a heart, and a small pink pebble—to add to a new fairy house.

Melanie shifted so she could pull the envelope from Aaron Bloomwood out of her back pocket.

"Do you think he really was only leaving that for Maya?" Daphne asked.

"He said this is an additional proposal."

"Of the marriage persuasion?" Daphne joked in a British accent, her chin dipped down in false seriousness.

"But of course," Melanie retorted, sounding more like a count with a funky loose tooth than anyone British. "Our bossy sister is awash in suitors."

"Are we going to open it?" Daphne whispered, leaning forward.

Melanie grinned, remembering the time as kids when they'd read Maya's diary and giggled over their sister's first kiss—which in Maya's words had been sloppy and unimpressive, leaving Melanie wondering what all the fuss was about. She had a feeling Maya and her fiancé, Connor, were solving that little mystery several times an hour lately.

"Shall we steam it open, read it, then reseal it?" Melanie asked. "Or do we own up to our snoopish ways and tear it open?"

"He said it was in regards to the offer, right?"

She nodded. Her lawyerly training could get behind the logic of where Daphne was going with this line of thought. "Technically, any offer is for the owners. And we have 50 percent of the voters present—if we don't include Mom in our count."

"He mentioned something about it being time sensitive?" Daphne leaned forward, eyes glued to the envelope.

Melanie ripped open the end and pulled a sheet of paper. In the process, a square of card stock fell out. Her sister came to sit beside her, picking it up.

"It's an invitation to the unveiling of their development plans! Are they nuts?" The scorn and disbelief in Daphne's voice echoed the disappointment Melanie felt as she read the short note. She'd been hoping for something intriguing, like a Nancy Drew mystery that she and Daphne could unravel. But this? This was just baffling and possibly insulting.

"Why was he so worried about whether she'd get this? And where is the proposal?" Melanie tossed the sheet of paper on the coffee table.

Daphne reached for the letter, then paraphrased the contents. "They're asking us to join them for supper, then enjoy a private tour of the island before the party where the plans will be revealed. They do say we can discuss any additional proposals at supper. There's nothing specific." She dropped the letter where she'd found it and swiveled her head to look out across the water that separated their place from Baby Horseshoe Island. "They want to woo us."

"I'm not up for wooing," Melanie grumbled, rubbing her eyes. The heat of the day, the three whiskeys, the hurt of Tristen's rejection and now this latest letdown were hitting her hard. She wanted a nap. She wanted her mother. "Do we have time to visit Mom on the way home?"

"Hmm?" Her sister blinked. "What?"

"Want to visit Mom on the way home?" The nursing home's official visiting hours would be over, but none of the staff seemed to mind the sisters coming by to see their night owl mother at unconventional times.

"I think we should go," Daphne said.

"Great. Maybe Simone can meet us. I want to tell her in person that if Maya has asked her to make more of those dresses for me, it isn't necessary. I don't want to hurt her feelings, but I'm done with Maya's attempts at revamping my appearance. You know?"

Daphne was still staring at the island across the way, lost in her own world.

"Mom?" Tigger came bouncing onto the veranda. "Can we buy

a Bedazzler? I don't have any more coins for my fairy houses and I need something. Fiona has one."

"Then ask to borrow hers, please." Eyes brimming with something that got Melanie's espionage radar blinking, Daphne turned and held up the note. "I meant this. We should go. Reconnaissance."

"Really?"

"They think they can woo us, but I say we go and gather ammo so we can shoot these pie-eyed, fat-headed, greedy rich cats out of the sky."

Tigger gave Melanie a wide-eyed look as if to say, *What did you do to my mother?*

Melanie grinned and high-fived her sister. For Daphne, that speech was as close to swearing as she ever got.

"I'm in! I say we learn what we can, then use it to halt Rubicore in their tracks. In the meantime, I'll talk to Mr. Valos over at the municipality. I bet he'd love to hear a presentation about Rubicore's plans from our side of the fence," Melanie said.

Oh, yeah. Things were about to get good.

Chapter Four

A small sports car purred down Tristen's driveway. He watched as it crunched to a halt by his front step, the early morning light flashing on its shiny red door as his ex-wife got out. "Really, Tristen? Gravel? You couldn't pave it or lay out all those fancy stones you drone on about?" She winked as she slammed her door, but he knew she was half-serious.

"They don't make a good driveway. Not with our winters. Where's the Escalade?" He'd special ordered her a fully-loaded Cadillac SUV, and she wasn't even driving it?

She gave him a look. "You really thought that thing was me?"

"It's what all the stay-at-home moms were driving."

"Yeah, well, that was before you sold me your half of the company. And just before an economic downturn. Thanks for that." The fire and ice in her voice would be enough to make most men's testicles crawl inside his body for protection, but for Tristen it was the anger flashing in her sapphire eyes that made his Adam's apple lodge in place, not allowing him to talk or breathe. The old Tristen had been into screwing people over in business, but never family. Surely she had to know the timing wasn't his doing?

He moved around the tiny car, which was definitely a bad choice for Ontario's busy, often rock-lined highways. What luck would she have against a tractor trailer, and how on earth were those sporty, low-profile treads going to keep her on the road in the middle of any kind of storm? Did she not comprehend how little rubber was connecting her to the highway? And traveling with their daughter—what was the safety rating on this thing? Did it even have side air bags?

His gaze drifted to his only mode of transportation, the truck. Definitely no air bags. He was going to have to buy a new vehicle if he planned to be driving Dot around. Possibly a Volvo. Or a Hummer. Those seemed pretty sturdy.

Working hard to calm himself, he tried for a welcoming smile. He pulled his daughter to his chest, noting that he'd committed a fatal error even before her body froze against his. He tucked her head under his chin nevertheless, surprised at how tall she was. Then he held her for an extra second, letting her know that he was that dad—a father who was not afraid to express physical affection, because he was *not* emotionally stunted, as his ex had stated so bluntly while delivering her petition for divorce.

Tristen released his daughter, noting that her upper-lip snarl was quivering, as though she'd needed that hug for months.

He really had to prove to them all that he could do this, didn't he?

"How's it going, Dot?" he asked. She'd added a green and an orange streak in her bangs—if you could call them that. It was more like a sheepdog shag covering the front of her head, swept forward to cover the left third of her face, ending in a point near her small, sharp chin, which she raised defiantly as he took her in. Half pixie, half sheepdog. He was going to have to be careful what he unconsciously nicknamed her.

"I like your hair."

The snarl was back, and her arms crossed over her thin chest.

"You look hungry," he added.

He caught the look from his ex-wife, who was equally thin,

and sighed. Women. They weren't all like Melanie Summer and willing to work it. That girl had curves like a modern day Marilyn Monroe, without the "I know I'm sexy" turn-him-off attitude. Ms. Summer probably ate without worrying about whether it was going to give her some padding a man might actually enjoy.

Why was he even thinking about her? She was the devil, tempting him back to the dark side of land developments. And no, that dark side did not have milk and cookies. It had beasts and quicksand. Snake pits and so much worse.

He grabbed Dot's luggage from the minuscule trunk and half listened while Cindy ranted on about what she thought their daughter needed. Just when he was about to shoo her away—forcibly if necessary—his ex-wife leaped in her car and tore out of the driveway without even a goodbye hug for the daughter she hadn't been separated from for more than a weekend in probably at least a decade.

"No lost love, huh?" he said to Dot, turning to find her gone. He found her on the stone patio overlooking the water, feet up on the outdoor furniture, head tucked low as she typed on her phone. "Want me to show you your room?"

"I'm not staying here."

"Well, I doubt your mother got you a room at the local inn, so let's go." He half turned, waiting for her to follow.

"I'm staying at a friend's house."

"Nope."

"The only thing that makes you my father is the fact that you knocked up Mom."

All right then.

Here was the first example of the hormone-induced lash outs the internet had warned him about. He supposed he no longer needed to wonder why his ex had peeled out of here. She was probably ready to hit every bar on the way back to Toronto, crying, "Freedom! Freedom!"

"Right. We do share biology. However, I also bought that phone you are using and took you to Disney World when you were seven."

She glared at him. "Mom bought me this phone."

"Where do you think the money came from, Missy Pants?"

His daughter popped up off the couch, livid. "Don't call me that."

"You liked it when you were three."

"No, I didn't. You only used it when you were scolding me."

That actually sounded fairly familiar.

"Mom works, you know. She spends hours on that stupid business you abandoned, just like you abandoned us." His daughter's chest expanded and contracted with emotion, and her eyes were damp as she fell back into the cushions, her face so close to her phone that he worried about her vision.

"All right." Tristen took the seat across from her. "Looks like we need to set a few things straight. Number one, I am your father and always will be." He swallowed hard, drew a deep breath and tried to forge ahead, but found himself unable to say the three simple words he knew she needed to hear. Cindy's words ran circles in his head. *Why can't you say* I love you? *Don't you think I need to hear it?* The words froze in his throat, unable to come out. They were too important. "I uh…" Nope. Wouldn't come out. "It's that four-letter word found in a three-word phrase, Dot." He cleared his throat. "I always have and always will feel that way about you."

Her shoulders hitched higher and her lips curled.

"Two, I'm glad your mom is getting out there and working. It's good for her. Three, that business is something I built from the ground up. It's called TriBell for a reason. When your mother and

I parted ways she got half of it as my spouse, and I sold her the rest. I didn't abandon it, but I admit that, yes, I ran from the city."

He had Dot's attention now. He could tell by the slight face tilt so she could catch glimpses of him, even though her attention was still aimed at her phone. How little she'd changed since she was a toddler. "I didn't intend to make you feel abandoned, but I understand how you might feel that way. And for that, I am sorry, Dot."

"Nobody calls me Dot."

"What do they call you?"

"It doesn't matter."

"You want me to call you Dot?"

She gave a tiny shrug.

When had she become a woman, with the mood-powered Tilt-a-Whirl personality that came with it? He bet Melanie wasn't like this.

Max roamed over, having noticed there was someone new present and Tristen wasn't simply talking to himself.

"This is my dog, Maxwell Richards III."

Dot's headed lifted in surprise, a smile starting before she caught herself, tamping it down.

"Quite the name, right?" He scratched the dog's ears as the furry beast checked in with him before heading over to see what Dot had to offer. She ignored him, so he plunked his massive head in her lap. "He's a Bernese mountain dog. Friendly. Lazy. Eats a ton. Craps like an elephant."

Dot blinked, holding something back. Finally, she peeled one hand away from her phone and gently patted Max's head. The dog nuzzled closer and lifted his brown eyebrows in such a pathetic request for love that Tristen could visibility see his daughter's heart melt. She scratched under Max's chin, then, realizing what she was doing, pulled her hand back, crossing her arms.

"He sheds," she announced.

"Year-round. So? Ground rules or show you your room?"

Dot heaved a sigh so severely exaggerated he had to bite back a smile.

He headed into the building, knowing she was sure to follow this time. Grabbing her luggage from the entry, where he'd left it, he led Dot down the hall to the guest room. He nudged the door to the ground-floor bedroom open, pointing out the nearby bathroom, which was their one and only, sandwiched between his bedroom and hers.

He placed her suitcases by the bed. "Need anything?"

"An escape plan," she muttered, falling onto the mattress, which bounced her back onto her feet. "This bed sucks."

"So then, a few ground rules. We eat meals. Three of them. Every day. At the table. Together."

"Don't you have a job?"

"I do. And I have to head out in an hour and you'll come with me. I'm not going to have any of those 'I'm not hungry' or 'I just ate' games in this house. It might work with your mother, but not with me." He gave Dot the I-mean-business eye and noted she appeared slightly shocked. He might not have been around much in the past seventeen years, but he noticed things. And now it was his turn to play parent, without worrying about his wife undoing it all while he was at work. "No sneaking out. Phone is left on its charger in the kitchen at bedtime. In other words, no calls or texting at night." Her mouth dropped open. "You need sleep— uninterrupted—and you're a teen. Sleep is mandatory."

"What is this? *Jail*?"

"Mean Daddy Boot Camp," he said with a smile. "You can get a job while you are here, if you're interested. You have your driver's license?"

She shook her head.

"Want it?"

There was a glimmer in her eyes, which had finally lifted enough he could see their familiar star pattern. She didn't answer.

"You can also borrow my bike. We aren't far from town. There's a nice library there. I can get you a library card if you want. I don't have cable or satellite." Her eyes grew round again. "I have internet. I'll get you the password. No porn. Surf safe and all that."

"I have data on my phone."

"Which will remain on its charger at night."

"People can watch porn during the day, you know."

"Good point. I'll be sure to look over your shoulder every so often." He touched the cool surface of an amphibolite rock he'd placed on her windowsill as an attempt at décor. The dark-and-light gray striations were swirled, making it resemble marbled fudge.

He turned back to his daughter, who was tapping through messages on her phone. "Do you have a boyfriend?"

Dot froze. "No."

"Well, no boys. I guess you could go on a date if I meet him first and say it's okay. But assume you can't have boys over or go to their place unless I know them and have given approval." Tristen glanced again at his daughter. How could she not have a boyfriend in the middle of her seventeenth summer? "Sure you don't have a boyfriend? No crushes or anything that I need to worry about? Maybe this friend you wanted to stay with? Your mother and I eloped when we were only a little older than you, you know. I know what teenagers do." He sat beside her on the bed. "So? Boyfriend?"

"I'm gay, Dad."

He didn't know whether to be relieved that there'd be no boys, or to allow the joy of hearing her call him "Dad" sweep him away.

"Gay, happy? Or gay, lesbian?"

"I prefer the company of females." Her arms were crossed, eyes daring.

"Fine. Amend the no-boys rule to cover girls of the girlfriend persuasion. And at least I don't have to worry about you getting pregnant."

"Ha, ha."

"What? It's true. A father's worst nightmare—your teenaged daughter becoming a mom while still in high school." Other scenarios filled his mind and he amended his statement. "Well, one of the worst. Although really, that wouldn't be too bad. It would just be hard on you, giving up your freedom. And teen pregnancies are fraught with risk, healthwise. What I mean is that it could be worse. I would like to be a grandfather some day. Just maybe not right away. You're not pregnant, are you?" Tristen placed a fist over his mouth and cleared his throat. Time to shut his word hole.

"Are *you* allowed to have girlfriends over?" Dot's dark eyes narrowed in challenge.

His mind flipped to the image of Melanie sitting on her motorcycle, and the way she'd given him attitude.

"Don't have one," he said simply.

"That's lovely. You didn't even stay with the woman you left us for?"

Tristen choked on his shock. "Excuse me?"

Dot glared at him, all her teenage hatred and hurt directed at him. It felt as though an evil cloud of black pain had been shoved in his direction.

"Your mother and I broke up because she was tired of me not

being around. Did she really tell you I was with someone else?" His voice was low, almost too quiet. He pushed back the anger, knowing where it would take him if he let it grab hold.

"I just kind of figured."

"Never assume." He directed them out of the room, his moves sharp, laced with pent-up anger. "Your mother and I came to the end of our ride together, that's all. Make sure you learn that lesson from us and communicate with your partner." He pulled Dot into a tight, partial hug before letting her go. He noted she took a large step away, but then slowly eased closer as they moved down the hall.

When they reached the end of the corridor, he stopped, blocking her way. "I know you probably don't want to know this, but there's never been anyone other than your mother. Well, in high school I saw someone else for a while. But when I met your mom, that was it for me. Nobody since."

"That's pathetic."

He wasn't sure if she meant settling down so young or the self-induced solitude. Either way, spending the last two years mostly alone had been good for him.

"Can I work for you?" his daughter said out of the blue, head cocked to one side.

The expression "damned if you do, damned if you don't" popped into Tristen's mind.

"I'm not working a lot at the moment. Some real estate on the side when others want a vacation. A bit of rock work. Nothing exciting."

"Fine." His daughter crossed her arms and reduced her eyes to slits, jutting out her chin. "If I fail it will be because of you."

Oh, look, the Tilt-a-Whirl was at work again. "Can you please explain?" he said, forcing himself to be polite.

"I flunked gym class."

"But you're an athlete." She had been part of the starting lineup in soccer since age five. It didn't matter if she had just entered the next age level and was the youngest on the team, she was always a starter. How could someone like that flunk?

"Whatever. I'll just drop out."

"No. Explain what you need."

She told him in one long breath, "I'm short the number of credits I need to graduate on time. I have to do summer school or work experience or I won't graduate. I missed registering for summer school."

"So, what do you need for that?"

"A job."

"Any job? How many hours?"

"I want to be a lawyer and the schools prefer law office experience, but anything would work."

Little spider feet crept up his spine. Law. *Melanie.*

Tristen took a deep breath and turned to head to the kitchen. "Let's have breakfast." He pivoted to face his daughter again, knowing, like a fifth sense, that an excuse was about to trip off her tongue.

"Nope," he said. "I'm a good cook, and I know you didn't eat on the way up. You're eating. Rule one."

It was time to get this parenting party started.

EARLY MONDAY MORNING, Melanie stood outside the municipality office of Mr. Valos, an old family friend. His secretary, Nora, who was her former roommate, had snagged her an early appointment—first of the day—and Melanie planned to share her fantastic arguments on why Rubicore couldn't continue their plans to destroy Muskoka. Mr. Valos would be convinced that he needed to put a lockdown on Rubicore's plans, and she'd skip off into the future, somehow finding her share for the cottage's taxes, and live happily ever after. The end.

Right. She really needed to figure out a solid plan for coming up with several thousand dollars over the next four weeks or she'd be the one responsible for losing the cottage. And that was not how she wanted to finally stand out in the Summer family. Being the only sister sent to Camp Adaker to be straightened out after their father's sudden death as kids had been bad enough.

Melanie pushed open the tall door to Mr. Valos's office. Who did they think was going to work here—giants? Yeesh. She padded across the carpet to the desk, giving the man a light hug of hello as he stood to greet her.

"Good morning, Mr. Valos."

Had he gotten shorter? Because that was a really awkward place for his head—below her shoulder and a bit too close to her boobs. He was holding her as though he expected comfort, his arms hugging her too tightly. It was the kind of awkward that made a person want to toss their cookies a little bit. He finally released her and she struggled to keep her smile from wavering. She needed Mr. Valos on her side.

"Melanie Summer!" He held her hands in his, stepping back to take her in. "You look well. I heard you'd moved back after school. How are you?"

"Fine, thank you." She smoothed the dress she'd worn yesterday. She figured if it worked on bikers, it might work on politicians, too. "How are you and Mrs. Valos?"

"Great. Just great. Golfing a ton. Got my par down by three points from last year."

"And your daughter, Jess?"

"Married!" He clapped his hands in glee and sat down, leaning back in his chair.

"Jess is married?" Well, that took the cake. If that girl could do it, then why wasn't Melanie getting any action? "That's wonderful."

"So, what can I do for you? Just stopping by to see my new office?" He held out his arms, showcasing the grand room.

"Actually, I was wanting to talk to you about a development slotted for Baby Horseshoe Island."

"Oh?" He turned to push the intercom button that linked him with his secretary. "Let's get Nora to set up an appointment."

"Actually, I'm your first appointment of the day." Melanie unbuckled her briefcase. "I'd like to discuss Rubicore and their proposed resort."

"Yes, great for jobs and tourism."

"Wonderful economic reasons to love a development," she said cheerfully. His hand left the phone. "Although possibly not so wonderful for the environment."

He laughed. "You been talking to that sister of yours? What's her name? Belle?"

"Daphne."

"Causes quite the ruckus, doesn't she? I suppose that's what happens when you lose your father so young. Such a shame." He shook his head. "A crying shame. He was so good at poker."

"I don't believe our father's death had anything to do with Daphne's passion for animals and the environment. At Halloween, if you'll remember when she was four—" Melanie laughed lightly, attempting to ease the edge from her voice "—she used to ask for donations for the no-kill shelter in lieu of candy."

"Oh? She's diabetic?"

"No." Melanie sat up straight and placed a stapled document on Mr. Valos's desk. "Anyway, about this development."

"Should have sent Belle to that camp for emotional kids, too. It did wonders for you. You're a lawyer now."

"Camp Adaker," Melanie supplied weakly.

"Yeah, yeah. That place. We'll see what happens with that, then, eh?"

The room felt as if it was spinning. She was missing something. Something important.

"What do you mean?"

"Well, it's on that island."

She'd been fund-raising for the camp almost every year since she'd gone there as a camper, and then as a counsellor. To say she believed in the camp and that it meant a lot to her was a complete understatement.

"What's going to happen?" she asked.

The man stood. "I'm so glad you came in to visit, Melanie. Great to see you." He placed a hand on her lower back as she rose to her feet, about to argue that she still had a few more minutes in her appointment time. He gave her a gentle nudge forward and she resisted, holding her ground, knowing that once he got her out of the room, it was over.

She needed reinforcements, someone who could sway Mr. Valos's opinion, since he obviously still thought of her as a grieving child.

"I'd like to talk to the town council at their next meeting, as well. There are some serious environmental concerns, as well as ones regarding heritage loss, bylaw infringements, parking, traffic, noise, lighting, and even the footprint, which, from what I've seen, will be quite significant. I—"

"Very nice. Very nice. Create a presentation and we'll see."

"I have one." Melanie held up her briefcase. She'd stayed up until four in the morning creating this presentation, then begged Nora to find a way to slide her into Mr. Valos's schedule. And for what? Him to kiss her out the door? Not a chance.

She dodged him and headed to his desk, where she placed her laptop on the reflective surface.

Mr. Valos stood at the open door, seeming confused.

Melanie smiled, not making eye contact, so he'd be less likely to try and stop her. "I have all the information right here."

Hearing Mr. Valos greet someone, she turned, full of smiles, hoping to woo another member of the council into hearing her presentation, especially since the next meeting wasn't scheduled for a while. Time was of the essence.

Her smile dropped, then picked up along with her heartbeat as she spotted a tall man standing in the door. Tristen. She didn't know whether to effusively rope him in, or be miffed that he'd refused to help. Either way, judging from the surprised look on his face, he wasn't here to play hero.

"Ms. Summer," he said with a slight nod. "I'm sorry, Vincent, I must have the wrong time. I'll check back with Nora."

Mr. Valos hauled him into the room by his shirtsleeve, seemingly with the opposite emotion he'd expressed while trying to drag Melanie out. "Stay, stay," he crooned, straightening the sleeve of Tristen's crisp dress shirt.

"I'm actually about to do a presentation about my concerns in regards to Rubicore's proposed resort development on Baby Horseshoe Island." Melanie turned back to her computer, waking it from sleep mode.

"This would be more appropriate at the next council meeting, Melanie. Ask Nora to be a dear and put you on the list, if we have time," Mr. Valos said in an authoritative, patronizing tone.

"And will there be any planning meetings between the municipality and the developers before then?"

"Oh, can't be sure," he replied, hooking his thumbs in his belt loops.

"Shall we ask Nora? I'm sure she must know." Melanie reached for his phone, lifting the receiver. "I'd hate for something to be approved that could endanger what everyone loves about Heritage Row. Muskoka is such a unique area of the world."

"I think I'll come back later," Tristen said, turning toward the door.

"Yes," Melanie chirped. "I believe we're going to need some time here, and since I know you're afraid of developments and developers, this might make you uncomfortable." She punched a button she figured would get her through to Nora.

Tristen gave her a parting glare, jaw clenched hard. He slammed the door behind him, making the framed pictures rattle.

"Ms. Summer," Mr. Valos said, his voice low with anger.

Oh, it was *Ms. Summer* now. Nice.

He gently took the phone from her and placed in its cradle. "Mr. Bell has been waiting to see me about a very important matter and I don't recall seeing your name on my schedule. I think it would be best if we did this at another time." He opened the door. "Mr. Bell. Please. Ms. Summer and I are done. Your time is valuable, and I apologize for the mix-up and to have kept you waiting."

Butt kisser.

Tristen reappeared in the doorway, his expression livid. Melanie had to admit it was a terribly sexy look on him. It tightened his jaw in a way that made her long to run her hand down it. Slowly. And maybe follow up with her tongue and some love bites. Oh, heck. She was going to need a cold shower if she kept staring at his jaw.

Focusing on the space just beyond Tristen, she said, "Mr. Valos, I feel Mr. Bell could provide valuable input on this issue. Should he deign to weigh in."

Silence stretched in the spacious room.

"Mr. Bell?" Melanie asked, hoping her voice didn't betray her desperate need to have him not shut her down. To help her out.

The man in question looked away and Mr. Valos gave an embarrassed cough.

Fine. She'd show the wimps that she could do this without them.

She snatched her briefcase from the desk and said, "I'll set something up with Nora—*again*—on my way out. Thank you for your time, Mr. Valos. Oh, and tell your wife that I would be happy to help her sort out the fender-bender she had last week if her insurance company is still giving her troubles."

Head held high, Melanie stomped from the room.

"Nora?" She snagged her friend on the way out. "I'm going to need another appointment. One where Mr. Bell can't shoo me out."

"I'm so sorry. He was early. You should have had another ten minutes." Nora's cheeks flushed as her long nails clicked across the keyboard. "Let's see what we can find."

"And can I get a slot at the next council meeting to do a presentation, too?"

"You bet. Just give me a minute."

Melanie hefted her briefcase, which was too light. Her computer. She'd left it in Mr. Valos's office. "Excuse me." She pushed open the door, not caring if she was interrupting some oh-so-important meeting between the two men.

"The land out by the highway. Did the rezoning go through? A client was wondering…" Tristen trailed off, looking away as Melanie strode back into the room.

She shot him a dirty look as she made her way to Mr. Valos's desk.

So much for Tristen leaving his developer side behind. The liar.

"Sorry, boys!" she chirped. "Forgot my computer."

"Dear, this isn't the best use of your time," Mr. Valos said gently, pushing her computer closer to the edge of his desk so she could grab it.

"Let me worry about how I spend my time." She gave him a bright smile and tried not to kick Tristen as she passed him again.

He kept his eyes averted, jaw set, but she could feel his attention follow her as she crossed the room. She wished she was wearing something more adorable than the same dress she'd worn when they'd met yesterday. Why couldn't she ever be that amazing woman in front of others? In command and in control?

And that better not be pity she saw in his eyes as he glanced up.

She glared at him and shut the door behind her, barely refraining from sticking out her tongue.

She needed to show that I'm-so-great-and-too-good-to-help-you man that she could do this. *Would* do this. Without him.

Chapter Five

Tristen walked the docks, eyeing the antique boats that had been entered in Port Carling's annual boat show while trying to clear his mind of Melanie Summer and the nasty look she'd given him as she'd stormed out of Vincent Valo's office. The guy had been a condescending prick and it had been nearly impossible for Tristen to sit there, acting as though he wasn't insulted on her behalf. The problem was that the real estate office he moonlighted for needed Vincent as he was the man who could get things rezoned faster than anyone else on the council. Today it had been Tristen's job to schmooze, and he'd walked right into that wave of anger coming from the woman whose image had kept him tossing and turning late into the night.

But now he was done work for the day, had let Dot loose on the boat show for a half hour, and had time to ponder an idea he wanted to try. Working with stone always cleared his mind and today he was counting on it.

He continued walking along the docks that wrapped along the one side of the small island park that had been cut off from the mainland by the larger steamship locks behind him. He remained on the lookout for the boat that had inspired his latest idea. It was a long shot, but he thought he might be able to use the boat's hewing, notching, and joining technique with stone. A way to naturally fit several rocks together without the use of anything but skill.

And there it was. The *Winged Goddess*. An exceedingly rare wooden boat from the 1930s. Tristen waited for a group in tennis whites to move past, stealing the opportunity to check out the boat while a woman wearing a baggy shirt and shorts had the owner distracted.

Wood was different than stone, but it was also surprisingly similar. You could alter it. Carve it into almost anything if you were patient and knew how to finesse it. But you couldn't just jump in and do whatever you wanted to any kind of stone. And sometimes, if you tried to do too much without paying attention to the individual rock's internal cracks and striations, it broke. Kind of like a marriage.

"Sunk her this spring," the owner was saying.

The woman gave a shocked squeak, and Tristen let out a huff of a laugh at her indignation and horror.

"Yep," the man continued. "Mouse hole I didn't notice when I put her in. I gunned it to shore when I realized I was taking on water. Sunk her less than ten feet from land. Boy, that water was cold!"

"You and the boat are obviously okay, though?" she asked, her voice kind and soft. Caring. Familiar.

Later. Tristen needed to focus on the boat. The voice could very well belong to a woman he was avoiding—and there were several.

Their conversation grew more distant as they moved to the other end of the boat to check out the supposed damage, and Tristen crouched by the bow, inspecting the woodworking techniques.

"Well, hello!" cooed a voice dangerously close to his ear.

That was *not* the same familiar one he'd heard a few moments ago.

He cut a glance to the side. Crap. Alice Estaire. Stalker extraordinaire. Okay, not stalker. Just overly friendly and clueless. Sort of like a puppy. She ran a finger across his shoulders. Not surprisingly, she found a knot and began kneading it. He stood abruptly, smoothly displacing her hands. Nice enough lady, but not the one for him.

"Hi, Alice."

She squeezed her arms together in a way that made her breasts push higher in her pink tank top. "I see you're back at the real estate office."

He gave a tight smile, turning on his heel to hurry away. "Lovely to see you. Must meet up with someone. Sorry." He nervously toyed with a polished stone in the pocket of his shorts and scanned the crowd for his daughter. Now would be the perfect time for Dot to show up. Striding down the dock, he made obvious phone-checking gestures. He felt bad for the way he'd brushed off Alice, but what was a man to do? They'd already had the it's-not-you-it's-me talk. She didn't take his hints, and if he was any more obvious he'd hurt her feelings. If he did that she might cry. And that would be uncomfortable for everyone.

At the end of the dock, still not spotting Dot, he paused beside an old schooner, taking in the way it had been put together. He still wanted a few more moments with the *Winged Goddess*, but didn't dare backtrack.

After asking permission, he took a few photos of the joints at the schooner's stern. Pretty standard and nothing exciting, but he felt the need to do something as he waited out Alice. A woman was bending to chat with a man sitting in the boat docked in front of the schooner, her laughter washing over him. That laugh. Melanie.

Beautiful, beautiful Melanie.

Tristen resisted the urge to run.

Away.

Fast.

"Beautiful lines," she was saying, her hands out as though fighting the temptation to run them over the boat's curves. A surge of jealousy swirled within Tristen and he tamped it down, crossing his arms, wanting to turn away but unable to. He couldn't possibly be jealous of a boat. How ridiculous was that? He faked further interest in the schooner as he watched her chat, animated and happy. In her element.

She was wearing scruffy, loose clothes, so unlike the dress he'd seen her in just forty minutes ago. Her face was open, relaxed. Was one of the Summer sisters Melanie's identical twin?

And yet he knew this was his Melanie. The same woman who'd had bikers eating out of her hand only yesterday.

"So Tristen Bell is into old boats?" she asked, coming over. Was she swaggering? He could swear that was a swagger. Why was she acting as though she had something on him?

She hated him. He'd seen it in her eyes, so why wasn't she avoiding him?

He glanced behind him, aware he was backing away.

"Funny," she said. "I hadn't guessed that—despite your truck. Although that thing is just *old*. Nothing like this boat." She did a little move as though she was a model showcasing the antique craft. He'd never seen a woman act sexier, even in that horrible old T-shirt that was much too large for her luscious form.

Which meant there was something wrong with Tristen's brain. Seriously wrong.

This woman had the potential to push him into something that could destroy him, and all he could do was stand there and smile.

Managing to snap out of the hold she seemed to have on him,

he said, "Was that a dig, Melanie Summer?" He sounded almost breathless, and cursed himself. Where was the suave dude he used to be? Had he inadvertently locked him away with his playmate—the monster side that had destroyed his life?

He couldn't be sure, but Melanie seemed half pleased to see him and half hopeful that she could find a way to shove him between the dock and boat, hold his head below the lake's surface and see how long it took him to drown.

The fact that her expression suggested his life was in imminent danger really shouldn't be a turn-on. But it was.

"A dig?" She placed a finger to her chin and stared upward, coy and cute. "Hmm. Possibly."

Oh, she was going to kill him. Definitely. Something scary had switched on within her and there was a flicker of the devil in her gaze. She wanted to get even for something. It was a look he'd received a lot back in Toronto for crossing people or signing contracts with new companies before his competitors even had a chance to say hello.

"They don't make them like they used to," he said, clearing his throat. He pointed to the boat in front of them. Then, hesitantly, and with enough time to second-guess himself, he jerkily leaned in to give her a light kiss on the cheek. "Good to see you."

She smelled good. Like cookies.

Her danger face melted and she blushed, unable to meet his eye. "You know it makes you sound like an old man when you say 'they don't make them like they used to.'"

He grinned. He knew he was supposed to stay away from her, but couldn't quite remember why.

Oh, right.

Land developments, possible relationship expectations, et cetera. She was so fun to toy with though. All he had to do was compliment her or show her a minor courtesy and she melted like sugar. The old Tristen would have used that against her in some way.

"I *am* an old man," he said. "Haven't you noticed?"

"Did you know that I happen to like older men? They are more stable and kind." She gave him a shrewd glance. "Usually."

"I thought you liked bikers."

"They'll do in a pinch, but I prefer men who are little more refined. And I must say, your manners are impeccable. Generally speaking."

There was a hazardous element to her words, but that flirty smile… She could punch him in the nuts, but if she gave him that smile he'd ask for a repeat.

Stupid, stupid man that he was.

His voice dropped. "Are you flirting with me, Melanie Summer?"

She turned away, addressing him over her shoulder. "Maybe."

Hello, flight control? Yeah, we have trouble on the runway. Despite being grounded it seems Tristen is gearing up for takeoff.

He took in her tatty outfit, carefully noting every worn detail. "You like old things?"

"I like things that are…*experienced.*" She turned back to him, not touching, but acting as though she would play with his necktie if he'd been wearing one. The idea did funny things to his groin.

"You are a beautiful and dangerous woman, Melanie. You would never need a man like me." He wanted to touch her, move close, tell the world that she was his and that this was their little corner of the planet, and to go away.

She laughed, a high flush dancing across her cheeks. "I'm just playing, Tristen. Besides, I'm sure you and your actions won't ever show up on anything but my hit list." She gave him a smile brimming with moxie, but something had changed her eyes. They looked less playful and devilish. More hurt somehow.

He pretended to pull a dagger out of his chest, while keeping a watchful eye on her. Maybe she didn't hate him, just the way he behaved.

Story of his life.

Had that aspect not changed despite two years of beating himself up over it?

"So, tell me, what do you like about antique boats?" She crossed her arms, suddenly serious as they stood shoulder to shoulder, facing the moored vessels.

"I'm sorry about Mr. Valos."

She gave a frown that brought her lips into a pout before she shook off his apology.

"So what do you like about them?" she insisted.

Tristen took a moment to change his focus from her and their games to the vessel in front of them. "They're like people."

"How so?" The crowd swelled and ebbed around them, bits of conversations floating past in waves. This was where he excused himself, found Dot, went home and didn't come out again until it was safe.

Likely around 2050.

Melanie's arms were still crossed protectively.

"Sometimes they shine in their age," he blurted. "They become better."

Damn. He hadn't meant to say something that sounded deep, but there was something about Melanie Summer that hit him hard enough to be uncomfortable. He wanted to learn more about her, but at the same time wanted to push her far away so he could breathe properly.

She nodded thoughtfully and went to sit on a nearby bench.

"Shouldn't you be at work?" Tristen sat beside her, arm draped across the backrest. So much for being able to breathe right. His arm wasn't around her, but he was close enough to feel the heat from her back seeping through the fabric of his shirt.

"I took the morning off."

"And what do *you* like about these old crafts?"

"Their stories," she said immediately. "Their history. They made it through when others didn't."

Why did it feel as though she was no longer talking about boats?

"Anyone ever tell you they can't talk?" he joked.

She swallowed hard, her neck lengthening as she jutted out her chin. "Shut up, Mr. Bell. You know what I'm saying."

"Sorry." The truth was that he did know. It just sounded hokey and he hadn't talked about anything real or deep in a very long time.

They sat in silence, the bench comfortable, just like the quiet between them. He wasn't quite sure what to make of it, seeing as she'd been angry with him only an hour ago.

"I thought you were done with developing?" Melanie stared at him, and he was fairly certain she was waiting for him to form a nervous tick, or generally reveal that he was, indeed, a lying schmo who wouldn't stand up for her.

Oh, wait. He'd already done that in Vincent's office.

"I am done," he said.

"Really?"

"Really."

"Then what about the land you were talking about with Mr. Valos?"

Tristen stretched his legs out in front of him, enjoying the shade from the large trees that grew on the grassy hill behind them. "Eavesdropping, Ms. Summer?"

"It was difficult not to when you were taking my appointment time." He could feel the anger from Vincent's earlier dismissal building within her again, and it was as though he was sitting on a volcano about to erupt. Time to bail.

No. He wasn't a chicken. He could use the old Tristen in a way that wasn't monstrous and stand up for himself.

"You took my appointment time and then didn't leave."

"I most certainly did not take your time." She drew herself up, eyes flashing. "And next time, grow some balls and be honest. If you don't want to help, then fine. But don't *lie* to me."

Oh, this chick was going down.

"For your information I am a *Realtor*, Melanie, and sometimes I inquire about zoning bylaws."

"And yet you can't give me advice about that sort of thing." She opened her small purse, pulling out her checkbook, voice cool as she said, "I see how this works."

"What are you doing?"

"You have to be paid to be helpful, obviously."

He took in their surroundings on the island, wondering how many of the people on the nearby sidewalks and docks were overhearing their conversation.

He stood, but didn't walk away. "I don't do that sort of stuff any longer." He squeezed his eyes shut when he saw the rejection in hers. "I'm sorry, Melanie. It's not about you. It's about me, okay?"

Dot loped out of the crowd, her sharp gaze taking in the two of them. Tristen slung an arm over his daughter's shoulders, pulling her into a half hug. She seemed both conflicted and happy by the embrace.

"Nice talking to you, Melanie," he said over his shoulder as he steered Dot away. They could take the path around the quieter side of the island where the small boat locks were located, then maybe take a shortcut up the hill past where the small museum was nestled, over the footbridge and then back to his truck and his much-needed solitude.

Dot planted her feet like Max did during hot-weather walks. "You didn't introduce me to your girlfriend."

Melanie quirked her head, then bent over, laughing.

Nice. Now he felt insulted. Why did this woman have to live on the same planet? Couldn't she move back to Mars or Venus, or wherever women were from?

"What's so funny?" he snarled. He tried to stare her down, but an elderly woman caught his attention as she moved toward him with her walker. Hitch the walker forward, drag the bum leg. Hitch, drag, hitch, drag. It was distracting. Especially given how she kept staring at him, unblinking. He stepped out of her path, but she deliberately turned toward him once again.

Not good.

Melanie, now standing, extended a hand to Dot. "I'm Melanie Summer. Pleased to meet you."

The old woman, now a foot away from them, cleared her throat.

"Oh, Mrs. Kowski!" Melanie bent over the walker, giving her a hug. "So lovely to see you."

"Did I hear you have a boyfriend?" the woman asked.

"No, ma'am, you most definitely did not," Melanie replied.

Tristen smiled. How many people called older women "ma'am" these days? Melanie had been raised right.

Mrs. Kowski glared at him and made a disgruntled sound. He reached out and shook her hand. "I'm Tristen Bell. Pleased to meet you."

"I'm sure the pleasure is all yours."

Ouch. A relation of Melanie's, perhaps? She had the same sharp tongue.

Mrs. Kowski started in on him. "What is wrong with you that

you won't take Melanie out for a lovely supper? A woman needs to enjoy as many good suppers as she can before they put her in a home and she's stuck eating strained peas and other foods that are affront to the term *meal*." She edged closer, almost nailing him with her walker. "You hear me, sonny?"

"Yes, ma'am."

"Mrs. Kowski," Melanie said. "The man will barely talk to me, let alone take me out for supper." She winked at Tristen. "He's always acting as though he's got a great big bug up his—"

"I talk to her," Tristen interrupted, clutching Mrs. Kowski's cool fingers. "Although I don't know why. And I do not have a bug up my—no. Never mind."

He was fighting for this crusty old woman's favor and wanting to win. Melanie Summer was trouble, all right.

"This is my daughter, Dot." He looked to Dot, hoping she would smile and charm the lady.

"You poor dear," Mrs. Kowski said to the silent teen. "*Daughter Dot.* Your father isn't one to think things through, is he?"

Dot smirked in collusion. Before Tristen could defend the name, Melanie was choosing sides, as well. "You poor thing."

"I resent that tone," he interjected.

"He made me have breakfast, and thinks that everyone should eat as much as he does."

Tristen bristled. Food habits were not good conversation territory for them right now. Getting her to finish her breakfast had just about done him in.

"I'd rather not talk about meals, thank you." Mrs. Kowski sniffed and headed for someone new to grouch at.

"I could tell you how to apply for legal emancipation," Melanie muttered to Dot out of the side of her mouth. "Then you can eat what you want, when you want."

"I heard that," Tristen said, trying to draw his daughter away.

"Really?" Dot's eyes grew rounder and she held her ground once again. "You know how to do that?"

"Please don't encourage her." What would Cindy do if Dot managed to pull that one off? He'd have to move farther away than Muskoka.

Melanie winked at him over Dot's head as the teen turned to glare at him.

"You know what legal emancipation is?" Melanie asked his baby girl, tempting her toward rebellion.

"I took a pre-law class in high school last year. I want to become a lawyer."

Melanie gave her a high five. "I'm a lawyer!"

"Get out!"

Yep. This was where things got bad.

Melanie grinned. "Which schools are you looking at?"

"I can't decide between McGill or Queen's."

"McGill? That's seven hours away." Tristen protested. Toronto was far enough. He needed Melanie to convince Dot that Queen's was the place to go, as it was only a little over four hours away.

Although, if every meal was like breakfast, he might just pack his daughter's bags and send her to school at the other end of the country.

"That's hardly far, Dad," Dot said with a smirk. "But I need more experience before I apply, as my marks aren't stellar. Something about being abandoned by my father a few years ago set me back." She whisked her shaggy mane out of her face to make sure both eyes could reach him with their death-ray glare.

"Yeah, not at the joking stage for that little misunderstanding yet," he muttered.

Melanie, as if sensing his desperate need to change the subject faster than a rocket could launch, asked, "Are you looking for a job or internship?"

"Either would be great."

"There might be an opening in my office." She pulled her phone from her shorts pocket and addressed Tristen. "Can I ask?"

"Oh my God!" Dot gave a little bounce that was completely at odds with her rocker chick style. She whirled toward him, hands clasped. "Please?"

He couldn't be the one to dash all that hope. And honestly, he hadn't seen his daughter this overjoyed since the trip to Disney World when she was seven.

But damn. More Melanie? That wouldn't end well for him.

Nevertheless, he gave a minuscule tip of his head, and Dot was in his arms, bouncing and squealing and generally making a scene, as well as bursting his eardrums.

"Thank you! Thank you!"

"Yeah, sure." He gave a sharp nod. "I'm going for ice cream. You coming?"

"Dad, teenage girls don't eat that kind of thing unless they're fat or something."

Melanie's cheeks flushed and she ducked her head so fast Tristen wanted to rewind the moment and erase it. A small voice in his head warned him not to acknowledge the comment, and to disappear. It was the same one that had told him to work harder when Cindy expressed that she needed more from him. It wasn't a very smart voice.

"Dot, just so you are aware, men don't like bitchy women. They like real women who don't mind putting food in their mouths."

Ah, man.

That didn't work.

His little parenting party had officially come to a grinding halt, and he was pretty sure he'd inadvertently offended Melanie while he was at it. He couldn't win, could he?

"I don't care about men," Dot snarled. "Don't you even *listen*?"

Her voice reached a crazy pitch and he cringed. Tilt-a-Whirl time. "Not that you care, I have a girlfriend now."

"So, I'll just text my boss and see what's available, shall I?" Melanie said, her voice tight.

"What? When?" he asked Dot. "I left you alone for twenty minutes."

"Just now." Her arms were crossed, her chin jutted. "Her name's Samantha."

"Um?" Melanie was still waiting.

"Sorry. Yes, Melanie," he said. "I appreciate it, and I'm sure my ungrateful daughter does, as well." He tugged Dot's arm, urging her away from what was quickly turning into a complete disaster.

"I do appreciate it, *Dad*." She dug in, refusing to budge. "I need to give Melanie my phone number. It's rude to just take off without even a goodbye."

"I didn't take off," he said, his voice tight with held back anger. "And I said goodbye."

"It's okay, I know your dad's number," Melanie said without looking up, her shoulders frozen in a way that told him she was trying to hide, so she wouldn't be dragged into their fight.

"You do?" The hope and curiosity in Dot's voice made him want to gag her.

"Yeah. A mutual friend gave it to me." She looked at him this time. Her eyes were different. Sad. Lonely. Rejected.

Again.

Who was he kidding? Melanie Summer sad, lonely, and rejected? Get real. She was nothing like him. She wasn't hiding away from the world. She was out there shaking things up.

Dot was staring at him, putting together random, unrelated pieces and undoubtedly believing that he was lying to her once again.

"I didn't just take off on you, Dot, so just leave it alone, okay?"

He stomped off, hoping she'd follow, so he wouldn't have to call Cindy and tell her he'd already lost their daughter.

TRISTEN TOOK A SEAT at his kitchen island as Dot grinned at him, momentarily forgetting the ice cream cone in her hand, and giving Max the opportunity to claim the melting treat with a well-timed flick of his jumbo-sized tongue.

Yes, Melanie had come through for his daughter, saving the girl's future with one text to her boss—a text that had just secured Dot a position as an intern.

And now Tristen owed Melanie.

In deeper by the moment.

Dot threw her arms around him, pulling him into a monster hug, before running to her room to text her friends about the turn in fate.

He looked at Max, who was eyeing Tristen's empty hands. "Sorry, pal. I ate my cone back in town."

The dog's brown eyebrows lowered and he dropped his hundred-pound frame to the floor with a thump that vibrated through the laminate flooring.

"How do you not break something when you do that?" Tristen muttered. Grabbing a handful of blueberries, he opened the patio door, trying to ignore the garbage barge speeding by. It was too small to be Shawn McNeil's. Plus Shawn always followed the speed limit, whereas this barge was trucking along as if rules didn't apply. Tristen went back inside for his phone, then dialed the number for the police.

"There's a large barge with demolition debris speeding through the bay outside Port Carling," he told the dispatcher. "The scrap is just about spilling into the water. Maybe it already has." Because of the way the barge was weighted down with the remains of an old cottage, its speed was that much more dangerous. Traffic near town was bad this time of day, especially with the boat show.

"We'll send out the marine patrol," the woman said before hanging up.

Tristen leaned against the deck railing. This was the second or third barge he'd noticed in the past day or so. He supposed the recession wasn't hurting people as badly as he'd thought, which would mean vacation properties might pick up again. Not a bad thing when a Realtor earned a decent commission, and most cottages in the area went for over a million hot ones.

He smiled and returned to the kitchen to sort out supper. He needed something good, celebratory, healthy, yet filling for a growing teenager. Something his daughter would eat without protest.

"What's her name again?" Dot asked, joining him in the kitchen, phone in hand.

"Melanie."

"Cool." She texted something, tucked the device away, then smirked. "Her name was right on your lips, wasn't it?"

"There's nothing between me and Melanie." He reached far into the fridge, maneuvering jars of pickles and jam out of the way.

"Why not?"

"Why should there be?"

"She didn't go running and screaming from you."

He pulled his head out of the fridge to stare at his daughter.

"Not much fashion sense, though."

"She has plenty." His tone was too curt, his defense too quick. He put his head back in the fridge, half wishing it was a gas oven.

"You totally owe her one. You should take her out for supper."

"Not going to happen."

"Why not?"

"She wants something from me."

"Ew! I didn't want to know that." The disgust on Dot's face made him smile. He was tempted to leave the misunderstanding in place for his own amusement, but knowing she would be spending a lot of time with Melanie, he didn't want inopportune comments popping out that might give the woman the wrong idea about him and his intentions.

Not that there were intentions. Other than to avoid her.

"She wants me to help stop a development. Advice and such, and I don't do that any longer. I'm happy with stonework."

Dot crossed her arms and twisted her lips doubtfully.

"I left the business. I'm here and have time now. Okay? I'm happy." He turned away and clanged some pots together. He *was* happy, dammit. He would continue to cut his old world from his new life—with the exception of Dot, of course—and it would remain just fine.

"You're a jerk."

"Hey!" He pointed a noodle scooper in her direction. "Watch your language."

"It's true. She totally just bailed you out and you can't sit down and tell her how to take down corporate Canada before they destroy the world? Nice, Dad. Real nice."

"I don't like your tone, young lady."

Dot stormed out and Tristen fought with the urge to go after her and yell until his voice grew hoarse. Instead, he sat at the table and clutched his head, because she was right. He was a jerk. However, where Melanie was concerned, he had absolutely no plans to remedy that fact.

Chapter Six

Melanie hunched over her computer and propped her head in her hand. Staying up late on Sunday night to create the presentation for Mr. Valos was finally catching up with her. Evidence: what had she been thinking, flirting with Tristen yesterday? He was the enemy. A big fat hot-and-cold, keep-to-himself, flustering, sweet hunk of man.

Oh, my. She was so doomed.

As she'd tried to sleep, his words about how antiques were like people and that they sometimes got better with age had repeated over and over again. If he hadn't said that, she was pretty sure she could have stayed mad at him. Instead, she'd jumped at the first chance to be helpful, and arranged an internship for his daughter, effective pretty much immediately. Something about cheap labor made her boss perk up. And of course, being lowest on the office totem pole, Melanie would be the one training Dot. Which actually worked out okay, seeing as the girl caught on quickly, giving Melanie hope that the two of them would find her desk's surface again. Under all the angst and dyed hair, Dot was actually kind of sweet.

"There's someone here to see you," the teen said, edging into Melanie's tiny office, her eyes round.

"Sorry, one day they will let the newbie have a bigger office."

Melanie, still seated, reached out with a leg to nudge a chair out of Dot's way.

Mrs. Star wanted to update her will in order to give her thrice-removed nephew, Benji Reiter over in Blueberry Springs, a share of the lawn ornaments she kept in front of her home. Melanie restacked the overstuffed file folders into a tower to her left, trying to carve out a space where she could take notes.

"You can send her in."

"It's, uh, not a her. It's a him," Dot whispered.

Aaron from Rubicore appeared in her doorway, a crisp black suit making him somehow look bigger. He was practically blocking out the feeble sunshine that made its way to her back office. Melanie wasn't sure why, but she got the impression that if this were a movie, he'd have blown her away with a bazooka by now.

"Hello." She walked around her desk and shook his hand. He squeezed hers too hard. Annoying. She needed to use those fingers to type. "Aaron Bloomwood, is that correct?"

"Yes." He turned and waved another man forward. A very large man. On a dog-to-human ratio he'd be a massive Newfoundland. "Your assistant said you are available."

Melanie checked her watch. "I have five minutes before my last client of the day."

"This is Mario LaToya, my personal assistant." Aaron gestured to the Newfoundland at his side. "Melanie Summer."

Mario nodded, his eyes so dark it was hard to know whether he was friend or foe.

She had a feeling he was more vicious junkyard dog than cuddly pound puppy.

Aaron took a seat while Mario remained by the door in a military "at ease" position. Melanie slipped behind her desk, feeling unexpectedly nervous.

"What can I help you with today?" She folded her hands, spine straight. "Oh, and I passed the invitation on to my sisters. Did Maya tell you we'd be pleased to attend? RSVP the four of us, please. Although she's not sure what the proposal is that you spoke of."

Aaron scowled. Not a big scary one, but big enough to show he was not pleased with her for some reason. Melanie would have thought he would be thrilled to hear the people he was trying to schmooze were willing to join the fun. You know, evil laughter, followed by fingertips being tapped together as the plan slipped into place.

"We were hoping to further discuss any concerns you have at the dinner prior to the party, but I hear you have immediate concerns." The scowl was gone, his face suddenly placid and friendly. Almost.

Melanie gave a noncommittal "Oh," and smiled encouragingly, hoping he'd show his cards. Or at least how many he was holding.

Impatience flickered across the man's face. "We would appreciate it if you talked to us if you have concerns. Allow us to alleviate them."

Melanie tilted her head as though confused.

Mr. Valos had ratted her out? But why?

Or was it Tristen? Maybe that was the reason he wouldn't help her—because he was already on the other team.

Dot hovered near the door and Melanie tipped her head, indicating she could close it. Instead, the girl continued to stand there, at a loss.

"We'd rather you and I discuss any issues you have," Aaron said, crossing his legs. "I am confident that reasonable people such as ourselves can come to an understanding without involving the municipality."

Mr. Valos. The sneak.

"I'll keep that in mind. Thank you for coming to see me." Melanie spun her chair to the side so her legs were out from under her desk. She placed her palm on a pile of folders and leaned forward, ready to stand, essentially dismissing him.

"I don't expect you to understand how cities, towns, townships, or other municipalities work, Ms. Summer. The paperwork and bureaucracy can become quite involved in a project of this magnitude. Our financiers could become upset if we encountered delays over something so small I could have resolved it with a simple conversation." Aaron stood, adjusting his suit jacket with a half laugh intended to suggest they were on the same side. "And you know how the government can be."

Mario puffed out his chest, arms crossed, legs wide apart. Those scary dark eyes still watching her every move.

"Oh, I didn't realize you had approval, Mr. Bloomwood. Congratulations."

Aaron smiled, not giving away whether he did or not. Damn.

"As a smart woman, you surely understand where I am coming from?" The developer leaned a bit closer. Not so much that he could be considered threatening, but with Mario behind him, that was definitely his goal.

Melanie laughed lightly. "Of course. I'm sure my sisters would love to have a chance to chat with you about the resort, and dinner is such a good idea." She held a hand against her chest, ignoring the fact that both men had moved closer. There really wasn't enough air in here. "And personally, I do wonder what will become of Heritage Row. It's so pretty, and I notice that one of the cottages is already gone. Only three left. Such a shame."

"It had termites."

"Oh, I didn't realize they came this far north. We'd better get our place checked. Thank you for the heads-up."

Aaron placed a hand on her desk, obviously seeing through

her charade. He met her eyes with a forceful glare. "Don't go to the municipality, Ms. Summer. Come to us."

Melanie swallowed hard, trying not to allow her smile to vanish the way the saliva in her mouth had.

"Ms. Summer? There's someone here to see you," Dot said, her voice wavering. Melanie sighed in relief at the interruption. Talk about timing.

She caught a flash of black leather in the doorway. Had Mrs. Star gone for a makeover or was this yet another unexpected visitor?

"Send her in," Melanie called to Dot. "These men were just leaving."

Instead of Mrs. Star, Ezra the biker from the Steel Barrel pressed his way into the small room, blocking Aaron's and Mario's exit. "Everything okay, Melanie?" His low voice rumbled with a warning that sent a wave of both fear and relief spiraling through her bloodstream.

"These men are leaving. Thank you, Ezra."

The biker narrowed his eyes, legs planted hip-width apart.

"Move," Aaron snapped. He took a step forward, but the biker didn't budge.

"I do hope you weren't harassing this young woman." Though Ezra was shorter than Aaron and Mario, Melanie had no doubt he could take them out in a truly gory fashion.

Rubicore's front man glared, pushing past Ezra, who still didn't move, causing Aaron to bounce off him and hit the door on his way out. Melanie bit her bottom lip to hide her amusement. Mario, following his boss, flashed her a curious, reassessing glance.

When the two men were gone, Ezra shut the door with a bang, and it bounced back open again. He took a seat across from Melanie, who had collapsed into her chair.

"You let me know if they're a problem and I'll take care of them."

"Thank you." She wasn't going to question how, just take solace in the fact that someone would keep her safe if need be. Not that she thought she might need to take him up on the offer, of course. Aaron was just being a pushy prick. Which told her exactly what she needed to know. There was a way to stop them, or at least seriously impede their progress.

She could take them down, but unlike yesterday morning, when she'd wanted to show Tristen that she could do it on her own, she knew she was going to need help. Plenty of it.

"What can I do for you, Ezra?"

"I need a divorce."

"I don't specialize in divorce law, but I could recommend someone for you." She flipped through her drawer for the business card of a local divorce lawyer.

"I want you."

Melanie glanced up in surprise. His voice was unexpectedly soft.

Standing behind him was Tristen, arms slack at his sides. He blinked, closed his mouth and stepped into the room.

Well, it looked as though everyone was coming to visit her today. Lucky duck. She knew she should have worn something more fun than her boring gray pantsuit. Not that she had anything more fun. She might have to break down and ask Simone for another dress, despite herself.

Melanie moved around her desk to usher Tristen out. "I'm sorry, Mr. Bell. I'm with a client at the moment. If you're here to pick up Dot, she can leave early."

Tristen's gaze flicked between her and the biker, who was sitting back, hands folded over his small paunch.

"Is this man bothering you, Melanie?" Tristen asked.

Was he kidding? Today was turning into pissing match after pissing match. There had to be something in the water, or else a bright, flashing sign outside saying Come On In and Mess Up Melanie's Day. "No, he is not." She enunciated the words carefully, not wanting to offend Tristen by pointing out how utterly ridiculous he was being.

"Oh my God, Dad," Dot said, joining her father in the doorway. "This guy just totally scared away some jerks who were giving Ms. Summer a hard time."

Tristen's face flushed red and he came closer to Melanie, making her step back. "Is that true?"

"What is this? Protect Melanie Day?" She gave a nervous laugh and moved behind her desk again.

"Some developer trying to silence the girl, I'd say," the biker drawled. "That the truth, Miss Melanie?"

She sighed and nodded. That about summed it up, although it sounded much more sinister coming from him. It kind of made her hands shake a tiny bit, something that her knees seemed to want to get in on as well.

Tristen was staring at her, his fists clenched at his sides, a vein in his forehead throbbing.

"She held her own," the biker said.

"Ezra helped," Melanie added.

Tristen was around her desk in a flash, his fingers gripping into her shoulders, his brow wrinkled with what could only be worry. "Did they threaten you?"

Ezra was up and cramming himself into the small space behind her desk as Tristen gave her a small shake to get an answer out of her. "Did they?"

"Back off," the biker warned.

Melanie wrenched her arms from Tristen's grasp, pushing her chair backward as anger rushed through her veins, setting her on fire. "You don't want anything to do with Rubicore, so bugger off and mind your own business. I can take care of myself."

"You're in over your head."

"At least I'm trying to make things better, and not running off scared."

"You need help."

"I don't need help, thank you very much." She crossed her arms. "I can do this without you."

"No, I don't think you can."

"Really? And what exactly are you going to do for me, Tristen Bell?"

He rushed from the room, his face a fireworks display of conflicting emotions, leaving Melanie to scratch her head.

"Wow, okay," she said with a laugh.

"You're a real jerk," Dot called after her father, before following him.

So Tristen was going to run away again. Why should Melanie expect anything different from the man?

She addressed Ezra. "Sorry about all that."

"So, can you help me?" the biker asked.

"Technically, yes. But I think someone who specializes in divorce would be better, if it isn't an amicable split." She dug out a few forms. "Whoever you decide to go to, filling these out ahead of time will help keep the costs down, since lawyers bill by the hour."

Mrs. Star appeared in the doorway, smiling and cradling a garden gnome. Grand Central Station had nothing on Melanie's office this afternoon.

"Hello, dear. Oh, I'm sorry. You're with Ezra. How are you, sweetie?" Mrs. Star reached into the room to rest a hand on his leather-covered shoulder. "Is your mother's ankle okay? I heard she had a spill."

"She's fine, thank you." He stood and offered Mrs. Star his seat. "I'm sorry I'm late, Melanie."

"Am I interrupting your appointment?" Ezra asked.

"Of course you are, my dear. I am not some Hells Angel waltzing in and expecting to be served, due to my intimidating behaviour."

Ezra gave a good-natured laugh and bowed gallantly. "My apologies, Mrs. Star."

"Are you here to get rid of that wife of yours? I heard the two of you were separating."

"I'm afraid so."

"Elsie owes me five dollars," the older woman announced triumphantly. "That's my sister," she added for Melanie's benefit. "She's over in Blueberry Springs, and says it's the best place on earth." Mrs. Star gave a snort. "That place has nothing on Muskoka. Wouldn't you say?"

Melanie slipped the divorce lawyer's business card into Ezra's hand, in case he changed his mind about hiring someone who knew what he or she was doing. At the same time, she studiously avoided Mrs. Star's attempt to get her involved in the ongoing battle between the woman and her absent sister.

The biker shut the door on his way out and Melanie relaxed. Back on schedule and back to normal.

"What was the kerfuffle out there about someone harassing you?" Mrs. Star asked with a severe look, almost daring Melanie to hide the truth.

"The developer out on Baby Horseshoe Island wanted to discuss things, that's all. He'd rather I chat with him before talking to Mr. Valos."

Mrs. Star snorted. "Mr. Valos couldn't help you save his own life. Now, what about that fellow yelling in the parking lot? What's he about?"

"What fellow?"

"He was yelling at two men, saying they needed to leave you alone." Mrs. Star was practically aquiver. "Does he like you? Is he your man? A fine fellow, defending you like that. Mrs. Kowski said there was a guy eyeing you at the boat show." Melanie's client pressed a palm against her bosom, eyes twinkling.

"There wasn't a guy eyeing me. Was the man outside with a teenage girl?" she asked, barely daring to let herself hope that much.

"Yes." Mrs. Star leaned forward, eager for her to confide all.

Melanie sagged into her chair with a sigh. Why was Tristen protecting her? Or was he only protecting Dot?

"He said they needed to leave you be because you were a lone woman and wouldn't cause them any problems."

"He did, did he?" She leaned forward again. Well, she might just have to show Tristen Bell that he shouldn't underestimate her. Just because he wasn't going to help her didn't mean she was going to roll over and not make a difference in this world.

TRISTEN SAT ON THE DOCK and closed his eyes, nudging Max's heavy body off his warm feet. What was Melanie getting herself into with Rubicore? And having a member of the Hells Angels defending her? The woman was in over her head and didn't even realize it. Normally, Tristen would walk away, but with his daughter working so closely with Melanie and rubbing elbows with her dangerous acquaintances, she could become a target, or worse.

He squelched the urge to take action, to destroy the enemy by any means, and in the process ground his jaw so hard a tension headache formed.

Dot paddled over on her pink inner tube, sporting the anklet he'd bought her for her thirteenth birthday. He'd almost forgotten about it. He'd spent hours looking for just the right item. A chain that was delicate, yet wouldn't break if she acted like a kid; a heart charm that was classy, but still spunky. Something she could wear anywhere, anytime, any age.

But maybe not swimming. He debated asking her to take it off, but was worried that, if she did, it might slip between the boards of the dock and be lost forever.

"You don't have to watch me, you know," she called. "Mom lets me swim alone."

"I happen to like hanging out on my dock, thank you very much."

"Holy grouchy pants. What worm crawled up your—"

"Don't use that tone," he warned.

"So, you enjoy sitting here, scowling at the trash barges going by?"

"I'm not scowling." He relaxed the muscles that were pinching his mouth.

"Yes, you are. You glare at them while they pass."

"Have you looked in the bay?" It was only a few hundred feet across, really just a cottage-lined bulge in the river before it wove its way through the Port Carling locks and into Lake Muskoka. "They're dropping debris, which is going to wash up on my shore. How am I supposed to get a thirty-foot fir beam out of the water?"

Dot shrugged, her attitude back. "Who cares?"

"I do."

"Then help Melanie stop the development. And I mean more than just yelling at those bullies in suits."

Tristen tried to pry his hands out of the fists they'd formed, but found he couldn't. The tension had spread all the way down to his thighs.

"Chicken?" she taunted.

He stood up, hoping to walk off the anger ripping through his muscles, making them burn. "You work for her, but I don't appreciate you getting involved with her development battle. You need to stay out of it, as it does not concern you."

"They're dropping stuff in the water I'm swimming in." His daughter's head tilted in a haughty challenge.

"Don't you dare get involved in this!" Realizing he'd moved to the edge of the dock and was glaring down at her, giving her the reaction she'd feed upon, he stepped back and forced himself to cool it.

Dot's fingers tightened on the edge of the dock as she bobbed in the wake from one of the barges. "Why are you being such a dick? You could squash Rubicore in, like, five seconds."

"Don't talk to me that way, young lady."

The teen gave an angry snarl, rolled off her tube and swam away.

"Stay close to shore."

He judged the distance between her and the barges. Given the location of the cottage on the outside curve of the bay, she had plenty of room before she ended up where the boat traffic naturally turned on its way in and out of town. But still, it was hard to see a swimmer, especially one far from shore.

Tristen checked his cell phone for reception, took off his watch and shoes, removed the small, polished black stone he carried in his pocket to remind himself that power, prestige, and wealth didn't equal a life worth living, and kept an eye on Dot in case she needed help. Having a teenager was going to make him prematurely gray.

That and the way Melanie kept popping into his life, taunting him to step into the world he'd left behind. He was a stoneworker now. One on the brink of being able to ditch selling houses, and start doing it full-time without digging into his billion-dollar nest egg. Call him crazy, but he felt the need to start this new life without his old money tainting it. An all new Tristen was being formed and he didn't need anyone or anything distracting him from the goals he'd set out for himself.

Dot continued to swim, rolling into a fluid back crawl, making her way toward shore, where the water was dark, shaded by tall trees. The exertion would hopefully work off the excess surliness and she'd return to the land of the normal. Then, he'd suggest she find a different law office to work in.

When Dot was close enough for him to holler at, he called, "How does someone with a stroke like that fail gym class?"

She pulled her head out of the water, not even out of breath as she replied, "What?" The snarky note in her voice was still there.

"Keep swimming, kid."

A few shingles nailed to a board drifted by, and he stooped to scoop it out. Max came over to inspect the object and Tristen found himself hoping Melanie would manage to put some stops and checks on the developer, if nothing else. Rubicore didn't care about the surrounding area, only their bottom line. And in a quaint, historic area such as Muskoka, it was a shame they should be allowed to act that way.

Dot's regular splashing faltered and she let out an anguished cry, which had her choking on water. Tristen went on alert, perching himself on the dock's edge, ready to dive in, arms out for balance as he watched for further signs of distress. As Max barked at his side, he mentally calculated Dot's location, in case she went under.

"Are you okay?" he hollered.

"No! I'm stuck to something!" Her voice was high with panic, her eyes huge. Tristen's legs burned with adrenaline as he shoved off the dock in a dive, arching far across the water in hopes of getting to her faster.

Then he was splashing across the lake, the inner tube under his arm, the weight of his clothes slowing him down as his cargo shorts' pockets filled with water. The tube interfered with his movements so he clipped its seam between his teeth and backstroked to where his daughter was treading water, struggling to keep her head above the waves.

"There's something under the water," she gasped as he came closer. Her eyes were black with panic. "It's caught my anklet."

"It's okay. I have you now." He pushed the tube toward her but she flailed, knocking it away as she went under. He grabbed her around the waist, trying to hold her up as he stretched for the tube, which was dancing away in the breeze. They went under together. Tristen kicked hard, his legs screaming. They were going down, along with whatever she was caught on.

He let go of her to try and dive, but she scrambled against him, hugging him so hard he lost the breath he'd been holding.

The water was deep, the bottom coming closer by the second. His foot hit a dark object under Dot. The fir beam he'd been griping about had decided it was time to sink to the rocky depths with his daughter attached.

Tristen twisted away from her, letting her use her energy against him as he bent to grab her leg. He yanked.

Nothing.

He was out of air. Dot's struggles were weakening. He shoved her arms out of his way and grabbed her ankle, bracing his feet on the old beam. It was too dark to find the clasp to her anklet. He yanked again. Then harder. Why had he bought such a strong chain? He was going to hurt her if he wasn't careful.

He fumbled through the darkness, unable to find what the anklet was caught on.

Dot was barely moving. He couldn't lose her. Not like this. Not ever.

He braced himself against the beam, knowing this would hurt Dot, but that it might be their only chance. Wrapping his hands around her ankle in hopes of minimizing the damage, he gave one last vicious tug, using his legs as leverage. The anklet broke beneath his grip.

She was free!

Kicking hard, Tristen pushed past his daughter, snagging her as he burst to the surface, her limp body clutched against him.

Tristen gasped and sputtered. His lungs fought to take in the sudden oxygen; his muscles speared by pain. Shore. He needed to get to shore.

His body weak, he kicked as hard as he could, heaving great gulps of air as he dragged Dot to land. After carrying her over the rocks set along the shoreline, he collapsed onto a bed of pine needles lowering her to the ground.

Her eyes were closed, her lips not nearly as pink as they should be. His fingers fumbled to find a pulse. He lowered his ear to her chest and checked for breathing.

"Come on, Dot. Breathe. Don't die." *Please don't die.*

Movement. Her chest expanded.

He rolled her onto her side, unable to take his eyes off the pulse at her neck, her nostrils' slight flutter.

Wake up.

After an excruciatingly long series of seconds that had him praying to every god he'd ever heard of, she stirred slightly. Then nothing. Max came thundering over, crashing into Dot. He barked twice, then licked her face. She coughed and sputtered, her eyes opening. Then she let out a wail, and Tristen crushed her against his chest as she sobbed in terror.

"I have you, Dot. I have you. It's okay."

Max nosed his head between them, licking Dot's face.

Tristen checked her over as he held her. The leg that had been caught was bleeding from a long gash, and there was an oozing, angry welt where he'd tugged off her anklet.

His baby girl.

He hefted her, Max barking at his side, and spun to head up the hill to his truck. "I'm taking you to the hospital."

A large wail escaped her.

"Are you hurt anywhere other than your leg?"

She clung to his wet shirt, her hands in fists. The water she wrung out of the fabric trickled down his chest. He wanted to shake her, get a full sentence, so he could slow his storming heartbeat and know she was safe.

"Are you hurt?"

She let out a sob, her body shaking in residual fear.

Tristen tightened his grip and hurried his pace. Someone was going to pay for this.

TRISTEN HELPED DOT into the law office. She had needed twenty-four stitches to her foot and ankle due to the developer's negligence, and it had taken every scrap of willpower Tristen possessed not to go marching over to Melanie's and ask her to start a lawsuit against Rubicore, even though it was almost midnight by the time the doctor had set them free.

Melanie wanted action? Well, now that Dot had been hurt, there was going to be plenty of action. And not just from Tristen. His girl was fired up and ready to take on the world, as well.

Look out, Rubicore.

"Oh, my." Melanie rushed to help Dot as the girl hobbled into the office's entry. "What happened to you?"

"I got caught," she replied in a shaky voice. "On some trash that fell off Rubicore's barge."

"Rubicore?" Melanie met Tristen's gaze.

"We're pretty sure," he said.

"It was under the water," Dot continued. Her vulnerability tore him up, and he had to suppress the urge to punch something in hopes of making the helpless feeling go away. "We need to go get them, Melanie. We need to make them pay. My dad is right—they have to clean up their mess."

Melanie cut him another glance. She was in one of those 1950s dresses again, blue this time, with white accents, and it was as sexy as all get out. His eyes kept being drawn to her cleavage, which was tasteful exposed, but ultimately a sexy curve that made him want to get her naked.

He had to be hard up for a lay. It was the only reasonable answer. Two years of abstinence was finally doing him in, because he was seriously considering a woman that a smart man would not take to bed. Melanie was not a one-night-stand sort of gal. She was the other kind. The kind he was definitely not seeking and therefore should not be eyeing.

They were waiting for him to speak, their expectation tangible.

"What?" he asked.

"Are you going to help?" Dot plunked her hands on her lips, that scary teenage persona flickering to the surface.

"Sure, let's get you over to your desk." He helped her along, purposefully misunderstanding her meaning, doubts niggling his mind. If he got into this Rubicore mess with Melanie at his side he would ruin everything. And he wasn't referring to Rubicore. He'd crush the developer, of course, but he couldn't be that dashing hero for Melanie and still be the man he wanted to be. The man he was now. The man who wanted Melanie, a sexy, smart woman, to desire him as badly as he feared he desired her.

Doomed. That was the word for it.

"No." Dot stopped moving. "Help with the development." She gave him an assessing glance, then reached for the killer ammo. Like an illegal arms dealer, she pulled the pin on his soft side's grenade. The hurt child card. Helpless, he watched it roll in. "They hurt me, Daddy."

Daddy.

Crap.

He was officially a ruined man.

"I know, Dot. But we…I—"

"What's the excuse, buster?" Melanie had moved up on him, arms crossed, fury pumping below her unflawed skin.

Double crap. He used to play hockey, but he hadn't seen his opposition closing in on him, ready to take him down. "Look, I don't have the puck, okay? So go after someone else."

Melanie narrowed her eyes. "You can't put the rookie with no experience on the ice and expect her not to get creamed. The team needs an experienced coach."

Triple crap. She was using sports analogies now? Add sprinkles and a cherry on his I'm-completely-and-utterly-screwed sundae.

He looked to Dot. She, too, needed him to be the man he'd become, not the monster he used to be. The man who could make her laugh and not scowl all the time. A father who was there. Not the man who strived to win at any cost.

Maybe he could sue Rubicore from afar.

"We need you, Daddy." Dot pulled on his arm, her eyes big. "We need you to be the scary guy who takes them down. We can't do it without you."

Both women might be harmless in appearance, but he knew they had a hard underside of manipulation and strength. While they were softening him, they were no match for an experienced manipulator like Rubicore, whose administrators had money, power, and prestige on their side and could buy out anyone—and likely already had.

Melanie and Dot couldn't do it on their own, could they?

"Imagine who else is going to get hurt if we don't stop them. I can't even go swimming anymore. What if something happens to Max? Or Melanie's kids?"

"I don't have kids."

"Who is going to stop them, Dad?"

Okay, first of all, it didn't have to be him. Anyone could raise a ruckus.

"We need you. You know what to do."

Unfortunately, that was true.

"We only have one chance. Time is limited," Melanie added quietly.

They were dog-piling him.

"I'm sure the municipality will do something," he replied.

"I called them this morning and I got a brush-off." Dot's chin jutted out and trembled. "You said you'd help. You said you wanted to crush their skulls like they were canned salmon bones." Her eyes brimmed with tears.

Oh, no. Not the tears.

He edged toward the door.

"You know people in the municipality, right, Tristen?" Melanie asked softly. She was following him. Stalking him with her pretty, sweet, and innocent persona. Nonthreatening but completely dangerous.

He *was* being a jerk saying no, and by now he had probably learned how to manage the monster he kept bound in the attic if he only helped in the background, right?

"We need you, Daddy."

His daughter needed him. How could he ever convince himself there was a choice in the matter? If she needed him, he was in. End of story.

Chapter Seven

This was bad.

Tristen had changed his tune and was eager to help, which was good, but he'd turned into an impossible bossy pants who wanted to take over and be in control.

"We need to get someone who can make sure they perform due diligence. Like a watchdog committee," he said, leaning against the couch back, making himself comfortable here in Trixie Hollow. They'd left Dot at the movie theater with her new girlfriend Samantha and had done a motorboat drive-by of Baby Horseshoe, seeing frustratingly little despite hearing loud machines working in the island's woods. They'd decided on a Nymph Island stopover to try and come up with a game plan.

"How do you find a person like that?" Melanie took off her glasses and rubbed them on the skirt of her dress.

Tristen stared at the fireplace's stonework, seemingly lost for a moment.

"Out here, in the middle of nowhere?" he said finally, coming back around. "Not sure, exactly."

Melanie sighed, wishing the frustrating man didn't smell awesome. She'd been ecstatic when he'd agreed to help, but now he was withdrawing, becoming distant and professional. She wanted the man who had charmed her at the boat show, the man with the passionate glimmer in his eye when an injured Dot had convinced him to help.

Part of Melanie wondered if he was having second thoughts about working with her.

She walked to the screen door that led out to the veranda and listened for a moment. "How can they possibly have a permit to be doing whatever they are doing over there? I haven't seen a thing in the municipal news."

"I'll write a letter to the council that you can use as your own," Tristen said, moving back to the garbage issue he seemed so stuck on.

"Why can't it have your name on it?"

"I thought you wanted to be the head of this project?"

"Why don't you want Rubicore to know you're involved?"

Tristen wouldn't meet her eyes as he began typing on his laptop. "I think you should also set up a few meetings to find out what is really going on."

"Mr. Valos still thinks I'm a useless teenager. We need someone with more sway." She gave him a pointed look, which was lost on him.

"I'm going to talk to the bylaw officer about the trash issue. I'll take the concerned-father approach."

"What can we do about the heritage they are surely destroying over there?"

"The garbage issue is long-term, Melanie."

"So is heritage."

"They are still going to be hauling trash once the resort is open. It's not something we want to see or have falling into our water."

"And the other environmental issues? Such as destroying habitat, creating noise and light pollution? This is a dark-skies area. Has that been considered in their plans? Will I be able to look at the stars with Tigger or will they have too many security lights running so we can't see the heavens? They'll totally denude the place of shady trees, I'm sure, and then have to run noisy air conditioners. Sound carries across the water. And a golf course—they're hard on the environment, especially along the shore. How did anyone approve that? Just the fertilizer and pesticides running off into nesting areas are enough to make me want to scream and lie down in front of a bulldozer." She sat down in a huff beside him, arms crossed. "I could go on, you know."

Tristen took a long, slow breath. "You're not going to stop this development, Melanie. The best you can do is ensure they stay accountable and follow the rules."

"Look at what they're doing! And nobody has the teeth or the backbone to stop them." She stood again, her anger exploding. "Why are you even here? For the stupid garbage issue? Because that's like asking someone to repaint a car that's going to crash into everyone's lives. You're going to pull out as soon as they clean up the bay, aren't you?"

Tristen's jaw tightened and he flexed his hands, finally settling them into fists on his knees.

"Oh, my word. You are." She wanted so badly to shake him her arms hurt from the effort of holding herself back. "I thought you were a real man, Tristen Bell. I can't believe you were going to use me like that."

He glanced up, eyes wide with surprise. "No. Melanie, I wasn't."

"You're not even one bit committed to stopping Rubicore. You've given up and rolled over." She leaned closer, his amazing scent wafting over her. "Are you committed to helping me, or not?"

"Melanie, I can't give you what you need. I can't be here all the time. I have a job."

"I asked you to *help* me. To do more than tell me things I already know, and write some lame letter."

He stood slowly, like a spring whose tension was gradually being released. "You asked for advice. I'm giving you advice. You can't attack all of those things without engaging in a massive all-out battle that will overtake my life."

"*You're* life?"

"Yours, too. Dot's. Everyone's. You don't have time to take that on. Taking this on is a full-time job for at least ten people with an incredible amount of knowledge and connections."

"You're telling me to give up."

"I'm telling you how you can achieve small wins."

"You've underestimated me, Tristen Bell. I am in this for more than a cleanup day at Rubicore's expense. I'm in this to play hardball."

"Rubicore plays dirty. They're big, smart, and have done this so many times they know every loophole there is. Take my advice and look for ways you can win something against them."

"I'm not doing this to validate myself. I'm shutting them down, do you understand?"

"Melanie, you can't."

"Yeah, well, if you don't believe...leave. I'm tired of people thinking I'm a nobody." She pointed to the door, her muscles trembling with adrenaline.

"You asked for advice and I'm giving it."

"You heard me. Commit to my plan to oust Rubicore or get out of my cottage."

"Listen to me." He held her arms as though he feared she was going to run away. "A company like Rubicore has so much money and power behind them—"

"I still believe in the power of grassroots movements, democracy, the legal system, and the power of right and wrong over money. I'm sorry you don't. Now, I'll ask you again. Please leave."

"You gave me a ride here."

She chucked her cell phone at him. "Call a water taxi."

"Melanie..."

"I don't want to hear it unless you are going to commit to showing these guys some teeth."

He lowered his brows, looking torn and broken. He stared at her phone for a few seconds, then with a sad shake of his head, carefully tapped in the number for the water taxi.

MELANIE WIPED THE TEARS from her cheeks. She was silly, getting upset over Tristen, but as usual she'd expected too much, got her hopes up, and boom. There it was: a man who wasn't that interested and wasn't able to support her in the way she needed.

Oh, but how his cheeks had created those dreamy lines on either side of his mouth when he'd frowned at her.

Melanie smoothed her new dress over her knees—Simone had insisted she take it as a gift—and wondered what she should do next. Save the cottage? Figure out how to take Rubicore down?

At least she and Tristen had discovered early on that they couldn't work together. It would have been awful if she'd gone to lean on him and found he wasn't there.

Sitting on the floor, she opened the old steamer trunk they left behind the couch facing the fireplace, and inhaled its aged smell. History. So much history. She stroked its dinged metal edges, then reached in to pull out her favorite item. Old letters scented with dust and adventure. It had been years since she'd last looked through the trunk, and she placed the bundle of old letters addressed to her great-grandmother in her lap, ready to enjoy the guilty pleasure of reading someone else's business and being swept away to another time.

The sloping handwriting of her great-grandmother's male pen pal had become familiar over the years and Melanie's eyes quickly adjusted to its swirls and the faded ink, making it easy to decipher.

She used to read the letters simply because they were a tie to her great-grandmother, Ada, and not because they made a lot of sense—not without her grandmother's side of the story. Skimming the first letter on top of the stack, Melanie sighed. This was a man who was committed. He was discussing a project they shared and how they were going to break ground in the spring. The letter writer was likely from northern Ontario, as he kept calling what must have been a cottage a "camp." Melanie flipped the envelope over, squinting at the postmark. Illegible. She read the signature again. That was tricky, because it looked as though it said Stewart Baker. But that was ridiculous. The only Stewart Baker she knew of had been an old Canadian movie star in black-and-white films—a man she'd heard about only recently. There would be no reason for a man like him to write to her great-gran about how they were building a cottage. Melanie laughed at the way her heart was racing. Ever the romantic.

Despite feeling silly, she skimmed another letter for clues that the pen pal was *the* Stewart. Nothing. A slight reading on the Swoonalicious Scale, but that was about it. The next letter mentioned Muskoka and a weekend spent at Windermere House. Another needle bump on the scale, but no real clues. Was this man the father of her illegitimate grandmother?

Melanie carefully set everything back in the trunk and stood, barely daring to breathe so she wouldn't break the pieces that were trying to float together in her mind. Standing, she grabbed her purse and the boat key. There was one easy way to find out if

Stewart Baker, the movie star, had spent time in the area. And if he had, then maybe, somehow, she could pin historical significance on the cottage and save them a few tax dollars.

Relieved to see Tristen wasn't still waiting on the dock for the water taxi, Melanie climbed into the family's Boston Whaler and set out across the water. She docked at the island where the museum stood, and climbed the small hill to see what she could discover.

"Stewart Baker, huh?" asked the curator, her longtime friend Christophe.

"Yeah. Do you have anything on him? Did he vacation here?" She held her breath, knowing her hopes would be unrealistically dashed if the letter-writing Stewart was merely a random man. And she had only half an hour to find out before Christophe locked up for the day.

"He did."

"For real? The movie star?"

Christophe nodded, his floppy hair dropping into his hazel eyes.

Melanie paused, thinking. She still needed proof whether the letters to her great-grandmother were actually from the movie star, especially since none of them mentioned movies, fame, or a career.

"Do you have any letters with his signature, by chance?" she asked.

"I don't think so. I'll check the archives. I have a few photos of him in there that I can dig out, for sure. In the meantime, why don't you start over there?" He pointed to a display a few feet away. "With last year's short documentary on old-time movie stars, I put up a few of the better photos of him and some other celebrities."

"What documentary?"

"It was on the CBC. It may be still viewable from their website." Christophe adjusted his glasses on his long nose. "Say, are you putting anything in the antique show this weekend? Daphne told me your collection is rotting in cardboard boxes."

"It's not rotting."

"I could sell a few things at my table if you'd like." He gave her a wink, tucking his shirttails into his droopy trousers. He'd been trying to curb her "hoarding habit" for years, telling her that antiques were valuable only if you sold them.

"Ha, ha." She gave a weak smile, trying to work through the tightness that had developed in her chest. If she sold her antiques collection she might be able to foot her portion of the tax bill for Nymph Island, but it wouldn't be easy parting with the old friends. And yet she knew she would do it without barely a second thought. Poor Hailey had carried the burden of their cottage for too long. It was time to step up and help out in any way she could. If Melanie had to declutter in order to do so, then so be it. It would be worth it. Her sisters and the memories held on Nymph island were worth more than any antiques. There would always be more to collect. There wouldn't always be a cottage that brought them all together.

"Yeah, I might," she said, finally.

Christophe's eyes widened and he hurried off to the archives, taking a second glance over his shoulder as though she was something to fear. It almost made her laugh.

"Yeah, I know," she called. Desperate times called for desperate measures.

The curator disappeared through a door and Melanie turned to find Tristen standing close, his phone held up for her to see.

She took a step back, hand on her chest.

He waved his phone, saying nothing.

She peered at the encyclopedia page displayed there, trying to stay as far away from the man as possible.

Stewart Baker. Tristen had looked up the man she was investigating? Was that creepy or charmingly helpful? And why hadn't she thought to pop the movie star's name into a search engine? Unsure, she glanced at Tristen, but found his expression unreadable. Grabbing the phone so she could scroll, she read about Stewart's life, death, and career.

"It was at the right spot," Tristen said. "Before you scrolled." His hazel eyes were flecked with a gold she only ever saw on the rims of her antique teacup collection. He gave her a tiny smile, as though they were having a secret conversation. Then he gave a small nod, at her questioning glance, and she knew. Tristen understood. What, exactly, she wasn't sure, only that he understood.

She handed him the phone, not finishing the article. "Why are you here, eavesdropping on my conversations?"

"I wasn't ready to go home."

"So, you followed me?"

"Actually, I was here first. I thought maybe *you* were following *me*. Came to apologize, perhaps?"

She let out a snort, her cheeks burning with sudden anger. "A little full of yourself, perhaps?"

His lips thinned. "Look. I know what I'm doing with this. You want me to help, then do it my way. Don't waste my time because your pride sits in the way."

"My pride?" She threw her head back and laughed. "You are such a big chicken it isn't even—"

He grabbed her cheeks in his roughened hands and pressed his lips to hers, hard. Her eyes flew open, heart racing. He was kissing her. Tristen Bell was kissing her, and my word. It felt good. Really freaking good. She reminded herself to shut her eyes, and once she did, she was lost. Her body fell against his, her palms mirroring the way he was holding her face, latching him against her until she was ready for him to stop. Which would probably be never. The kiss deepened and her hands drifted down from his face to his chest. Her fingers stopped when they hit his belt. He was a trim, lean, solid piece of rock from the neck down. As hard as the rocks Dot said he worked with. And Melanie wasn't even talking about that something between his legs that was nudging up against her thighs.

Holy macaroni.

Tristen stepped back, breaking their kiss. Her eyelids fluttered, unable to fully open after having her circuits blown.

"I'm willing to help you, Melanie, but it has to be on my terms. I can be a valuable member of your team."

Team. She didn't even have a team. Well, she had Dot who was eager, but inexperienced. Daphne, who seemed less and less interested in charging off after Rubicore in regards to the environmental impact, and Maya spouting off about economics, and Hailey lost behind her camera, thinking photos would save the day. Melanie sucked as a leader, if that was her team. They didn't even have a game plan and she was not taking Tristen's, which was to play helpless and get steamrolled.

"Do you want me to be part of your team, Melanie? Yes or no?"

There was an edge to his voice that made her turn her back to him. She threw up her hands, wondering if kisses would be part of his terms. "Whatever. Okay, whatever. I don't care, just don't ask me to roll over and play dead."

"Stewart Baker built one of the cottages on Baby Horseshoe Island."

"Heritage Row?"

"It didn't say, but maybe the curator knows."

Melanie studied Tristen. "Would you have told me this if I'd said no?"

"It sounds as though the man spent a lot of time in the area."

"Why are you being so helpful?"

"I'll be helpful with Rubicore, Melanie."

"I didn't mention Rubicore."

"You didn't have to."

Christophe joined them, handing Melanie an envelope full of black-and-white images. "I've got special gloves over at my desk that you can wear when you look at these."

"Thanks."

"Do you happen to know which cottage Stewart Baker owned?" Tristen asked.

"JoHoBo." The curator winced. "Sorry, Missy's Getaway, now."

"Stewart owned JoHoBo?" Melanie perked up.

"Back then it was the Rusty Pelican. His family had it built in 1900, if memory serves. Stewart would have been about ten at the time, but he had quite the fortune already. He was *the* baby or small child in the first silent films. The cottage doesn't look anything near the same since renovations. Can't believe the council allowed that." Christophe tsked quietly. "By the time I heard they'd applied for a permit to gut the place, it had already been approved. Anyway, Stewart's production company really came into its own during the First World War. When he passed away in the fifties he was an icon. And rich as sin." The curator winked and, with a nod, backed away to his desk.

Melanie paused. There was something wrong with the timeline. Maybe Stewart wasn't the clue she was looking for.

"What?" Tristen lightly touched her elbow. "Is something wrong?"

"I felt as though I was close to something."

"Maybe saying it out loud will jog your mind into making the connections."

Melanie pushed her glasses up her nose, wondering why he was being so helpful. She'd kicked him out of her cottage less than an hour ago. And men thought women we confusing.

"Ages ago, my great-grandmother was given Nymph Island, which included the cottage, Trixie Hollow. But we don't know by whom, or why. I was thinking it was Stewart and that maybe they'd had a relationship, but there's a twenty-year age difference. It's just…I can't imagine my great-grandmother being a mistress or having a sugar daddy."

"That was her photo on the mantel at your cottage?"

Melanie nodded.

"She was pretty. Like you. I could see it."

There was a fondness in his eyes that made Melanie's heart swell, even if she didn't quite believe the compliment. Why was he buttering her up? She ran a hand through her curls in frustration and bent to read the caption under a black-and-white photo. Something about a governor at a grand opening.

"Who is that?" Tristen pointed to the picture.

"Some governor."

"No, beside him. In front of the steamship."

Melanie shot straight up, then bent to stare at the grainy image. It was hard to pick details, so she leaned back, squinting at it.

"Isn't that your great-grandmother? And Stewart Baker?"

Melanie placed her fingers over her mouth. It couldn't be. She snapped a photo of it and the caption to text to her sisters, careful not to use the flash. "You know how many times I've been in here and never noticed that?"

Her great-grandmother had known the movie star. The letters were the real deal. But what was the story? The tale she could use to claim heritage status? Everything had lost its story, like the teacups she'd found stashed in a dusty old box in the back of a Parry Sound antiques shop. Those cups had to have a provenance. They were black-and-white nymphs, fashioned in a style that was tacky yet fascinating. Commissioned. Rare. Priceless.

Why was she thinking about her cups?

Because she didn't know their story, either, and she'd always felt they should be connected to their island somehow.

"Why would someone give her a cottage? Was she keeping secrets for someone important? The governor? Stewart?"

Tristen listened, leaning against the display, arms bulging under his shirtsleeves, pulling at the material.

Who was her great-grandfather? Melanie had always imagined him as a World War II hero who went off to war and didn't come back to his pregnant girlfriend, as story that was common enough. But what if it was one of these men? What if her grandmother had been a secret, illegitimate baby?

"What mystery are we trying to solve?" Tristen asked.

Everything.

"If Trixie Hollow has heritage significance we can get a tax break, and we won't have to sell it to Rubicore."

"Wait. Sell it to Rubicore?" The air crackled around Tristen.

"They made an offer, but we're not going to take it."

"Were you going to tell me this?"

"We're not taking the offer, so it doesn't matter. I'm going to save the cottage." Somehow. *Teacups.*

Why did they keep popping up whenever she thought about the cottage? Was it the nymph connection? So many mysteries. So few solid clues.

"But they want something from you," Tristen said. He was standing close, his eyes digging into hers. "That changes everything. You fighting them will be a personal affront. This is dangerous."

"It's not *dangerous*. You're being dramatic." She pulled him farther along the display, glancing at photos. "Come on, help me. If we can find something we can pin on Heritage Row, too, then Rubicore can't destroy it. See? Everything is connected."

"That's what I'm worried about."

Melanie gave him a disgusted look.

"You've got to hit them in the pocketbook," he said. She could tell he was trying to be gentle. He was also trying to tell her how to fight Rubicore again, and hinting she couldn't win. "Stories about long-gone lovers isn't enough to stop these guys. It has to be something that drives fear into the masses, like public safety."

"And is it fear that finally made you want to help me and my sisters?"

"Yes."

Their eyes met, neither of them blinking.

"And?"

He remained silent for a moment, then sighed. "Look, Dot got hurt. She almost drowned." Tristen sagged, his strong frame suddenly seeming smaller, his expression exhausted. He let out another sigh, eyebrows furrowed. "Do I need another reason?"

"Yes."

He looked up. "Yes?"

"Selfish reasons aren't enough. It has to be noble."

"How very romantic of you."

"Catch me if I swoon." There was no humor in her voice. "I need your help, Tristen, and I know you want it your way. I get that. But we've agreed to work together. *Again*. And you can't shut me down every time I want to take another route on *top* of yours. We'll do it your way, but we're going to do some of my things, too."

"Don't let it sidetrack you or detract from the main strike. The hit we know is going to make a dent." He pursed his lips in thought. "You're going to need stories—something people can tie into."

"You just said that won't work."

He gave an exasperated sigh. "I mean in real life."

"Long-gone lovers is real life."

"We need to stick with this century so folks can relate to it. Something that will stir people up but still hit Rubicore in the pocketbook."

Maya was right. If something wasn't connected to the here and now, nobody cared. Melanie suppressed the urge to cry at the futility of it all. She was wasting her time. And for what? To delay the inevitable? As Tristen had said, Rubicore would get their way. She'd be better off if she sold everything she owned to save Trixie Hollow.

Chapter Eight

Melanie was in his space. Specifically, she was in his bedroom, but she wasn't dressed in lingerie. At least if she was, it was covered by her 1950s sex appeal dress. He should have told her to stay in the living room while he came to retrieve his laptop.

After hearing from Dot that Melanie planned to go to a party held by Rubicore, he'd asked her to meet him at his place after work to sort out a strategy. But something was off with Melanie. When he'd left her at the museum last night she'd looked dejected, but he'd thought she was still on board. But now it was as though she'd given up, and he was finding himself more invested in the fight against Rubicore than she was.

He moved them to the outdoor patio overlooking the water, and offered her a bottle of water and a seat. He waited until she was comfortable, then settled on the other side of the small coffee table.

"First off, why do you want to go to the party?" he asked.

She shrugged. "Free food."

"And free booze?"

She rewarded him with a small smile.

"You okay?" he asked.

She gave a half shrug.

"Well, tomorrow night, just keep quiet. It'll be difficult, but go with the intention of listening. Watch for the unsaid things between the men. They're going to try and play you and your sisters. Possibly divide and conquer. Distract you, woo you, perhaps try to switch your attention to something that isn't related to them. Give you another target to fight against."

"Right. Reconnaissance." Melanie shifted, her legs long and tempting. The passion to fight Rubicore was gone and she seemed smaller and lost somehow.

"You need someone to go with you," he said.

"To the party? My sisters are going with me."

Tristen ran the heels of his palms down his quads, working out tension left over from his early morning run around the museum's island. The way she was acting, he was afraid Rubicore would get her and her sisters to sign a noninterference agreement or something that would bind her, leaving her unable to fight when she got her spirit back. While he couldn't go with her, as Aaron would immediately know what they were up to, maybe he could convince someone else to go along to keep them safe. But who?

"Someone who knows Rubicore's games," he said.

"You."

He watched as conflicting emotions moved across her face.

"Not me. Aaron knows me."

"You're enemies?"

"I wouldn't say enemies, exactly."

"Your hesitation says there's a story."

Her smile was welcoming, beckoning him to talk. Nuh-uh. She would have to find a less tough nut to crack.

"Nothing but boring backstory."

"You know what I love most about the *Winged Goddess* at the boat show?"

Bait. It was bait.

"I love that the owner left the boat's subtle signs of age," she said.

"Poor restoration and lack of proper storage, care, and maintenance," Tristen interjected, knowing he was being a jerk. But he also knew it was likely his only defense against the attack she was lining up. She was going to give him a heart-softening story and set him up for the kill. Just like Dot did. No way to stay clammed up without being a total dick. He admired her for it, even though it sucked being on the receiving end.

"You must be a good lawyer."

She ignored him, carrying on, her voice a soothing balm. Putting him in a trance before the attack, and heck, he didn't even mind. "I can stare at that boat for hours, always seeing something new. Unlike most of the other boats that show up there, it still has a few dings, respecting the fact that they mark the passage of time, its history and stories. They show what it's been through. It's wholly unique. They haven't covered up what most would try to hide."

"And?"

She moved to sit beside him. Her body pressed against his shoulder, not in a take-me-now-big-boy sort of way, but rather a let-me-in way. "I like backstory, Tristen Bell, and if we are going to work as a team you need to quit hiding from me."

"I'm not hiding."

Dot stomped onto the patio, grabbing a diet something from the fridge. He needed to stop buying that crap, as it would give her a tumor.

"Have you cleaned your room?" he asked, grateful for the interruption.

"I just got home. I was *working* all day." She plopped into the nearest chair, her legs splayed over its arms, her back contorted in a way that made his nerves scream in terror.

"Sit properly. You're going to give yourself spinal problems."

Her mouth moved with what he was sure were silent insults as she swung her legs to the floor.

"Studies show diet stuff isn't good for you. Plus, a teenager doesn't need to be worrying about dieting."

"I'm almost an adult," Dot said. "I could apply for emancipation."

"Don't start."

"I'm going to town to get signatures."

"I told you to leave it."

"It's for a petition, *Dad*."

"For what?"

"I *told* you already."

"Watch your tone."

She held in an eye roll. Things had been getting better between him and Dot since she'd begun working with Melanie, but there were still times when he wanted to ship her back to Toronto.

"Is that the trash petition?" Melanie asked.

"Yeah."

"I dropped a letter off at the municipality and sent one in to the paper, too," Tristen said.

"I'm going to town," Dot said.

"If you're taking my bike, don't forget a helmet."

Once Dot was out of earshot, Melanie said, "You shouldn't harp on her about diet stuff. She's probably really sensitive about her body right now. Seventeen is still an impressionable age."

"She seems pretty tough to me."

"The way you talk about what she puts in her body will have a lasting impact."

Melanie's cheeks were flushed. Were they were dipping into her backstory instead of his? If so, very nice.

"Did your dad say things when you were a teen?"

"No." She tipped her head down.

"Then why do you feel I have such an impact? She needs to eat better."

"Show her how. Talk about it. Don't order her."

Tristen clenched his hands, trying to quell his anger. He appreciated Melanie caring, but this was his life, his daughter, his job to raise her.

Melanie said in a rush, "I know she's with you only for a month, but you're important to her. Her experiences now—including those with her body and food—are shaping the woman she'll become. If you're not careful, you could have a serious impact on her self-image." Melanie began gracefully ticking things off on her long fingers. "On her self-esteem, confidence, self-worth. She needs to know you love her however she looks. That you support her and that you're there for her."

He cleared his throat, unsure what to say. This was getting kind of touchy-feely.

"Show her she has the power to take on the world."

There was that passion he'd been looking for. Irresistible.

He leaned over and kissed Melanie.

When she didn't pull back, he deepened the kiss. Her lips were perfect against his, soft cushions, her mouth wet and warm. He cradled her head, making love to her mouth in a way that took him back to his teenage, lust-fueled years. A woman hadn't turned him on like this in forever. Not even Cindy.

And to think that only moments ago he'd been peeved at Melanie.

She pulled back, her cheeks flushed.

He held her forehead to his. "That was really sexy, what you said."

Her whole body flushed with the compliment.

"You're blushing worse than a lobster."

She straightened the hem of her dress, pulling out of his grip, unable to meet his eye. "It's not often that men kiss me to shut me up." Her gaze met his and he was struck by the power behind it. If he wasn't careful, he'd be a goner. But right now, that seemed like a tantalizing promise rather than a threat.

He reached for her, his thumb resting in front of her ear as he drew her head close again. Her earring tickled his palm. He waited a beat, and her chin tipped up. She wanted another kiss. He could oblige her. No harm, no foul.

"Ew!" Dot's voice was laced with disgust.

Melanie leaped back and Tristen sighed, resting a hand on her bare knee, a knee he didn't want escaping just yet.

"What do you need, Dot?"

"I didn't need to see that." The disgust was still there.

"What do you need?" he repeated, more insistently.

"I have to go to the far end of town to see if Samantha will help, and there's no air in the back tire."

"I said no girlfriends unless I was present."

"No, you didn't. You said I couldn't go to their house unless you said it was okay. I'm just picking her up."

"The pump is in the shed."

Dot disappeared, but the mood on the couch was broken. Tristen leaned back, his arm draped over the back of the sofa so if Melanie relaxed, she'd be in his embrace.

She stood. "I told Daphne I'd take care of Tigger—my niece—tonight. Did you have any more advice for the party?"

"Yeah, don't go." He hooked her index finger with his.

"My sisters and I—"

"I meant right now."

Her perfect mouth popped open, then shut. She looked away, her brow furrowed, her finger dropping his. "Don't play games, Tristen."

"No game. Stay."

"I'm leaving." She was backing away, spooked. "Tomorrow night, I'll keep my mouth shut and ears open." Her hands were shaking, but she hesitated, seemingly at war with herself.

He forced himself to stay seated, to not chase after her. "It was just a kiss."

She bent over, so close he thought she was going to pick up where they had left off. He smiled, waiting for her to land.

"It is never. Just. A. Kiss," she whispered.

TRISTEN HAD THOUGHT about Melanie all night long and woken with a raging erection that was difficult to ignore. What was he supposed to do with her? He couldn't send her out to the wolves on her own for this dang party. But if he went, it would ruin the entire element of surprise, which was the only way they'd win against a company like Rubicore.

Around four in the morning he'd come up with a plan. Not a perfect plan, as it meant putting his pride and dignity on the shelf, as well as asking his daughter for a major favor that had likely made her throw up in her mouth when she'd finally stopped laughing at him.

He knocked on the door to Melanie's rather small house, feeling hopeful.

She opened the door, her bathrobe tucked tightly around her curves. Her hair was in an updo and she smelled like nail polish. She was going to the party. Good. And she was smiling in surprise, but was it because there was someone odd at her door, or because she recognized him, even though he was dressed in women's clothing?

Speaking to her might be a problem, he realized, as she waited for him to do so. He held a hand to his throat and used a light, raspy voice. "I'm so sorry, I'm losing my voice. Do you happen to know where number 85 is?"

Melanie paused, thinking, then leaned out the door, one eye on Tristen. She pointed vaguely up the street.

He laid a hand lightly on her elbow and thanked her.

She jolted, head tilted back like a horse about to rear. "*Tristen?*" The pulse at her neck was throbbing madly.

"Hello."

Melanie sniffed the air. "Is that Katy Perry's new perfume?"

He gave a dejected sigh. "Yeah."

She stared at him, her fingers resting against her neck, her other arm wrapped tight around her middle.

"You didn't recognize me, right? I mean, at first?"

"No. You look very..." Melanie's eyes trailed down his tight red dress, to the second-hand heels, then up to the short blond wig he'd borrowed from Dot. He felt like a drag queen with foundation and powder layered on so thick over his close-shaven cheeks, but Dot had assured him that nobody would recognize him and that he didn't look half bad. "Um...different," Melanie said. "Pretty good, actually." Her eyes drifted over him again.

He was going to have to be crazy vigilant about keeping his knees together, not adjusting himself, keeping things tucked in place, and generally acting as though he was the real thing, but it looked as if he might have found a way to make sure Melanie stayed safe at the party.

"We're good then. I'll go with you."

Her shoulders shook and she put a hand to her mouth as though trying to hold in a bubble of laughter. Finally, it bubbled up and burst forth. The seal broken, laughter flowed like lava until she was bent over, gasping for breath.

"Nice." Tristen turned away, hands on his hips. He flicked out the skirt of his dress, not used to the way it tickled his newly shaved legs. Apparently that move fueled the fire, as she only laughed harder. He whirled, fed up. He hadn't denuded his arms and legs of hair for nothing. He only had a few hours until his five o'clock shadow would be begin to peek through the makeup—there wasn't time for this. "You can't go to this thing alone, Melanie. You need a man to go with you and keep you safe. You need me."

She sobered up as though someone had thrown her in an icy lake.

"You are not going alone."

"The more I stare at you, the more you look like a really big man squeezed into a form-fitting dress that might pop off you at any moment like an overstretched rubber band."

"You didn't recognize me." He wasn't sure if it was the conversation or the dress, but he was definitely feeling like the girl in this situation.

"No, you can't come." Her voice was firm as she subtly backed into the house.

He placed a hand on the door so she wouldn't be able to shut it on him. "I am going with you, Melanie Summer, and that is that."

A woman appeared behind Melanie and flinched so abruptly she almost fell over. "A drag queen? Wow, you don't see those very often."

"Maya, not now," Melanie said, her voice filled with impatience.

"No, really. And wow, that tight dress is both scary and sexy." Maya analyzed him, scratching her head. "The square neckline makes your shoulders way too broad, though. You'd look drool-icious in a suit." Her eyes ran down him and he could have sworn she licked her lips.

"Tristen Bell," he said tightly, extending a hand to her.

Melanie's sister gave him a wicked grin. "I knew you looked familiar! Wait until Connor hears about this."

"Please don't," Tristen said with a grimace, as the woman took a picture of him with her phone before he could stop her.

"He wants to come to the party," Melanie said. "He doesn't seem to think I can handle myself." Her arms were crossed, her mouth set.

"Good plan." Maya didn't glance up from her phone, as she was surely sending the photo to Connor. Tristen took the device, deleting the photo and text before she could send it off into the universe.

"Wow. You have massive hands," she said as he handed back the phone. "Keep those tucked away or everyone will know you're a man." She turned to Melanie. "I need to help Daphne finish getting ready. You're next, Mellie Melon. Don't take too long."

As the sister vanished into the house, a small child came bounding out. She launched herself at Tristen, squeezing him around his stomach so tight he thought he might involuntarily lose his lunch. Which was pretty impressive, seeing as that should be well digested and along its merry way by now.

The girl released him and bounded up a step, then looked him in the face before giving a shriek of terror.

Melanie swept the child into her arms and whispered something into her unruly curls. The girl's terror-mortis eased.

"I thought you were Lady Gaga." The girl eyed him again. "I wrote her a letter asking if she'd come visit for my mom's birthday. It's in a couple of weeks."

"I'm not Lady Gaga."

"I *know*."

He cleared his throat. "My name is Tristen Bell."

"My auntie doesn't like you. You won't help her."

"Tigger..." Melanie said in a warning tone, her cheeks pink.

"This is my niece, Tigger. No secret is safe with her."

"Will you help her?" The girl's eyes were so big and round Tristen felt his heart ping.

"I am trying, but your auntie is making it very difficult."

The child thought about that for a moment while the auntie in question stiffened beside her. He could feel her becoming defensive.

"Do you have candy?" the girl asked. "Auntie Maya's boyfriend, Mr. MacKenzie, always has some. And Auntie Hailey's boyfriend, Mr. Alexander, he bought me this dress." She twirled, making the skirt flare out. Maybe Tristen should have worn something more like that. It would hide his narrow hips and maybe not show off his physique as much. Although he might look like a scary version of Little Miss Muffet. And that was not a cool look. On anyone. Well, unless you were under the age of about seven.

"Do you?" the girl prodded.

"Tigger, let him be." Melanie tried to shoo her into the house.

"It's okay. I think I have something." Tristen hurried to his truck and dug through the glove box, desperate to win the girl over, in hopes it would help Melanie change her mind about him coming to the party. He sorted through the random rocks he'd collected, choosing a cold, pink stone before rejoining the gals on the step. He held out his closed fists. "Pick a hand."

The girl lightly tapped his right hand. He opened it to reveal the heart-shaped pink quartz.

The little girl squealed, her eyes bright as she snatched the stone, then held it to her chest. "For *me*?"

"If you'd like it, yes. It's pink quartz and I found it while working in the Parry Sound—"

"My fairies are going to *love* it!" She whirled, bouncing into the house. "Mom! Look what the man gave me!"

"That made you popular." Melanie crossed her arms and leaned against the metal railing.

"I do what I can."

Had he scored a point with her? It was difficult to tell.

"Is she going tonight?" He didn't expect danger, but he knew how distracting a child could be when professional bamboozlers were playing their game. In fact, he wouldn't be surprised if Aaron used the little girl's presence against them, sweet-talking them into signing a noninterference agreement, twisting everyone's words and intentions, knowing the women wouldn't create a fuss in front of Tigger. Tie their hands, duct tape their mouths by using their own family against them. He'd seen that happen more often than he'd like to admit. Find a soft spot, then utilize it to one's own advantage.

Loud laughter came from the house, practically shaking the windows.

"Her mom hired a babysitter."

"Good." One less Summer to worry about.

"Tigger is certifiably awesome."

"Just like the other females in her family."

"But I don't think that a party is appropriate."

They stared at each other for a moment.

"Don't play me," Melanie said.

"I'm not. You *are* something else, Melanie. And I'd like to come and help you. I won't cause a scene, but in order to help, I need to know what kind of games they're playing. Which punches they might pull. It's in everyone's best interests."

"Tristen," she said in a gentle voice, likely meant to let him down easy.

"You can't go alone, Melanie. There are no ifs, ands or buts. End of story."

"It'll be fine."

"No, it won't. They will try and bulldoze you."

"I'm stronger than you assume." Her hands were on her hips, her cheeks flushed.

"I know that, but I also know how these men work. Plus I have a pretty good idea that you would do whatever it took to protect your sisters. You're a loyal sister, missy." He chucked her gently on her chin. "Let me come along and be your wingman. I can be the heavy, if you need one."

"They'll figure out who you are."

"I'll be quiet and hide in the back, unless you give me a sign."

"You still sound like you."

"What about this?" He lowered his voice so it was husky and had a come-hither quality.

"Okay, that just messes with my brain."

"You like that, baby?" He gave a little sway and nudged his fake chest up against her. She laughed and looked away.

"You are too much, Tristen Bell."

"I won't make a scene, I promise." He put up a hand, knowing he was getting close to a yes. "Scout's honor."

"And are you a Scout, Mr. Bell?"

"Okay, so I never was. But I am a man of my word. Take me along. I can redirect conversations or create a screen or distraction. Whatever you need."

"Nobody ever notices me, so a screen isn't really necessary." She pointed at him. "Don't argue with me. I know my life. I am invisible and nobody would notice if I got in a boat and never came back."

"I would notice. Let me come along and keep you safe."

Melanie sucked her cheeks in. "If you are worried about my safety, then you shouldn't come and put yourself at risk. You have a daughter. I have nobody." Her voice went low and his heart ached for her. How could she feel as though she had nobody? She had the whole world eating out of her hand. Everyone from bikers to little old ladies were ready to defend her. She lived in a house that was currently shaking with laughter.

He gently cupped her cheek, worried she'd pull away. He looked deep into her blue eyes. "You really can't see yourself, can you?"

"Tristen…" She pulled away.

"No." He tightened his grip so she couldn't escape. "You're like those antiques you talk about. Unique. Special. You've made it through life, and instead of breaking and getting worn from the challenges that have been thrown at you, it's made you better. Given you a shine and a sparkle that makes you valuable and sought after by those who know what to look for."

She leaned into his touch, her weight gently resting against him. "And are you looking, Tristen?"

His familiar line escaped. "Always looking, but never seeking."

Her posture stiffened as she caught his meaning. She turned away, and he knew he'd lost her again. He was a man used to being in control, but with Melanie, being in control was darn near impossible.

Chapter Nine

Melanie stood on the dock, uncertainty causing her to hesitate. Patio lanterns hung on a wire strung above, and an antique water taxi waited for them. Tristen was at her side, doing heavens only knew what with that skirt of his. In the end, she hadn't much of a choice about him coming to the party, after Daphne exited the house, all smiles and welcoming, having heard he'd given Tigger a stone. For the first time in days, Daphne was acting like her old self, and Melanie had quickly relented, allowing Tristen to come play superhero.

"This is really twisted," she whispered to him now. He had stopped adjusting his clothes and was smoothing his wig repeatedly.

"Why?" His daughter's perfume wafted over her instead of his usual cologne as he leaned close to hear her.

"Just very twisted." She wondered what he'd done to prevent a male-like bulge from appearing in the front of his dress. Being attracted to a man who was currently wearing women's clothes was messing with her mind every time she started to check him out—which apparently was a new, unbreakable habit of hers.

"Right," he agreed, his voice rough.

"Shhh. You're talking like a man."

"How do you stand these heels?"

"How did you even find those? Your feet are enormous."

"Used clothing store. I like your dress."

"Okay, we are not doing this."

"Doing what?"

"The whole girl thing where we compliment each other on things, to see where the other one shops, while secretly thinking we could do better in some small way."

"Women do that?"

"Yeah, and good luck getting your hands on this dress, buster. Simone designed it for me specially. One of a kind."

"I can tell. It looks as though it was made for you. It hugs your curves in a way that shouts to the world that you are all woman."

"I can't decide if I should shove you in the water or thank you."

"A kiss would be fine."

She glared at him and he laughed, rich and low.

Remind her again why she thought this silly man was sexy?

"Ooh. Nice outfit, Tristen," Hailey called, joining them on the dock.

Melanie shushed her sister with enough vim and vigor to catch Aaron Bloomwood's attention as he arrived. "*Trista*," she reminded her sister.

"We're so glad you could be our guests tonight." Aaron appeared at Melanie's elbow, his white suit looking very *Miami Vice*. The sky behind him was streaked with pinks as dusk settled in, a storm on the horizon. Perfect weather to go hang out on an island with the enemy. A cool breeze ruffled Melanie's dress and she shivered, bringing her arms around herself. Tristen had his own wrap—provided by Maya, to help mask how broad his shoulders were—around her in seconds, and she turned to give him a round-eyed what-are-you-doing look. He was going to blow his cover before they even got to the dinner.

Melanie slipped the wrap off her shoulders, handing it back to Tristen as Maya, laughing, with fingers pressed just above her cleavage, complimented Aaron on his attire, thereby drawing his attention away from the garment exchange.

Aaron reached past Melanie—invisible, thank you very much —and clutched Hailey, giving her a cheek kiss. Another for Maya. Daphne. And even Tristen.

"See?" Melanie whispered to him, as their host waved Mario over.

"See what?" he whispered back.

"Never mind," she grumbled. Of course he wouldn't notice that she was invisible. He'd gotten a cheek kiss of approval from their host. If anyone was to guess who was the man in drag, it would likely be her getting the votes. It didn't help that Maya had given Tristen some body language lessons, including how to do the sexy, swaying hip walk. If Melanie were a man, she'd be all over Tristen. She hadn't asked what he'd slipped down the front of his dress, but he definitely fell in the well-endowed bombshell category.

"And who do we have here?" Aaron's attention was stuck on Tristen. Not good. He wasn't supposed to notice Tristen. If Aaron figured out that the woman he was ogling was actually his old cutthroat competitor from Toronto…no, Melanie most definitely did not want to think about that, nor the possible consequences.

Mario was leaning in, drawn to Tristen, as well. Aaron's guard dog was wearing an impeccable black suit that disproved the theory that black was minimizing. In fact, the man's bulk might actually be enhanced. His scowl definitely had been. Well, until he'd seen Tristen. Now he was all smiles.

"You are so very tall," Mario said, his voice deep and accented.

Tristen placed a hand on his chest and gave a bashful eyelash bat that made Melanie want to barf, especially when she saw how well it worked on Mario.

"This is our cousin Trista," Hailey said. "I hope you don't mind her coming along tonight?"

Maya gave their host a lovely smile and Hailey moved to clutch his arm, adding her own lovely smile.

The man didn't stand a chance.

"Perfect," he said. "The more the merrier, if she doesn't mind us talking business?"

Tristen gave a demure shoulder shrug, which seemed to satisfy Aaron. The way he was studying Tristen's shoulders made Melanie uneasy, however. "I like strong women. Do you work out, Trista?"

Tristen swallowed hard and Melanie hoped Aaron failed to notice his large Adam's apple.

"How much can a gal like you bench press?" Aaron looked as though he was going to give Tristen's arm a squeeze, but Melanie stepped in, deflecting him.

"Oh, is this the boat we are taking? It's simply exquisite. I do love antiques. Was this in the boat show?"

Aaron frowned. "Oh, uh, yes, I think so."

"Shall we set out?" she asked brightly.

"I suppose we should, since everyone is here."

Mario began ushering them into the boat as Aaron began a sales pitch on how wonderful their evening was going to be. Tristen waited for Melanie, hand extended to allow her onto the boat first. She gave him a pointed glare and a shove, forcing him to go ahead. It was endearing how gentlemanly he was, but he was going to blow it. Big time.

Tristen sat beside her on one of the boat's bench seats, giving her leg a quick squeeze. "You okay?"

She gave a barely there nod.

"We can leave early."

Melanie pulled her shoulders to her ears and scooted over.

"You're breathing on my neck and sitting too close. It's like we're lovers, not cousins." This was not the time to enjoy how near he was.

"I thought women acted all cozy." He drifted farther away and she immediately missed his body heat. Tristen glanced around the boat's cabin, then grabbed his bra under his fake breasts and heaved it back and forth, like a cow with a major itch trying to relieve the agony on barbed wire.

"Oh, my word, would you stop that?" Melanie smacked his arm, loudly enough to make Hailey turn and stare.

"You two okay?" she asked, a crease forming between her brows. She'd straightened her hair and it fell over her shoulders in a glossy wave that made Melanie envious. Self-consciously, she ran a palm over her own curls, hoping they weren't frizzy, but knowing there was a fair chance they had sucked a good portion of the evening's humidity from the air, adding to its volume. She was definitely going to look like a drag queen by the end of the night.

"We're fine," she said.

Tristen clasped his massive hands in his lap and Melanie sighed, waiting for the inevitable disaster to hit.

THE WATER TAXI DROPPED them off in a small inlet where a screened-in room sat nestled along the shore. The lights inside, reflecting on the dark water's moving reflection, beckoned in welcome. It was a private restaurant that Melanie hadn't even known existed. A whole other world.

"Oh, Nate's," chirped Tristen. "Love this place." He gazed at the building as though taking in a long lost friend. "Incredible garlic bread." He took Melanie's hand and helped her out of the boat. She shook her head and let him. They might be able to teach him how to walk in heels, but apparently some habits were too ingrained. And if she was honest, she was secretly glad of that. He turned and helped the rest of the sisters, going so far as to playfully scold Mario for not being a gentleman and forcing "Trista" to step in.

The man had the grace to look sheepish, and hurried ahead to hold the door to the restaurant for the group, as the wind picked up.

Melanie sat through the meal, watching as Aaron and Mario sucked up to her sisters and Tristen. She was pretty sure they weren't succeeding. Daphne had a glazed smile. Hailey was playing with the light and shadows caused by her dessert fork under the chandelier's glow. Tristen was spending more time trying to avoid Mario's admiring looks than offering quiet commentary. Only Maya seemed half-interested. She was nodding politely, fist under her chin, adding the odd, "Is that so?" But even she didn't seem to be into it.

"When will you be breaking ground?" Melanie asked.

"As soon as everything is in order," Aaron replied, barely sparing her a glance.

"Will that be long? Summer is almost over."

"We're doing all we can to expedite the process."

"I hear the permit process can be very time intensive. Your investors must be frustrated."

Aaron gave her a glance, falling back into a rehearsed speech full of glitz and innuendos. Basically, he was using "look at this and ignore that" misdirection—the very thing Tristen had warned her about and was common in the courtroom. Add in a few reassurances meant to placate them and that about summed up Aaron.

"It must be so exhausting dealing with all that bureaucracy," Maya said. "I hope you know someone in the municipal office who can help you expedite things." She was toying with her fork, watching the men from under her lashes in a way that made Melanie wish she could do that without looking mentally deficient.

Aaron smiled, but didn't give more than with a noncommittal shrug and another canned reply.

Tristen hissed in her ear, "Can you believe this?"

"Yes."

"How stupid do they think you are?" He adjusted the linen napkin laid over his lap. "On principle, you should storm out of here. They won't say anything unless it is part of their prepared speech. I know I promised to remain silent, but I really think I should intervene."

"Don't you dare."

Maya topped up the men's wine, filling her own glass as well, which was swiftly swapped with Daphne's when they weren't paying attention. So far, by Melanie's count, the men had had about four or five glasses each and Maya about two. Daphne, however, was starting to look a tad tipsy from helping her out. Melanie wiggled her fingers at Daphne for the full glass, which made its way down to her. She set it in front of Tristen. This would be his third or fourth, as she'd placed a few glasses in front of him when the men insisted the sisters drink up. "This is how you help out."

He sighed and took a delicate sip so as not to smear his lipstick.

Maya tried a few more ways to get the men talking, leaning forward as she laughed at an inane joke.

"He's staring down Maya's dress!" Tristen hissed under his breath. He shoved his chair back and slammed the wineglass onto the table. Melanie quickly placed a hand on his arm.

"Are you okay, um, Trista?"

The sisters shot them panicked looks.

Tristen cleared his throat and Melanie quickly asked, "Did you need to powder your nose?"

"Yes. Excuse me."

Tristen's eyes widened and he half sat as he realized where he'd have to go in order to keep up the pretense.

Melanie took him by the arm. "Let's go, sweetie." She led him away from the table, adding merrily over her shoulder, "Poor gal can't hold her wine! But she'll be a blast later!"

The men laughed and waved them away, their attention already back on Maya.

Hoping Tristen might have some strategy ideas, she accompanied him to the ladies' room. She watched as he pushed open each stall door, an irrational bubble of laughter squeezing its way up her chest. "Did you *shave* your legs?"

"Yes." He tugged the red fabric of his skirt out of her grasp as she sought a better look. "I think it would be rather obvious that I am a man if they were to see—" The bathroom door swung inward and a woman stumbled in, her cheeks flushed. Polly Pollard. Hailey's old bestie from school—well, before Polly had decided to go the find-a-rich-husband-and-become-a-trophy-wife route and Hailey the struggling artist route.

Tristen, quick as a whip, supported Polly to keep her from falling. The woman giggled and reached up to place a hand against his cheek. "Oh, now aren't you just the homeliest but sweetest thing."

Tristen gave her a watery smile.

Polly, noticing Melanie, lurched into her arms. "Mellie…!" she crooned. "I've missed you. How *are* you?"

"Great."

"I have to tinkle, okay? Nice catching up with you."

Tristen helped Polly into a stall, shooting Melanie an amused look.

"So?" Melanie asked. "Are you going to keep it together out there or should I put you in a taxi?"

Tristen pulled her away from the occupied stall. "They're totally blowing sunshine, and aren't falling for bait." He pushed his hands through his hair, knocking his wig askew. "You're in over your head."

She lifted the edge of his wig, trying to pin it back in place, hoping the task would keep her from unloading her frustration with Rubicore onto his shoulders. A man like Tristen just might make her frustration his own problem, and try to take down the men who were causing it.

Tristen grasped her hands, stopping her ministrations. "You need to be careful. Aaron's made life difficult for his enemies. He's playing hardball out there. This is a big project, no matter what he says. Someone has put a lot of money on the line. If you have any secrets in your past, then it would be best to let this thing go."

Melanie, still toying with Tristen's slicked back hair, said softly, "I can handle this. I have no secrets."

"What about your sisters, your mother, your niece and her father? *Your* father?"

"He's dead. Has been for years."

"But what about everyone else?"

Did her family have more secrets? Hailey and their mother hadn't told anyone about the cottage's tax situation until last month—and now it was almost too late to make the payment. Their great-grandmother had been gifted an expensive cottage and had had a child out of wedlock. Was the cottage a bribe to stay quiet? How many secrets *were* in the Summers' past?

Melanie shoved the last hairpin in place and Tristen let out a gruff, "Ow!" as it jabbed him.

"Sorry."

"Oh, honey." Polly slipped out of her stall, her dress snagging on the latch as she weaved her way over to Tristen. "Get the hormones." She waved at his fake hair and makeup. "This is too high maintenance. My half-brother's dad got it done." She put a hand to her crotch as though lifting her nonexistent junk. "Whole kit and caboodle. It's no wonder Josh got in trouble as a teen. Talk about confusing. Dad becomes Mom."

"I think that's a terribly good idea, Trista," Melanie exclaimed.

Tristen shot her a look and shook hands with Polly, giving her a bright smile, and Melanie felt a surge of unwanted jealousy. "Trista. Pleasure to meet you."

"Well, Trista honey, you get this all taken care of and live your life as you were meant to live it, okay?" She leaned close, looking sad and aged. "That's so important."

The woman sashayed out of the room, sending a flirty glance over her shoulder at Tristen, who seemed to have his eyes glued to her pert nether regions. Something was up with Polly and her marriage, that much was evident. But there was no way she was getting Tristen.

Melanie grabbed his face, dragging his coral lips to hers. She pulled him forward, excitement mounting as he deepened the kiss, his body pressed tight against hers. His fingers tangled in her curls as he tipped her head back, exposing her neck. He kissed down the length of sensitive skin, heading to her cleavage as voices grew louder in the hall.

"It's never just a kiss," Tristen whispered, his lips against her throat, his warm hands releasing her slowly. His voice was a delicious form of sex appeal that she wished she could rub all over her body.

She straightened her dress and stepped to the door, passing a woman who gave her an odd, questioning look as she entered.

Melanie took her spot at the table, Tristen beside her. She felt riled up and frustrated. What was happening between them? She glanced at him, then away. She'd kissed a man wearing drag. She was half-drunk. What kind of espionage person drank on the job and took a make-out break?

Noting her arrival, Hailey did a double take, and Daphne started dabbing at her mouth like crazy.

Tristen turned, and Melanie saw that his lipstick was smeared.

"Oh, sh—" She quickly dropped her head and rummaged for a tissue, swiping at her lips to remove all lipstick, hers or Tristen's. Knowing her cheeks were burning, she took a deep, calming breath before daring to look up. Hailey was distracting the men by pointing to the small restaurant's beams and talking about light, shadows, gray space and who cared what else; she was keeping them from getting any odd ideas about Tristen and Melanie.

They still had to get through a party after this. A long, agonizing party.

As surreptitiously as possible she indicated where Tristen needed to fix his lipstick, and he took care of it as though they were playing some sort of mirror game.

"You look beautiful tonight," he whispered.

"Shh."

He was enjoying this.

She focused her attention on the chandelier above, struggling to keep her temper in check. What was it about him? He was so... so damn *tempting*. And she was not the type to be tempted. Not by someone like Mr. Hot and Cold.

"You're not that sexy, you know," she murmured.

"I totally am."

The room was warm. He was too close. She wanted to grab him and kiss him. Beg him to take her away somewhere private.

At the same time, he was dressed as a sexy woman—she needed to push him far, far away.

The wine was messing with her mind.

"So our proposal," said Aaron, interrupting her thoughts, "is that you stay out of our way and we'll do our best not to cause interference with your island. Be good neighbors. And as thanks for putting up with us, we'd like to offer you free lifetime golf memberships at our resort."

Under the table, Tristen gripped Melanie's leg—so hard she let out a squeak. Did he think she was dumb? There was no way she and her sisters would fall for that.

"After you kill all the wildlife in order to make it, and pollute the water with the chemicals off your perfect greens? No, thank you," Daphne mumbled, arms crossed.

"Golf is boring," Maya stated.

"There's more," Aaron said, his smile cranked tightly in place. "Discounts to our boutique."

"How about a job?" Tristen asked lightly. "I could use a job."

Aaron paused a moment too long. In the silence, they could hear the restaurant's old windows rattling as the storm picked up.

"Hiring from outside?" Tristen asked sweetly.

"Well, we…" Aaron floundered. "It's a very delicate procedure, starting a new resort, and we have a team in place who is experienced in getting something of this magnitude off the ground."

And there it was. Tristen flashed Melanie a wink. It was a big project, after all. As well as fairly typical in terms of them bringing their own experts and staff. Eventually, they might hire locals, but that would be a ways down the road. And even then the hiring pool would stretch far and wide, with no preferential treatment going to townsfolk. If anything, they would get the menial jobs and that was all.

"That's why you want our island. Staff housing," Maya said, her eyes meeting Melanie's.

"Will you be sourcing supplies locally? What is your footprint in terms of shipping pollution?" Daphne asked.

"We have our distribution chains in place," Aaron replied.

"So, that is a no," Tristen clarified. The lights above them flickered as an errant breeze filtered through the room.

"Please, have more wine. I'm sure we can come to a settlement and find a way to work together."

Settlement. Were they offering cash? Melanie immediately thought of their overdue taxes. Her family could use cash, but not from Rubicore. The only thing they should be doing with this company—which planned to take what was great about Muskoka and ruin it—was stop them.

"Shall we get out of here?" Tristen asked.

Melanie was breathing hard and she knew she had to be glaring at the men. But there was no way she was leaving. There was a lot more to find out.

TRISTEN FOUND HIMSELF staring at the model of Rubicore's resort plans, his mind shifting into an old gear that wasn't nearly as rusty as he'd assumed it would be. As the party buzzed around him, he stepped gingerly around the three-dimensional mockup of Baby Horseshoe Island, his feet sending spikes of agony searing through him as he analyzed the plan for potential issues.

So far, so good. It was evident Rubicore had put some time and thought into it. He wondered who they'd found for an architect. The proposed buildings had a classy, yet rustic look to them. Although Heritage Row was nowhere to be seen. Were they going to demolish the cottages, or relocate them? How would Melanie react when she noticed?

Beside him, she was pointing out problems, stating concerns about the watershed and so forth. The problem was, she seemed to be focusing on things the public honestly wouldn't care enough about to get behind, and Rubicore could simply slap Band-Aids on. They needed something big. Bigger than hiring local. Much bigger.

"What are they going to do about parking?" Hailey asked.

"I hope the dark sky legislation extends to the island," Maya said wistfully, her cheeks slightly flushed. "I like being able to see the stars when I'm on the dock."

"What about water quality and degradation issues?" Hailey asked. She nudged Daphne, who so far hadn't said a word.

"Sewage, noise pollution, an increase in traffic…" Melanie was still listing things off to her sisters.

Tristen sighed. Directing these women into following one solid plan—assuming he ever found something good for them to attack—was going to be like herding sheep with an air horn. It didn't help that he was exhausted and slightly tipsy. Being a woman and remembering all the rules was tiring. His panty hose was digging into his waist and the wig was itching like crazy. How did Melanie and her sisters appear so comfortable, milling about, chatting with other partygoers?

"We're going to go freshen our drinks," Hailey said, then departed with the other sisters, leaving Melanie and Tristen alone.

"Can we go sit?" he begged. The first hour of the party he'd followed Melanie like a lost pup as she had made the rounds, chatting and catching up with what felt like half the room, and introducing herself to the other half.

"Thank goodness these plans haven't been approved yet," Melanie said, hands on her hips.

"Actually, they were approved this afternoon," said Mr. Valos, joining them. He grinned down at the model as though he was a puppet master and this was his show.

Yep. It was time to step out of this mess. Dot could drink a big ol' case of Get Over It. Things were not good here. And the more involved Tristen became, the more likely it would be that he'd let the monster out of the attic.

Yet he couldn't make himself move away from Melanie's side. And he was pretty sure it wasn't because she smelled like coconut.

Mr. Valos clasped his hands behind his back, looking pleased. "It will be such a lovely resort. Such a wonderful thing for Muskoka. I can't wait for them to break ground at the end of August and see this dream come to fruition."

"Break ground?" Melanie's voice rose in disbelief. "There hasn't been a public meeting to hear objections. There's a process. This is Canada!" She was starting to yell, and Tristen gently tapped her arm, but she yanked it out of his reach.

"Now, Melanie," Mr. Valos said uncomfortably. "Let's not create a scene."

"You and the council are just going to have to sit on your rubber stamp of approval until the public has had a chance to weigh in on this."

"Now, Melanie..." Vincent repeated. His patronizing tone made Tristen want to shove his fist into the man's face. Angled just right for maximum destruction, of course. "The meeting was changed to accommodate the vacation times of some of the council members. They work hard, you know."

"Whoa." Melanie held up her hands, a dangerous look on her face. "Tell me you haven't already had the meeting."

Mr. Valos tugged at his tie, cheeks flushing with guilt.

"There was nothing in the paper stating the meeting time and date had been changed." Melanie was moving closer, as though she was going to attack the man.

"Mel..." Tristen warned.

"I sent a notice to the paper." Mr. Valos was drawing himself up.

"Then why did I not see it?"

"Too late to print, perhaps?" Tristen asked, barely remembering in time to use his female voice.

Mr. Valos blinked rapidly. Guilty. He'd probably sent it in, washed his hands and carried on.

That meant they'd just lost a big one to Rubicore and the municipality. Now the developer could proceed, as well as claim innocence on its part in terms of due diligence not having been performed. The municipality could issue an apology. Rubicore could hand out some free memberships. Over. Done.

Rubicore was probably bribing councillors, and the old Tristen probably would have done the same with such a costly project. But he had to admit, standing helplessly on the other side of that fence made him pretty damn angry.

"I don't see Camp Adaker in these plans," Melanie said. Her chest expanded as she caught on to what had happened: the camp was gone. Quietly swept off the table when nobody was paying attention.

"Well, Rubicore does own it. I suppose it is their prerogative. Now, if you'll please excuse me. I must go chat with the premier."

"They bought the camp?" Melanie caught Vincent's arm. Her voice was weak, and for a second Tristen wondered if she was about to faint.

Mr. Valos replied, "Years ago."

"But..." Melanie's face scrunched in a way that Tristen figured was a pretty good indication she was holding back tears. "I've been fund-raising for Adaker since I stopped working there as a counselor. It's a charity. Nonprofit. How could they buy it?"

Oh, boy. This was where it got personal for her.

Mr. Valos paused. "It's closed now. Didn't you hear?"

"How could they close it?"

"They didn't want the campers near all the construction, and felt it would be best to shut it down."

"Forever?"

Valos shrugged.

"I think it's time for us to leave, Melanie." Tristen glanced toward the exit and a woman in a pastel suit smiled, making eye contact.

"Have you seen the full plans?" she asked as she approached, allowing Mr. Valos to slip away. The woman wore a Rubicore name tag and began spouting off wonderful facts about the resort. She pointed out the parking plans, and Melanie, who seemed stunned by the news about the camp, allowed Tristen to pull her away. He just about had her out of range when she dug in her heels again.

"I'm sorry," Melanie said to the woman. "What did you say?"

"By creating more parking in port, we will not only solve our own parking issues but also create more public parking in the downtown core of Port Carling." She beamed expectantly.

"You *what*?"

Oh, he knew that tone. Someone was about to have their nuts handed to them in a gift bag.

"Parking," the woman chirped, oblivious. Probably because she didn't have nuts.

"I'm sorry, but this looks like the island where the museum is. You must mean the snippet of land that is across the road from the locks?"

The woman glanced over her shoulder, seeking help.

Tristen sidled up behind Melanie, not caring if he was standing protectively close. He wasn't going to risk missing a thing. That was his jogging island they were messing with.

"But how are you going to get cars onto the island?" he asked in his best Trista voice. "It's foot traffic only, and you'd be ruining the island's charm, changing that. It would involve major construction to get cars out there."

"A ramp. Now if you look at the—"

"I'm sorry. A ramp?"

There it was. The much-loved, small island park was going to be levelled and covered in asphalt, with sections of it carved out to moor an increasing number of boats. Currently, with the walking path around its circumference, the old log cabin museum, mature trees, as well as being a stopping point for the *Segwun,* it was picturesque, quiet, and so entirely Muskoka.

And about to be demolished in the name of progress.

His temperature rose, and he could tell the news was having the same effect on Melanie. Adding a vehicle bridge to the island would also create a traffic mess on the hill that joined one half of town to the other. In their fight against Rubicore, they'd quite literally found their hill to die upon and he didn't know how he was going to manage the fight without becoming a monster. And the more he got to know Melanie, the more he worried that his monster side would scare her away.

"Sweetie, let's take a picture of these beautiful plans," Tristen cooed, hoping Melanie would take a massive chill pill and follow his lead. He could feel Aaron's eyes drilling into them from the group he was chatting with, several feet away. "The parking is going to be so *helpful* for the town."

Melanie slowly changed her tune, shoulders relaxing. "Here, let me hold your purse for you, Trista."

Chapter Ten

Tristen listened to the man on the other end of the line explain who he was. "Sorry, with which paper?"

"*Toronto Star.*"

"And what did you need?" He prepared himself for questions regarding why he'd left Toronto. Had someone seen him in drag last night? He swore one of the men in the cluster chatting about golf had recognized him. Were things about to get nasty?

"You are Tristen Bell of TriBell Developments?"

"No, not any longer."

"You were before you sold your shares to your ex-wife, Cindy, is that correct?"

"Yes, but what is this about? Is she okay?" Scenarios of things going wrong with the company flooded his mind. Media storms were difficult for any business owner and he hated the thought of his ex, who had held the reins for only two years, being in the middle of something that could severely rock her boat as well as her bottom line.

"Your daughter is Dorothy?"

"Yes."

"And you are dating Melanie Summer?"

"What is this about?"

"You have concerns about a development led by Rubicore in Muskoka?"

"What business is this of yours?"

"That will be all. Thank you."

"Wait!" Tristen braced himself with a hand against his stainless steel fridge. "What is this about?"

"Just fact checking, sir. Have a nice day."

Fact checking.

Tristen pulled the phone away from his ear and stared at it, the dial tone humming.

This meant one thing. War. And the first shot fired by Rubicore was going to be a big one.

MELANIE STOOD IN THE HEAT of the midmorning sunlight bouncing off the window beside her, loving the way it warmed her after the too cool air-conditioning in her Bracebridge office.

"You need to back off," Tristen said. He'd pulled her away from her desk, where she and Dot had been trying retroactively to get last week back on track—a lovely way to spend a Saturday morning. If he hadn't seemed so stormy, Melanie would have been a tad excited at his take-charge attitude.

"It's not safe," he said.

"Had a side of drama with your morning coffee, I see?"

Tristen snatched her by the arms. "Listen to me, Melanie. I'm dead serious. I got a call from a reporter this morning and they are fact checking personal stuff. This is the beginning of it all. They are already twisting my life into something that is going to look really bad."

She whipped her arms out of his grasp. "Maybe it is a positive article—ever think of that?"

"There are a thousand ways to interpret the truth, and none of the ones that will hit the papers will be the way I see my life. That

I can guarantee." The lines around his eyes softened before crinkling again with worry.

"How do you know?" she asked. "Maybe they will see you the way I see you."

"Because. I've lived it. Nice stuff doesn't sell papers, Mel."

Mel. She liked the way that sounded.

"You'd better not have secrets," he continued, "because if you do, they will be everywhere."

"Not this again."

"They will aim to destroy you and everything that matters to you. They want to hurt you so bad you won't be able to get out of bed and face the world, the day, yourself. Do you understand? This isn't a game, it's war. Psychological, emotional, everything. Nobody gets between them and their buck. Nobody."

Melanie tipped her chin up, hating that the world had left him so jaded. "I have no secrets, Tristen Bell."

"Everyone has secrets."

"Well, I don't."

"Any embarrassing situations?"

Of course. She was human. And a woman, as well. Who hadn't had their period start at an inopportune time? But she didn't expect *that* to make the news.

"They will pick you apart like crows over roadkill."

"I can handle it and the exposure will be good. In fact, a war of words could be a positive thing. It will get us some publicity and I can bring up the parking issue. People won't side with the nasty big corporation that owns all but one of the cottages in Heritage Row, and has no plans to save them or turn them into a museum. And yes, I asked."

He grabbed his hair in frustration and muttered something under his breath.

"I'm a big girl, Tristen. I can handle whatever they throw at me, and besides, I won't be alone."

Tristen took a large breath as though preparing to say something else. She headed him off. "An old friend of mine works with the local paper and he'll be receptive to spinning some David versus Goliath stuff. Quit worrying." She gave Tristen's shoulder a squeeze. Man, he was a big guy. One day, she'd like to feel those big strong arms around her.

She turned to walk back to her office, but Tristen snagged her hand, stopping her, desperation edging his voice. "People are going to get hurt."

His eyes were fraught with storms again. She stepped forward, tapping his chest with a finger. "You know who is going to get hurt? Rubicore."

"What about your niece?"

"Totally unrelated to this."

"Nothing is unrelated. They were asking about Dot, and I can't have them tearing her up. You know I can't. They can rip into me, but not her."

"I understand that and I can see how much you care for her." Melanie smiled, hoping he wasn't heading in the direction she feared he was.

He lowered his head and when he looked up again, his eyes were dark with regret. "I have to bow out. I'm sorry."

"No." After he'd gone to all the trouble of dressing up in drag, which she'd figured showed great dedication to the cause, all it took was the possibility of a stupid newspaper article to scare him off? It had to be something bigger that was scaring him away. It had to be something about her. In some way, she wasn't amazing enough to keep him by her side. "You can't roll over and play dead. Dot wants to be involved in this. It's important to her. We need you." Crap, Melanie's voice was quavering. She couldn't lose him. When he was around it all felt possible and she felt safe and strong.

"I'm sorry, Melanie. I want to do this for you, but I can't reconcile the two sides right now. I have to protect my family."

"Is this about Toronto and your ex-wife?"

"This is about being a good father." His jaw was set, the muscle below his ear bulging.

"But their garbage hurt Dot."

"They're cleaning up the bay. I talked to council this morning."

"She's dedicated to this. She can handle some lying newspaper articles."

"It's my job as her father to protect her. I haven't always, but this time I can."

"Have you thought about asking her what she wants?"

"She's a kid. I'm her dad." His voice was getting louder, his cheeks flushed. "I've been through this before and I'm not doing it again."

"I thought you were a man who cared about more than yourself." Melanie chin wobbled as she fought back tears. She was so worn-out from keeping her chin up, shoulders back. Pretending to be the confident woman she had never been on the inside. And for whatever reason, Tristen just made her want to curl up in his arms and let it all out, which was so completely infuriating. She'd been doing just fine until she'd met him, but now that he was around, her life felt empty when he wasn't there.

Which was stupid. The big jerk.

"I thought you were a man who was strong enough to stand by me when the going got tough. Apparently I was wrong."

BACK IN HER OFFICE, Melanie pushed her trembling fingers through her hair. How had she let Tristen become so important in her battle? It felt as though he had pulled the rug out from under her by quitting, even though he'd barely done anything other than nag at her about hitting Rubicore in the wallet, and pointing out the obvious parking thing. But it had felt nice knowing he was on her side. And now she was alone again, to battle a company so much bigger than she was.

Sitting, she tapped a pen on the stack of waiting case folders. She needed help from someone who could get the word out about what Rubicore was planning.

"Was that my dad?" Dot asked from the doorway.

Melanie adopted a smile that fell flat. "Yeah."

"Why was he wearing his you're-in-trouble face?"

"He's out."

"Of what?" Dot caught on a second later. "What? He's giving up? He's going to let Rubicore win?" The teen fell into the chair across from Melanie, her face lined with anger, followed by disappointment. "But why? I thought the parking thing was a killer."

"He's spooked."

"Are you sure? My dad eats companies like Rubicore for breakfast."

"The papers called him this morning to fact check some stuff, and I guess he's just worried that things are going to get messy. He's trying to protect you."

Dot let out an exasperated sigh. "I don't need protecting and why does he always leave when things get tough?"

Melanie had already heard the story of Tristen leaving his family, his company, his city. It had seemed so odd before. A strong man like him taking off? But now, after seeing the haunted look in his eye, she understood that there was something in Tristen's past that was big enough to scare him into making a run for it even now.

She sighed. "He's trying to protect you." Melanie wished he was interested in protecting her, too. But she knew if their positions were reversed she'd do the same thing and pull out in order to protect Dot. "But messy doesn't bother me. I'm going to figure out a way through this. They aren't going to destroy a beautiful island on my watch. Are you still in?"

"Yeah."

"Good, because I could use the help." Melanie stood. "What do you say to an extended lunch and then working a bit later to make up for it? Think your dad would be okay with that?"

Dot's eyes shone with excitement as she followed Melanie to the door. "Are we going to go kick some butt, Ms. Summer?"

"We sure are. With or without your father. And the first place we are going to start is with someone who can give us a voice. If Rubicore's getting the papers involved, then we need to fight fire with fire, right?"

They walked through Bracebridge, turning into the office where Rick Steinfeld, a reporter friend of Hailey's, worked.

Melanie strode across the room, stopping to place her hands on Rick's desk, leaning forward. "How would you like to be in the middle of a media storm?"

He dropped his pen and tipped his chair back, all ears. "You know I would."

"Is Austin Smith still in town?"

"Whoa. Mellie, are you sure?"

"Why? Who's Austin?" Dot asked, practically bouncing at her side.

"Paparazzi. Major snoop," Melanie said.

"Awesome."

"And who is this?" Rick asked, sizing up the teen.

"Dot Bell."

Rick's head quirked. "Daughter of Tristen Bell?"

"Yeah." She crossed her arms as if to say *I'm not him.*

"Someone was asking about you."

"Who?" Melanie demanded, feeling fingers of dread working up her spine.

"Not sure. I overheard another reporter talking to someone." He scanned the open office. "He's off today. So, what are you two up to?"

"Rubicore is going around telling everyone that their big resort is going to create jobs in the area, but I happen to know for a fact that they don't plan to hire local, nor shop local. And preserving Heritage Row is not in their plans for their resort on Baby Horseshoe Island. They own Camp Adaker—which is also not in their development plans. They want to turn Port Carling's island park into a parking lot, and have the go-ahead, since the municipality didn't perform due diligence before approving Rubicore's proposals. They're ruining the environment. Noise, light, air, water, garbage—"

Rick, who had been taking notes, paused, hand held up. "Whoa. Back up a tad. These are a lot of serious accusations."

"They are ruining everything that makes this Muskoka."

Rick fiddled with his pen. Finally, he rubbed his eyes and let out a sigh. "Look, I don't mind helping you guys with your battles. I really don't. I've helped Daphne bring a lot of things to light, but my boss is getting tired of me always taking the environmental slant."

"Then focus on the other stuff. The parking lot issue is something that everyone can get behind."

"What did Rubicore do to you, Melanie?" he asked quietly.

"This isn't a vendetta. They're just…ruining things."

"Look, I know it must be difficult watching them change everything on the island across from you, when you guys are having a tough time. But making these sorts of accusations publicly could get you in a lot of trouble."

"It's not that." Her throat was filling with tears. First Tristen and now Rick? He was supposed to love crazy stories like this.

Someone in the office behind Rick called his name and he held up a finger, excusing himself. He entered the office and closed the door. A moment later he reappeared, unable to meet Melanie's eye.

"I'm sorry, I can't help with this."

"What? Why?" she protested.

Rick glanced toward the office behind him, then scrawled something on a scrap of paper. He spun it around so she and Dot could read it.

Major advertiser.

"No," Melanie whispered. "You have got to be kidding."

Rick slowly shook his head.

Tears of frustration welled up, blocking Melanie's ability to speak. Grabbing Dot by the arm, she led her onto the street.

"I don't get it. What does that mean?" the teen asked.

"The developer is advertising with the paper, so they can't say anything untoward, as it might sever their financial ties."

"That's so stupid!" Dot exclaimed.

"I know." Melanie paused, thinking. "But it might also explain why the public meeting's date change never made it into the paper."

Dot's shoulders had slouched forward. "Now what?"

"We have a case, but no help. I think it's time to get creative."

TRISTEN'S TABLET CLATTERED onto the countertop and he thrust a hand out to steady it. He froze for a second, then let out a breath.

This was not good.

He'd warned Melanie that her secrets would be exposed. He'd warned her and she hadn't listened. She'd ignored him and now everything was starting to crumble.

And it wasn't just her family secrets, it was his, too. His was the name people knew. He made the story juicy. Rubicore had taken a preemptive shot across their bow. They'd slammed her. Slammed him. Slammed everyone they could get their hands on who might be connected to the Summers.

He clutched the counter and lowered his head. His cell rang and, seeing that it was Cindy, he figured he might as well get it all over with now.

"Dot is *gay*?" his ex-wife yelled, before Tristen had a chance to say a word.

"Yeah, she is." He pinched the bridge of his nose. He didn't even consider that Cindy might not know that little tidbit.

"And I have to read it in the Sunday news? My mother called me this morning. I was enjoying a nice relaxing moment and now this. What did you do to her?"

"I didn't do anything to her."

"I'm coming to get her. You're a lousy father and you're destroying her."

"Some studies suggest that three percent of the population is considered homosexual or bisexual."

"*What*?"

"Three percent of—"

"Don't you see, Tristen? You're going to *destroy* her. This is just like when I kicked you out. Everything was in the news. I couldn't trust anyone."

"I know."

"How do you think she feels, being publicly outed? She's just a kid."

Tristen's jaw popped as he ground his teeth together.

"How is she? Does she know?" Cindy asked, her voice wobbling.

"I haven't talked to her yet." Tristen's ribs hurt from holding in the rage, the urge to slaughter whoever had revealed his daughter's sexual preferences to the media.

"And who is Melanie? Is she the other woman?"

"She is not the other woman." He could handle the allegations that he and Melanie were together and about to take down Rubicore. That wasn't a problem. The other stuff, however, went deep and would only get worse.

"She's the lawyer Dot has been working with, isn't she?"

"Yes."

"Is she gay? Did she turn Dot?"

"I don't really think it works that way, Cindy." Tristen sagged against the counter, absently rubbing Max's ears as he nudged his snout against Tristen's thigh. "Take a deep breath."

"Don't tell me to take a deep breath. This is my daughter. You need to stop this, Tristen. You need to pull the plug. That woman is unstable."

"Melanie is one of the most stable people I know."

"That woman had to go to a troubled teens camp."

"She worked there, Cindy."

"She was a *camper*, Tristen."

He paused, thinking, but failed to see Melanie as a troublemaking youth. "I think the camp helps kids who have been through a trauma, too, Cindy." Melanie had mentioned that her father had died. Maybe there'd been a bad accident.

"Don't make excuses for her, because I don't care. I don't want Dot around her."

"Have you considered that the papers might be wrong about some things? Were they right when they said I left you because you were more concerned about getting manicures than helping out with the business?"

Silence.

"Tristen, I don't like Dot being in the media. She's our *child*. We need to protect her."

The room felt too quiet. His world too narrow. Tristen braced himself against the fridge, pressing his forehead to the cool stainless steel. She was right. He'd failed Dot once again.

"You do whatever you need to do to get her out of the spotlight. You hear me? I'm running a reputation-based business and your name is still associated with it even though you obviously don't give a shit. We're still connected, Tristen, and I don't want my name in the news unless it's about me storming the business world."

He clicked off the phone and turned to see Dot standing in the doorway.

"So I'm gay, huh?"

"That's what the papers say."

She shrugged and opened the fridge, pulling out a wedge of brie. Stress eating, or had his chats about not worrying about every single calorie finally taken hold?

"Are you okay?"

"I guess." She spun his tablet to face her. He watched as she read, her expression changing from interest to anger. "What a load of bull. I hope Melanie slams them back."

"The best thing to do is not retaliate."

"She won't take this lying down. Not Melanie. She's tough."

But was she tough enough? That was the question.

And what kind of man was Tristen for sitting back, waiting to see if she was?

Dot's expression grew darker. She looked at the tablet again. "Dad?"

"Yeah."

"Rubicore is owned by Aaron Bloomwood, Jim Hanna, and Mistral Johnson?"

"Apparently."

She gave him a quick, fierce hug. "Thanks for backing out of the fight, Dad. Thank you."

"What are you talking about?" She was upset with him earlier for telling Melanie he could no longer help. And now she was thanking him? He really didn't have the energy for her mood swings right now.

"Ohmigod." Her face paled. "We have to stop Melanie."

"I already tried, she won't budge." He glanced at the tablet for answers on why his daughter was suddenly so upset. "What's wrong?"

"What's wrong?" Her voice was pitched so high he was sure dogs would come running. "If Melanie ruins Rubicore it'll destroy my girlfriend's family! The Hannas will be put in the poorhouse and then Samantha will break up with me!"

"Back up a step." His heart clenched. His daughter had been sleeping with the enemy? Well, hopefully not *sleeping*. But still. All those rules and promises he'd made to watch over her, and he didn't even know Dot's girlfriend's last name? He was a crappy dad.

"Jim Hanna is her *father* and you've told Melanie how to annihilate the company. You always screw everything up." Tristen braced himself as Dot's unbridled anger came rolling in. "That's why Mom's business is failing. Because she's too nice, not like you."

"TriBell is failing?" Tristen's world tilted. His family was in trouble? "How bad is it?"

Dot crossed her arms, shutting him out. "It doesn't matter. Mom will solve it, like always. Not you."

"I can't stop Melanie, but I'll do whatever I can to help you and your mom."

There was no way he could help Melanie now—even from afar—but maybe there was a way he could show her he still cared and that it wasn't personal.

Chapter Eleven

Tristen wandered through the indoor antiques show, lightly touching tables, his mind elsewhere, his mood edgy. He needed to find a way to show Melanie that him backing out of the Rubicore fight wasn't about her. After the way the papers had slammed her, he figured she had to be hurting something fierce. And while he'd warned her that this was going to happen, he still felt as though it was partly his fault for not protecting her somehow. Fights like this forged strength in some, while breaking others, and he wasn't sure which way Melanie would go.

Scanning displays bearing antique place settings, tablecloths, and trinkets, he kept an eye out for something unique. Something that obviously had a story. An underdog antique that nobody except Melanie could love. The right gift would tell her that she wasn't alone, that he saw her and believed in her even if he couldn't be at her side slinging arrows into any foe that dared come near.

He stopped in front of a table, doubting himself. He was falling into old habits. Gifts when the woman needed his time and presence. Wanted the impossible.

"See anything you like?" asked the lady watching the table's shellacked items. Nothing had the right energy. They were glossy, done up, their history hidden under fresh varnish.

"Not yet. I think I'll know what I'm looking for when I see it."

"Just like with love," she said, shooting him a wink.

The next table had toys and teacups.

"Over a hundred years old," the man said, passing him an old jack-in-the-box. The vendor looked familiar. Christophe. The museum curator. "And these teacups were found in an old ice shed here in Muskoka. Perfectly preserved." He lifted a cup and held it out for inspection.

Tristen turned it over, then set it down again. Too flowery. He had a feeling Melanie didn't like antiques that were too pretty.

"I can make a deal on anything from this half of the table. However, this side I'm selling for a friend, so unfortunately no deals." Christophe waved his hand toward an odd assortment of china that had seen better days, but had a certain something that caught Tristen's eye.

"You hear about the museum's island?" Tristen asked, bending down to study the strange collection of teacups that were lined up along the edge of the table.

"The bastards. Think they can just move that old log cabin as many times as they want, and it will still be okay."

"Sorry?"

"The log cabin? The part of the museum that was moved in from Glen Orchard in the eighties? This was supposed to be its final home because of its age."

"You aren't going to fight it?"

The man looked dejected. "What can I do? Nobody cares about that stuff."

"You should talk to Melanie Summer. She cares."

Christophe gave a rueful smile. "She's a good kid, but I'm not sure she can pull this one off."

Tristen ignored the remark, trying to keep it from getting under his skin, where he knew it would fester. The monster wanted out, wanted to roar at everyone in her way. It wanted to clear the path and present Melanie with a nice little castle, every problem swept away. Solved. By him. Using force, if necessary.

Tristen turned over an ugly cup that had faint cracks in its finish, and read the markings on the bottom. They weren't familiar, but he certainly recognized the tremble that had crept into his hand. He carefully set the cup down, knowing how rare it must be with its simple black drawings of nymphs. The price for this one cup could be well over a hundred bucks. He glanced down the row. Over a thousand dollars perched along the edge of the table. He gently nudged the cups back, hoping to keep the collection safe from children roaming the indoor market.

"How much is this cup with the nymphs? I know someone who might like it."

"That one's quite rare and unusual. We think it was commissioned, and have been trying to trace its origins for some time." Christophe studied the bottom of the cup, after shoving his glasses farther up his nose. He checked the price list beside him. "Two hundred and fifty. This one's price is nonnegotiable."

"Two-fifty? For one cup?" Tristen stared at him. The man had to be kidding, right? The thing was hideous. Christophe set it down again, and Tristen reached for it. "I'll take it."

Melanie would probably smash it at his feet. One cup. Two hundred and fifty dollars. He'd lost his mind.

A young child skipped up to the table and reached out to snag a cup. Tristen batted her hand away, causing one to teeter. He righted it, then quickly piled the teacups up in front of Christophe. "I'll take them all."

They needed someone who would keep them safe.

"That is…" Christophe paused to calculate the purchase price, eyebrows raised. Catching himself, he added quickly, "I'll wrap those right up. Cash, check, debit, or credit card, sir?"

Tristen handed over his credit card, keeping an eye on the

crowds milling about. One jostle and this history would be gone. Destroyed. He felt like a new dad trying to protect his offspring from a herd of stampeding gazelles.

He rubbed his brow. They were only cups. He didn't even like frail and delicate things. He smashed rocks, for crying out loud. He probably couldn't even drink out of these dainty little teacups without crushing them in with his big hands.

And yet he was willingly going to dip into his untouched Toronto account to cover this ridiculous expense.

At home, he unloaded a ton of granite he'd picked up before hitting the show. He heaved the heavy stones as far as he could into the bush, struggling to exhaust the energy fuelling the emotions roaring through him. He wanted to protect Melanie, though he barely knew her. He wanted to put on his old suit and kill Rubicore. Not just give them a limp or send them away. *Kill them.*

Panting, with sweat soaking his T-shirt, he stared into the underbrush. The rocks were unloaded, but had been tossed so far and wide it would take hours to ferret them out from under the fresh mulch of crushed ferns and saplings.

His arms ached from the effort, but he felt good. He'd make it through another day. And right now, that was all that mattered.

After a shower, he unpacked the teacups on the granite kitchen island, doubting himself and his intentions.

Dot, milking lake water out of her shaggy bangs and onto the floor, laughed at the cups. "This could be the definition of hideous. Wow." She carelessly held one up to the light.

"Didn't I tell you not to go swimming without me?" He snatched the cup and carefully set it down beside the box.

"It's fine. I was in the shallow area."

"There is no shallow area. The bottom drops off right away."

She shrugged. "I didn't know you liked antiques."

"Quit changing the subject. No more swimming without me. And I'm more into boats. And rocks. Not china."

"Rocks aren't antiques."

"Prove it."

She rolled her eyes, a small smile playing at her lips. "Fine."

"Good." He stared at the cups, unsure what to do. Was it too much to give them all at once to someone you hardly knew? Should he wrap them individually? Chuck them back in the box and then shove it at her as though it was old junk he couldn't be bothered with?

Dot fingered the receipt. "Three thousand dollars?" She stared at him, eyes wide. "You know I'd like a car, right?"

"You can earn one."

"Right. So you can buy ugly cups." She gazed around the simple home. "Mom said you have billions. Why..." She curled her upper lip, eyeing the hole in his old sock where his big toe peeked out.

"Why don't I spend it?"

"Yeah."

"So I can buy ugly cups." He grinned and shoved the box of cups into the middle of the island where they'd be safe.

Silence stretched between them and he could feel that Dot wanted to talk.

"Why are you bailing on us?" she asked.

"I'm not bailing on you. I'm just... It's complicated."

"You know I don't care what the press says."

"Your mom does."

"And since when do you listen to Mom?"

"I'm trying to do better. I don't want you getting hurt, Dot."

"Kind of too late for that." Her eyes darkened and the way she turned her shoulders, he knew she was about to flee. He pulled her into his arms, hugging her, unable to speak. Unable to explain.

"I'm sorry, Dot."

"For what?"

He held her by her shoulders, watching her expressions change like the seasons.

He was sorry for a lot of things. For not being around more. Not understanding that Dot's mother didn't need gifts and gestures to know that he'd loved her. For having to bail on Dot and Melanie in order to try and keep them safe. For not being man enough to deal with everything. For having a monster in the attic that he couldn't seem to control unless he hid out and smashed rocks all day, cementing them together as if it was his life he was piecing back together.

"I guess we can do it without you. I mean, that whole island parking lot thing is going to get everyone riled up, right?" She appeared so young, lost and in need of reassurance.

"You bet, Dot, you bet." He pulled her into one last quick hug, then released her, knowing what she didn't—that Christophe had already given up.

Tristen opened the fridge, staring at its contents. Max came to his side and sat, looking expectantly into the fridge with his sad eyes. "So?" Tristen asked. "Eat out tonight?"

"I totally want fries and a big greasy hamburger," his daughter exclaimed.

"You read my mind," he said with a smile.

"Can we go to McDonald's in Bracebridge?"

"I was thinking of a real restaurant."

"McDonald's is real."

"I'll think about it."

"Is that a yes?" She clapped her hands, eyes sparkling. Just like when she was a little girl. He'd missed so much over the years. But he wasn't missing it now, was he?

"Get in the truck."

"Are you sure that will get us there?" she teased, hurrying to the door before he changed his mind. "I heard about Melanie having to save you. Maybe you should only drive it if you have her or a mechanic with you."

Tristen laughed and pushed Dot out the door. If nothing else, things were finally coming along between the two of them.

MELANIE STRUGGLED TO pry a reporter away from Daphne as they bullied their way into the restaurant to get Tigger a sundae. The girl had waited patiently as the two sisters had tried to talk sense into Mr. Valos, going so far as to interrupt his Sunday tee time in order to do so. Talk about wasted breath. The man had to be receiving something under the table. Either that or he really just didn't care about doing what the taxpayers paid him to do.

And then, as the three of them had walked across the McDonald's parking lot, a swarm of reporters had descended. Cameras were shoved in their faces along with microphones. Questions were shouted. The Summers couldn't get back to the van and had made a break for the restaurant's doors, but reporters had blocked them, closing in. Melanie had never been claustrophobic, but this nearly did her in.

Daphne turned to face the cameras, tucking Tigger behind her. Melanie struggled to get to her side, but the reporters, sensing her sister was about to give them a sound bite, jostled her back.

"Rubicore needs to have a public meeting outlining the results of their environmental impact study, which should include waterway traffic patterns and their impact. This is a basic right belonging to the citizens of Port Carling, and Rubicore has failed to honor that right." A gust blew Daphne's light cotton dress against her small frame. She seemed so vulnerable trapped against the closed door. Melanie shoved a man out of the way as a new round of questions were flung at her sister. Daphne was used to talking to the press, but Melanie could see the fear lingering in her eyes, and Tigger was trembling, clutching her mother's skirt to her face.

Melanie stomped on reporters' feet, dug in her elbows and used her tall build to plow her way to her sister's side. "Please, we have no further comments." She felt as though she was a lawyer protecting her client as she ushered Daphne through the restaurant door, backing them up slowly.

"Daphne!" shouted a reporter from the rear of the cluster. "What do you have to say about your daughter's birth father applying for custody?"

Instantly, her sister's small form pushed against her back. "Keep going," Melanie warned.

"My dad?" Tigger asked, her voice small and curious.

"No. Say nothing." Melanie shoved her sister inside the restaurant and straight into the arms of Tristen. He whisked Daphne and Tigger away, calling to the manager to take care of the reporters. Melanie let the door swing closed, then blocked the entrance, arms crossed. Her body shook as she stared down the reporter on the other side of the glass.

"Mistral Johnson has filed for full custody," he shouted through the partition. "He wants his daughter back."

CAREFULLY, MELANIE JOINED Daphne and Dot in the booth, her butt sliding across the hard plastic seat. Her sister was trembling, staring blankly out the window. Melanie placed a hand on hers, hoping to help settle her.

"We'll sort this out, Daphne."

Tristen took Tigger to the counter to order her the promised sundae. Melanie gave him a reassuring smile when he didn't look away from them. There was something in his eyes that made it hard for her to breathe right.

"He's going to take her? Why now?" Daphne's eyes were full of pain, her face a mask of confusion.

"He won't. He can't. You've been a good mom. He can't just sweep in and take a daughter he's ignored for years." However, Melanie also knew the man had rights that he could ask the courts to honor. And with him being well off, when Daphne was a struggling single mom, the courts would likely give him whatever he asked for.

Daphne blinked back tears and Melanie whispered, "I'm so sorry. This is all my fault."

Tristen had been right. But she'd had no concept of how bad it could get.

"I'll call everything off, okay? I'll apologize to Rubicore in the papers. Tigger is more important than a development."

"Um, not to interrupt your guilt fest," Dot said, speaking up, "but hasn't Daphne been in the news a ton for environmental stuff? It might not be because of Rubicore, right?"

"Tigger's father is part of Rubicore," Daphne said quietly.

"What?" Melanie had to force herself to lower her voice. "When did you learn this?"

"Since forever. He inherited his share from his father when he turned twenty-one."

"Why didn't you tell me?"

"No wonder he's pissed," Dot commented with a surprised laugh.

"You can't quit, Melanie," Daphne said. "This would have happened between me and Mistral anyway. And Rubicore doesn't exactly have a great environmental record. You can't keep quiet just because of me."

"I can't let them take Tigger."

"*They* aren't going to. Mistral and I will talk. We'll figure things out. It's unrelated, as far as I'm concerned." The determination in her sister was welcomingly familiar.

"Is this why you were weird about fighting Rubicore?" Melanie asked.

Daphne paused, as if trying to decide how much to divulge. "They only care about money."

"That's true." Tristen interjected. He stood by their table, waiting for Tigger to finish chatting with a nearby family about ice cream and sugar.

"I'll be your lawyer, Daph. I'll make this right. We won't lose her. Not even for an hour a month."

Mistral was going to lawyer up with some hefty legal guns from the city. Melanie would have to find some smart tricks and loopholes. Quickly, if she planned to keep her niece in Muskoka.

"I don't get why he wants her all of a sudden," Dot said, her upper lip curled in confusion.

"This isn't about Tigger," Tristen replied. "It's about making the Summers pay for going up against Rubicore. He likely doesn't actually want the kid."

Daphne's mouth turned down, tears in her eyes.

Melanie squeezed her sister's hand. "We'll stall the custody proceedings until we've killed the development. Then he'll drift off and forget about it." Presuming he wasn't the type to do the whole vendetta thing when he lost, of course. "Okay? Chin up."

Her sister tipped her face upward with a sniff. "I can do this. Positivity. Being a mope brings no flowers or sunshine."

"Damn right," Tristen said, a stitch developing between his brows.

"Mom?"

Daphne wiped away a tear and replied, "Yeah?"

"Why is there a man taking pictures of our van?"

TRISTEN CROSSED HIS ARMS, trying to figure out how he was going to keep the two Summer sisters safe. Dot took Tigger onto the stone patio to play with Max, who was going ballistic trying to keep everyone away from Dot, as he'd been doing ever since the near-drowning incident. He was a guard dog, but only where she was concerned.

Tristen pulled up a stool at his kitchen island and addressed Melanie and Daphne. "You're going to need a security guard. Both of you."

It was stupid to have brought them here with the reporters snooping after them, but what else was he supposed to do? When the private eye had been not-so-privately snapping shots of Daphne and her vehicle to, no doubt, build a case against her as a mother, Tristen had realized they had to find a quiet place to come up with a pretty serious game plan. When Connor happened by—and incidentally prevented Tristen from breaking the PI's camera in front of the women—he'd poured the Summers into Connor's car and said to meet him at the first place to come to mind—home.

But now they were in his house, with a major media storm brewing, and he'd pretty much placed himself in the middle of it. Funny how it didn't bother him as much as he figured it should.

"I'll see if Evander de la Fosse is available." Connor began scrolling through the contacts in his phone. "Hailey and Finian used him and said he was good."

"Whoa…wait." Daphne raised her small hands. "Security? No. This is getting out of hand."

"I agree," Tristen said.

"This can be resolved with peace, love, and understanding," she continued. "We need to sit down and discuss things, not escalate them. Running scared attracts the wrong kind of energy. We need to rise above this slander and arms race."

"Arms race?" Connor looked up from his phone. "You want him armed?"

"No!" Daphne let out an exasperated sigh. She began explaining the impact of violent energy to Connor and Tristen blocked her out, his attention on Melanie. She'd noticed the box of haphazardly repacked antique cups on the counter. Gently, she picked up the nymph cup, staring at it as though it were a friend she thought she'd never see again.

"Ugly, huh?" Dot grabbed three oranges out of the nearby fruit bowl, while Max gave Connor a preemptive growl and slid his large body between Dot and the group of adults. "Dad's got exquisitely poor taste. Come on, Tigger. I'll show you how to juggle."

"Not in the house," Tristen called after them, not taking his eyes off Melanie. Her cheeks had flushed and she swallowed hard before slowly raising her gaze to meet his.

"They made me think of you." He pushed the box in her direction. "I saw them at the antiques show."

Melanie was clutching the nymph cup against her chest. "But these…" Her eyes lowered to the box, her free hand flipping back the wrappings as she took inventory. "These are really rare, Tristen. Exceedingly rare."

He wanted to say, *Like you.*

He could feel the others staring at them, the earlier discussion over war and peace having faded away.

"You get a security guard in place?" he asked Connor.

"I'm not sure Daphne is ready for that," his friend said carefully.

Daphne, eyes narrowed, feet planted firmly apart, had her small hands clenched into fists. Every fiber in Tristen's being told him to step away if he wanted to live. He only hoped the men who ran Rubicore felt the same way.

TRISTEN STOOD AT THE patio door, sipping a cup of decaf and watching Melanie. She had been standing on his back deck gazing at the bay below for almost an hour now. Arms crossed, clutching the teacup. Every once in a while she'd sigh, her shoulder drooping. Then, over the next few minutes, they'd rise up again.

He figured it had to be something big. Bigger than yesterday's headline that had claimed the two of them were dating. The paper had run a less than flattering photo of Melanie alongside one of him looking, quite frankly, dashing. It was meant to hurt him and his reputation, but he couldn't help but think it must have hurt her, too.

Connor had driven Daphne and Tigger home, Melanie not answering when they'd called to her. Daphne had told Tristen to give her some space, as she was likely working through something big, and she'd asked him to drive her sister home when she returned to planet Earth.

He'd never seen anything as interesting. Never seen a woman just…think. Men, yes. But women…not so much.

Finally, after an hour of letting her stew things over, he joined her in the growing dusk to see if she needed anything. Privately, he'd been wondering if she'd been having some sort of standing seizure. But she turned, eyes shadowed, fully conscious.

"How's Daphne?"

"She left."

"Without saying goodbye?" Melanie took a hesitant step toward the house.

"We called to you, but you were…thinking. I can give you a ride home if you're ready."

"I need to go there."

Had she taken a hit to the head? "Yeah, I'll take you. Ready?"

"No, Baby Horseshoe."

"That's private property, Melanie."

"I know. It's okay. I won't do anything stupid." She took his hand, still clutching the cup as she lead him down to the boathouse.

He followed her directions out to Baby Horseshoe Island, an argument constantly on the tip of his tongue, but unable to be released. There were so many reasons not to go there. She pointed them between the island and a smaller one, and finally to a boathouse that looked as though it was trying to get up the courage to finally bend all the way over and dive into its watery grave. Her island. Tristen let out a relieved breath and docked his boat before she could ask him to trespass on the neighboring shore.

Melanie moored the boat with ease, then disappeared into the dark. He called to her, uneasy about raising his voice so close to the enemy.

"Coming?" she asked, hidden in darkness.

He found the footpath and followed her up the hill. Small solar lights cast just enough of a glow to reveal tree roots poking out of the earth a second before he could trip on them.

Lights flicked on in the cottage and he paused, admiring its rustic charm, before heading up the wooden steps and onto the wraparound veranda.

Melanie shouldered her way out a screen door. She held up one of the cups he'd given her, the one she'd been holding while doing her thinking earlier. "Where it belongs. Nymph Island."

"How about that?"

"It's a sign."

"Of what? Apocalypse due to mythical creatures?" He was losing patience.

She passed him a can of beer, cracking one for herself. She poured part of hers into the cup and toasted him before lighting a lantern above them.

"The whole 'sign' thing is a long story," she said finally. "But basically, I was selling all those cups in order to save this place from a tax sale." She took a seat in a wicker armchair. "But you bought them as a gift. For me. These things were not meant to leave my hands, it seems."

"Wait. Back up a second. Did you just say I bought stuff you were trying to get rid of, and then gave it all back to you?"

"Technically, I didn't want to part with them, but I'm getting kind of desperate. I didn't think anyone would actually buy them, the price was so ridiculous." Melanie moved to the railing, gripping it as she leaned out, gazing toward Rubicore's island. "I owe you three grand."

Tristen rubbed the back of his neck. "No, I think this is the way it's supposed to be." They sat without speaking for a long moment. In the distance, there was a dull roar and whine of a motorboat. Birds had turned in for the night, leaving it quieter that he'd have thought possible. Quieter even than his place. "So? Was it enough?"

"The money?" She shook her head. "Getting closer, though. The cottage..." She turned quickly, watching him in the light of the lantern hanging above. "Do you believe in destiny?"

He shrugged. This was where she showed her crazy side and he ran for the hills, relieved they'd only shared a kiss, right?

"That things happen for a purpose or a reason?" she asked hesitantly. "That maybe there is some sort of energy pulling us along so we are where we're supposed to be at the right time?" There was something in her tone that suggested she might not believe in destiny.

She was a lawyer, after all.

"Daphne is always talking about it, and my analytical, logical mind just rolls its eyes and groans. But now..." Melanie inhaled shakily. "I kind of..."

"You feel it?" he prompted. He dropped his eyes. Crap. He was buying it, too, wasn't he? But the fact was, in that huge sale of literally thousands of items, he'd not only found the teacups she was selling, but bought them for her. "Did I buy all the cups you'd put out?"

"Every single one."

He pulled a hand down his face. Maybe they just had similar tastes. Tastes in ugly nymph cups. Or...more likely, Melanie was so unique that everything about her stood out in a crowd.

"I've never felt as though I belong," she was saying.

He finished his beer, setting the empty can on the coffee table. Confessions? Oh, hell. He couldn't do this.

Yes, he could. He was trying to change. He could prove to her that he was a good guy who listened, instead of shutting her down by telling her that everyone felt that way. Easy.

"Never?" he asked.

"Everyone walks around as if they have this great purpose and meaning, and know what they want and where they need to be. They're all so blissfully *happy*." He almost laughed at the vehemence behind her words. "With this thing with Rubicore, I feel like I can make a difference. That I am the person who needs to put a stop to it all." She sighed, hands on the railing as she cast her gaze out into the darkness again. Head bowed, she let out another heavy sigh. "But I can't. I just can't do it. I can't be the one."

Tristen relaxed in relief. Thank goodness. She was backing out. Now she'd be safe again and Dot could stay working at the office she so dearly loved.

Melanie turned to him in the soft light of the lantern and he surprised himself by walking to her side, running a hand into her thick hair and pulling her into a kiss.

He needed her. Not for any reason other than to simply have her. To find out what it was that made him toss and turn in the night, dreaming of her and that special hold she seemed to have on him.

Her fingers tangled in his hair, her hands wandering down to his chest, then his waist. She let out a moan of contentment as he sucked on her lower lip, his hand cupping the roundness of her full breast. She tugged on his belt, ruining any resolve he might have about being a gentleman, his mind set on finding a place to devour her fully. He lifted her in his arms, carrying her inside the cottage where he could make her his.

She directed him to a bedroom and he lowered her onto the high bed, placing himself on top of her when she didn't let go, her kisses urgent. Her slender hands moved over his skin like fire, hot and consuming. Her kisses left traces of moisture down his neck and he lost himself in the moment, hoping he could be everything she needed to feel right again.

Chapter Twelve

Melanie pushed her mother's wheelchair toward the flower-painted minivan she'd borrowed from Daphne. Her knees still felt shaky from the intensely passionate sex she'd had with Tristen last night. She hadn't meant to jump his bones, but after the teacups, then taking her to the island where he'd listened to her woes it had been as though a breaker had been flipped when he'd kissed her. In that moment she'd wanted nothing more than to have utterly, mind-blowingly amazing with the man. And she had. He'd met every urgent thrust, moan, and kiss with his own, digging them in deeper and deeper.

And now she had to deal with the consequences of having a one-night-stand with a man who had been very clear from the start about not seeking a relationship—while she was.

But the sex. Man, that had been simply out of this world and her body got all trembly and hot with want just thinking about it.

She was in too deep with Tristen after one night of sex. Just like that.

"You all right, Melanie?" her mother asked as she helped her into the passenger seat. "You're sighing a lot."

"It's all good," she said brightly, checking the time. She had forty minutes before she had to be at work, and hoped the doctor was on time for his first appointment of the week. Pushing the empty wheelchair around the van, she loaded it in the back, then gave a little shriek as a man popped up beside her, camera aimed at her face.

"Back off!" she yelled. Her cry caught the attention of the nursing home's caretaker, who ambled over, rake in hand. "You okay, Melanie?" he called.

"This man is harassing me."

The photographer backed away, hands raised. "Not infringing on anyone's rights."

The caretaker glowered at him, giving his rake a shake when the reporter went to move closer to Melanie. She ducked into the van, squealing the treadless tires as she left the lot, taking several hard turns, hoping to squelch any ideas of him following her.

"What was that about?" Catherine asked, clutching the armrest. With her left side affected by a previous stroke, she was having trouble staying upright.

Melanie slowed the van, her breathing shaky. "Sorry. A photographer was getting in my face." She checked the rearview mirror. How long would it take for the reporters to figure out that she was giving up the fight? That the risks to her family were too darn high, and she'd back off? Like she'd told Tristen last night, she couldn't be the one.

"What is that thumping sound?" her mother asked.

Melanie checked the dash. An amber light showed a flat tire. She slammed the heel of her hand against the steering wheel. "Damn it." She pulled over in a quiet neighborhood and got out to check the damage. All her heavy driving had created a leak in the driver's side rear tire. She took a long, slow breath, trying not to let it get to her.

It was a fairly quiet road, and so far nobody had discovered the flower-painted silver Caravan. If she was quick about it, she might be able to have the tire changed before anyone caught up with them.

She glanced up the road, half expecting Tristen to come to her rescue, as she had with him only a week ago. Only a week and he'd crept into her world so solidly.

"Are you okay, Mellie-Melon?" her mother called, as Melanie opened the hatch to look for the jack and spare.

Her lower lip trembled and she pulled in a deep breath to steady herself. "I'm going to change the tire."

Everything she touched was falling apart. Rubicore was going to ruin Muskoka. Daphne's life was being turned upside down. Tristen and Dot had been smeared in the papers. And now this.

She dropped the spare on the ground, groaning as it refused to bounce.

Flat.

Melanie stared at the tire, deciding what to do. She could call a tow truck, if she used some of the antiques money to pay for it. The problem was it felt completely wrong taking the cash, even though Tristen was a billionaire. The teacups were probably to appease his guilt for bailing on her and now he was going to think the sex had been a thank you. And it hadn't been. It had been something so much more.

Always looking but never seeking.

That's what he'd told her on his doorstep when he was dressed in drag. How much more clear could he have been? He didn't want what she wanted.

Melanie heaved the spare back into the van and slammed the hatch closed. Looked like they were driving on the flat. Consequences be damned.

"That was fast," her mom said.

"The spare is flat."

Stupid Tristen. The way he'd swept in and rescued her, Daphne, and Tigger when the press had closed in yesterday…way too out-of-this-world dreamy. And she kept wishing he'd kiss her again. Once, twice, forever.

She hated him.

He was the right guy in all the wrong ways. Or was it wrong guy in all the right ways?

Either way, she was great at falling for the wrong man.

"Are you okay?" Catherine asked.

Lowering her head onto the steering wheel, Melanie sighed. "Do you believe in signs?"

"Yes. You don't?"

"I didn't."

"You do now?"

"I let something go and it came back to me." Not that it mattered. It was just a coincidence.

She and Tristen may have had sex on the island but it didn't mean they were about to fall in love. Especially since neither of them believed in destiny or any of that hokey stuff. She was letting her mind get away from her.

And honestly, if she was him, she would be running away. It had to have hurt his pride a few days ago to see the sensational headlines that he, Tristen Bell, all debonair in a tuxedo, was dating her, all disheveled in a holey Camp Adaker T-shirt. She was a Sasquatch. He was in the McDreamy league.

Why was she even thinking about that? About him?

It didn't matter. He was done and the papers would soon grow tired of it all.

"I sold the Nymph Island teacup along with some others," she said, picking up the conversation again, "for an utterly ridiculous price, and someone bought them and gave them to me as a gift."

"Destiny," her mother replied with a certainty that should have comforted Melanie. "Who is the man?"

"Nobody."

"Nobody?"

"He has a daughter and he's divorced and he's just not...not into me. But he's special." Damn. Now she was going to cry.

"Oh, honey." Her mother laid her hand over Melanie's.

What did she have in her life? A crappy old falling-down cottage that had forced her to sell her beloved antique teacup collection, which had been returned to her for all the wrong reasons, meaning she needed to return the money. She had a developer ruining the cottage's view, as well as its peace and quiet. Taking down every stitch of heritage, story, the very things that made her island feel like Muskoka. Life was simpler there. It was as though she was visiting an older time, when women like her were sexy with their curves. And Rubicore was ruining it.

Plus, they were giving up on Adaker, the one place that hadn't given up on Melanie. A place that had made her feel better about the world during a time when she'd no longer believed it was possible. They were taking that away from other children, and that wasn't right. And for what? So the rich could romp and play and pretend there were no problems in the world, while they destroyed the habitats of rare animals that lived on that peaceful, treed island.

Rubicore had betrayed her. They hadn't told her who she was fund-raising for.

And now that she had publicly pointed out all the ways Rubicore was a sneaky corporation whose owners didn't give a lick about anything other than money, they were attacking everyone she loved. They were razzing Finian, a man who had come out about his gangster past and the promises he'd broken to fix his old neighborhood. They were all over Hailey and her previously failing business—saying it was taking off only because she was dating Finian and not because of her talent. They were calling Maya a money-grubbing siren who had hooked Connor and convinced him to sell his corporation, in a move that had stunned Bay Street. It had even brought Mistral out of the woodwork and into a custody battle for a daughter he didn't want. He was trying to uproot the best thing in everyone's lives—Tigger.

Tristen had warned her and Melanie had gone ahead, anyway. What kind of person was she for doing that?

"Talk to me," her mother said lightly.

"Everyone...I..." *Fight through it. Don't cry.*

"Is this about the newspapers?"

Melanie nodded, not daring to speak.

"They have been brutal, haven't they?"

Great, even her mom read the stories. What did she think of her daughter ruining lives, while not making a difference in the world? It was all for nothing.

Nothing.

"Don't you see?" Catherine asked. "You've scared them."

"They're being cruel to the people I love."

"That's because you got close to something good and juicy. Why else would they care about people like us? What did you find that they don't want the world to know about, Melanie? There is something wrong happening here, and they know you are onto it."

"You think so?"

Her mom's blue eyes shone with pride. "Go get them, Melanie."

"I can't. What about Daphne?"

"You fight this battle. She'll fight her own."

"I can't, Mom. I can't do this to everyone."

"We are tough enough to withstand this, Melanie."

"I might not make a difference."

"You won't know until you try."

Melanie sighed impatiently, thinking maybe her mother didn't get it. "But there's going to be pain."

Catherine laughed merrily. "Where there is something worth doing, there will always be pain. Don't let that stop you."

"But…" She swallowed.

"We all want you to do this. Do you understand? This is *important.*" Her mom added quietly, "Not just anyone can do this, but you can."

"But what about Tristen? What if I ruin his life? All these secrets are being thrown out there."

"Secrets, when revealed to the world, have a funny way of losing their scary edges. Think of it as airing out his closet and setting his skeletons free."

"Mom, I'm practically dancing across the world's stage with everyone's skeletons right now. I don't have the right to do that."

"Those teacups came back to you for a reason. Don't waste your time feeling sorry for yourself and worrying about everyone else. It's time for us to deal with our own problems. That's not your burden to bear, and you don't have much time to set things right with this developer. We're counting on you to be our voice, Melanie. Don't let us down."

MELANIE MANAGED TO GET Catherine to her appointment in time, then the tire patched during her lunch break. She'd then called Daphne after work to see if she would be up for an impromptu protest outside the municipal offices over Rubicore closing Camp Adaker and her sister had agreed.

The crowd of people had grown steadily, with Hailey's old friend Polly even coming out to support them. It had turned out the camp meant a lot to Polly as well, her half brother, Josh, having spent time there as a teen. She was eager to hold a gala and put her fund-raising prowess to work, if need be. And if anyone could raise awareness—especially among those with money to spare—it was Polly.

While they might not be able to convince Rubicore to keep the camp running on Baby Horseshoe after their resort opened, the public attention would hopefully force the corporation to reopen the camp elsewhere in order to save face. And as long as the camp continued its excellent work, then Melanie would at least feel she had accomplished something in all this big mess.

But she wasn't done with Rubicore. Not by a long shot. Her mother was right. This was her battle. And yes, Tristen was right about making the developers feel it in their wallets, but Melanie also knew she could make them bleed with a thousand paper cuts. She could be that bee that drove them crazy, wasting their energy swatting when she buzzed here, there and everywhere.

She grinned, feeling so evil and yet so alive. Taking down a nasty corporation one small step at a time was a nice dollop of awesome sauce on top of the in-your-face sundae she was serving up for Aaron Bloomwood and his crew.

Checking her watch, she figured she could likely catch the Fredericksons over on Baby Horseshoe Island before they turned in for the night. She'd love to see Tristen to get a gauge for how he was feeling about her, but she knew if she could convince the owners of Salty Dog, the last privately owned cottage in Heritage Row, to make a heritage claim, it could possibly help protect the rest of the cottages, even though Rubicore owned them. Time was of the essence.

Mr. Frederickson, his bald head glinting in the evening light, met Melanie on the short path leading from the dock to the rustic cottage.

"Melanie, I thought you'd mistook our place for yours. To what do I owe the pleasure? Did that man your sister Maya was seeing finally drown, trying to swim around the island? I haven't seen him in days."

Melanie laughed. "No, Connor is fine, Mr. Frederickson. He and Maya have been working out of his new place lately. They've started a business together. Even got engaged."

"Give them our congratulations."

"Thank you, I will." She inhaled the pine scent of the island and said, "It's quiet tonight."

"I complained to the municipality that those knuckleheads were working too late into the night and disturbing others."

Melanie held back a smile. A thousand paper cuts. She barely resisted the urge to hug the man.

"Mr. Frederickson? Have you and your wife put any consideration into claiming your cottage as a heritage site?"

He let out a snort. "And have the government breathe down my neck every time I want to fix my leaky plumbing? No, thank you. Plus, we have enough tourists coming by and gawking at the place as it is."

"I understand," Melanie said with a nod. She needed to chat him up, then slowly bring him around. But it would take time. Time she didn't have. "The taxes sure have gone up around here lately."

His head tipped back, taking in the tall pines lining the path. "I'll say. Up almost a third that one year." He shook his head. "Can't believe how many people lost their cottages. Good thing I have a decent pension. How are you gals doing?"

"Barely holding in there. I've actually been looking into the heritage angle for Trixie Hollow."

"And why would you want the government telling you what to do with your own property?" His tone said it all—*I thought you were smart, but now? Not so much.*

"Between you and me, Mr. Frederickson, we are this close—"

Melanie placed her index finger and thumb a fraction apart "—to losing Nymph Island in a tax sale. If we declared it a heritage site, then not only would we get a tax break, but we could get the likes of them—" she angled her thumb at the large Rubicore Developments sign that was pounded into the recently leveled bedrock, where they planned to build a helipad "—to leave our place alone."

"Are they bothering you?" Mr. Frederickson's brow was furrowed, his arms crossed.

"They want our island to house staff. I'm pretty sure they'd pull down Trixie Hollow and build something big. Take out all the trees. Increase traffic between the two islands. She's one of the last original cottages in Muskoka that has been mostly untouched, you know."

"There aren't many of those left." He glanced back at his own place on Heritage Row.

"I don't know how they got a permit to take that fine old cottage down," she said, referring to the missing one. "I thought that sort of thing had to go through the permit process, where the public had a chance to speak up about it."

"Full of termites, they said."

"Oh?"

"Came to our door saying they might spread if they didn't destroy the place. I said by all means take it down."

"Hmm." Melanie nodded as though she sympathized, but inside she was screaming. Why didn't they fumigate the place? Surely Mr. Frederickson wasn't that far out of touch? "You've heard they've closed Adaker this year and have no plans to reopen it?"

"I'm sorry, kid." He dropped a hand onto her shoulder, making her feel small. "I know that camp was good for you, but it was old. A lawsuit waiting to happen. A pile of timber waiting to ignite at the first hint of lightning."

Melanie drew herself up. "Why don't they build a new one? I'm sure a big corporation could use the tax break. And it was a nonprofit charity."

He nodded. "Never a problem housing that camp on the island."

"Have they made an offer on your place yet?"

"Yep."

"Us, too. It was insulting."

She really was going to have to sell every last one of her teacups—again. Because at the end of the day, the cottage mattered more than her collection. If she could sell them once, she could sell them twice.

"I wish I had something to prove our cottage has cultural value." If she could finally find the kingpin piece and get a tax break, her sisters might consider the cut to their annual taxes as her contribution to the debt.

Melanie inhaled, trying not to panic. Less than three weeks to pay up or the cottage would be seized. Three. Weeks.

"Its age isn't enough?" Mr. Frederickson asked.

"Sadly, no. Although if you and the rest of Heritage Row go, we'll be that much closer to being the last of the original cottages in all of Muskoka." She winked at him, trying to keep her desperation at bay. "Will you consider making yours a heritage site?"

He shook his head. "Too late now."

"It's never too late."

The lines around his mouth deepened in a way that made her sense something bad was in the works. Had he and his wife accepted Rubicore's offer?

Mr. Frederickson held up a finger. "I have something... Yeah."

He nodded thoughtfully. "Let me see if I can find it. It's been in the cottage since we bought it twenty years ago. I think it may have come from JoHoBo, back when it was called the Rusty Pelican. Sorry, it's Missy's Getaway now. I can never keep up with all these name changes. Hang on."

Rusty Pelican? Stewart Baker's cottage? Melanie resisted the urge to follow Mr. Frederickson into his abode and ransack it for clues. The man returned moments later with a package wrapped in an old, thick plastic bag.

"I think this has something to do with Nymph Island. Maybe you can use it for your heritage claim."

A HARLEY RUMBLED PAST Tristen toward Melanie's law office, its engine's reverberations rattling through him. It stopped in front of a waiting man wearing black leather and chains—the bearded guy from the Steel Barrel. Great. Tristen had simply wanted to drop off Dot's forgotten cell phone, maybe say a quick hello to Melanie to see how she was doing since quitting the Rubicore battle and then head out to Rosseau to give a quote on mending one of the village's rock walls.

Who was he kidding? He wanted to ravage Melanie at her desk. He hadn't seen her since their skin-on-skin escapade two days ago and he'd thought of little else since.

He should march in there and let her know that he respected her. That it had been fun and that he was willing to have more life-altering, mind-blowing, sweaty sex with her anytime, anywhere.

No. He should walk away. Melanie wasn't the one-night-stand type and going in there would give her the impression that he wanted something more, something deeper.

He stared at the motorcycle, fighting with himself, as it rocked

"Gangsta's Paradise" out of its speakers. The song took him back twenty years and for the first time in his life, Tristen felt old. And white. Really white. But mostly old. Too old to be standing outside a woman's place of work trying to summon the courage and a good enough excuse to go in and say hi.

The rider, wearing something bright and colourful, released the handlebars, shifting back on the bike as slim hands unhooked the helmet's chin strap.

An old-style dress. Intricate chain maille choker. No leathers.

The music died as Melanie turned off the bike, her laugh ringing through the street's early morning silence, hitting him in the chest. Why was she riding a chopper? She should be safely behind her desk reading legal clauses. Not riding a bike with handlebars up near a giraffe's ears.

She was going to ruin him.

No leathers. No. Leathers.

He unclenched his fists, hoping he hadn't cracked the screen of Dot's phone, then resumed walking. Trying not to look up, he caught sight of Melanie shaking out her hair, the helmet gripped between her hands, her moves slow and deliberate.

Hot damn.

His steps faltered. There was something different about Melanie Summer this morning. The weight that had been resting on her shoulders seemed to have lifted. Was it merely the effect of a good motorcycle ride? No, it was her hair. The curls were gone. Her brown locks were straight and glossy, flipped up at the ends like a Stepford Wife.

She caught his eye and flashed him a smile. He swore a woman never looked sexier.

Remind him again why he was holding back?

Right. A strong woman with moxie to spare didn't need a man like Tristen. Well, that idea bothered him. A lot. Bothered him as much as the way her prim and proper appearance was bad, bad, bad for his mind. He wanted to take her home, even if he had to carry her the whole way.

He needed to stop pulling back. Stop being a chicken where she was concerned. Two years of licking his wounds was long enough. They were both out of the Rubicore fight. Tristen no longer had to worry about the monster coming out and scaring her. He could be himself. His new self.

He rubbed a hand over his brow and walked closer. He didn't want to talk to the biker, but wanted Melanie all to himself. Wanted to ask her out. Touch her skin. Make love to her mouth.

"Hey," he said, managing to sound casual.

"Hey, Tristen. You remember Ezra?"

"Yeah, hey." He gave a chin lift in the man's direction. "What's up?"

"Melanie just took Marley for a ride. Marley the Harley."

"Is that why you weren't wearing any leathers?" Tristen asked Melanie.

She laughed and rolled her eyes in amusement, as though she couldn't believe he was being such a prude.

He was tempted to withdraw his remark, but had promised himself he was going to stop pulling back. This was him. Right here. Protective. She could take it or leave it.

"He has a point," Ezra said, eyeing Melanie's attire in a way that made Tristen want to block the biker's view. "One truck taking a corner too close, or someone not checking their mirrors…" He slapped his palms together. "Happens too fast and too frequently."

"You should buy a car," Tristen blurted out. "With air bags."

"Wow. You guys know that I already have a mother filling the role of worrywart, right?"

Ezra laughed, his gnarled beard bobbing against his chest.

"What about a father? Seems to me you could use one of those, Lemonade."

Tristen crossed his arms and glared at the man. If anyone was going to use cute nicknames and protect Melanie, it was him, not Biker Dude.

"Okay, well. This is getting awkward." Melanie handed the helmet to Ezra. "Thank you for letting me try Marley. She was awesome. But you might not want to let me do that again."

"Why's that?" he asked.

Tristen leaned closer.

"Because I'll want one," Melanie said, giving the biker a conspiratorial elbow nudge.

"That's my girl." Ezra slung an arm around her shoulders with in a jingle-jangle of chains.

"Melanie Summer! Was that you squealing those tires?" A small woman with a plume of graying hair strode up to the group, her finger waving.

"Mrs. Star. How's your sister in Blueberry Springs?"

The woman brushed off Melanie, who was closing in for a hug. "Don't you sweet-talk me, you young thing. Those two-wheeled contraptions are death traps."

"Yes, ma'am," Melanie said.

"Well?"

"She was doing me a favor, ma'am," Ezra interjected.

Mrs. Star cocked her head at the man in leathers, and Tristen found himself holding his breath. The pleats of her skirt flicked back and forth as she stormed over to poke the biker in the chest.

"Don't you go pulling a lovely, innocent young woman like Melanie Summer into your Hells Angels business, you hear?" She smacked Ezra in the gut with her handbag. "I'll tell your mother what you've been up to."

"Yes, ma'am." The biker gave a small, submissive bow.

"Now come with me. I need your help."

Ezra gave Melanie a chaste cheek kiss, then escorted Mrs. Star into a store nearby.

Wow. Maybe the biker wasn't so scary, after all.

"I hope I'm like Mrs. Star when I'm retired," Melanie said.

Please tell him she didn't really want that.

"So full of energy. She's awesome."

"And about to castrate a member of the Hells Angels."

Melanie laughed and steered him into the law office, her body bumping up against his as they went, no seeming awkwardness due to their night together. "I have something I want to show you."

He tried to remind himself that she likely wouldn't be showing him what his gutter mind had imagined, but given the polka-dot dress she was wearing, he'd probably allow her to drag him to hell and back, with a smile on his face.

Melanie was vibrating with excitement and he couldn't help but think that maybe it was leftover adrenaline from her motorcycle ride with no leathers. The woman was nuts. Crazy. Insane. Energetic. Inspired. Smart. Creative. Sweet. Determined. Lovely.

He loved her.

Whoa. Stop that train of thought. He did *not* love her. He was simply intrigued. She was interesting and caught him off guard, and kissed and made love like a devilish whirlwind, that was all. Nothing more. Absolutely nothing more.

"Check this out." She unwrapped an old plastic bag and set a stack of papers and photos on her desk. He came around, perching on a corner of the desk, staring at her. She was gorgeous. Eyes sparkling and wonderful.

She waved a photo in front of him.

Right. She wasn't an image he could get lost in for hours. She was real. He pried his attention away from the pearly skin of her long pale neck and glanced at the black-and-white photograph.

"It's Stewart Baker," she said.

So it was.

Tristen placed Dot's phone on the desk and angled the faded picture to get a better look at the background. "Is that your cottage?" The trees were short and the structure fairly new, but it was obvious he was looking at Trixie Hollow, with the rocky outcropping visible behind it.

He shuffled through the rest of the photos. There were ones with Melanie's great-grandmother and the movie star in couple-type poses, arms around each other, gazing into each other's eyes. In the background of some was Heritage Row, looking rather spiffy and fresh. New.

"What is this?" Tristen flipped over a photo of a baby, checking the back for a name.

"It looks like my grandmother, but then all babies seem the same to me. I haven't had a chance to check it against the photo my mom has."

Tristen squinted at the faded ink on the back, the swirly writing making it difficult to discern.

"I keep thinking that maybe Stewart Baker was the father. My great-grandfather. But I don't have proof." Melanie handed him a stack of papers. "There are receipts, too. Stuff being commissioned."

Puzzling his way through the stack, Tristen couldn't figure out if he was missing clues, or if he was still rattled from seeing Melanie ride a bike belonging to a member of the Hells Angels. Or maybe it was more due to the fact that he was waiting for her to mention their night together.

"I can prove now that those letters are from the movie star,"

Melanie said, "and that he and Ada had a romance of some sort. That has *got* to lend some significance to Trixie Hollow, right?"

"I don't know if your great-grandmother dating a famous person makes your property significant, Melanie. How does that provide cultural value?"

She sighed heavily.

The receipt he was holding felt thick compared to the other papers. Using his thumbnail, he carefully pried two thin pieces of paper apart. The hidden sheet held a drawing that made him close his eyes to refocus before looking at it again. Finally, he held it up to Melanie.

"Isn't this your teacup?"

Melanie paled, her fingers shaking as she took the sketch. She swallowed before reverently placing it on the desk in front of her. "An assessor said it was one-of-a-kind and had likely been commissioned approximately a century ago."

"By Stewart, apparently. A nymph cup for Nymph Island, possibly? A place where his lover stayed?"

"I found this in the archives over at the land title office." She handed him a photocopied deed to Nymph Island with Ada's name on it. "Do you think Stewart gave her the island?"

Melanie's eyes glittered with excitement and Tristen focused on the papers again, trying not to think about the last time he'd seen her eyes glitter like that—while moving over top of him gloriously naked.

With these new clues, you could connect the random dots, make a few assumptions and possibly end up with an argument for cultural significance. But there were some pretty big leaps on the path to making this all into a claim, and he believed the heritage board would want a solid, indisputable trail.

"You know that pursuing these leads might uncover secrets from the past?"

"I know! It's so exciting." She pulled an envelope from her desk drawer. "I almost forgot. This is for you."

He accepted the envelope, opening it in front of her. It was a check. The full cost of the teacups. "What is this?"

"It's not right for you to buy them in order to give them back to me." She wouldn't meet his eye and he knew it was about something more.

"I wanted to buy them. I did. I wanted to give them to you. I did." He handed the check back to her, but she wouldn't accept it. "What's the real issue here, Melanie? Is this about me and the Rubicore fight?"

"No."

"Then take it. I know you need it. I won't miss it." Yep, that was the wrong thing to say. "I didn't mean it like that. I just mean… can't I help you out?"

"Money only complicates…things."

"Things?" He had a feeling she was hinting at their night together, but he couldn't be sure.

"I'm not keeping the money."

"Yeah?" He ripped up the check. "Try and force me to take it."

Her shoulders dropped a hitch. Then she sat in her chair, got out her checkbook and wrote him a new check. She handed it to him, one eyebrow raised in challenge.

He could be a jerk and rip it up like he did the last one, or he could find a new and more creative way to help her out. If he put his mind to it, he bet he could find a way to get that three grand for the teacups back in her pocket—one way or another.

He took the check and pocketed it with a grin. "At least you aren't fighting Rubicore anymore." He paused as something clicked in his mind. "Wait. You aren't going to try and block Rubicore with this heritage claim, are you?"

Her eyes shone with the truth.

"You said you were out, Melanie. Done." His voice was too loud, too harsh.

What was with this woman?

She wouldn't meet his eye, cheeks flushed. "I changed my mind."

He pinched the bridge of his nose and sighed. The old squeezing sensation in his chest was back.

"I'm going to claim heritage significance for Trixie Hollow and put in lots of info about Heritage Row. It's called that, so why on earth wouldn't they protect it as a heritage site?" She waited for him to look at her. "But no, I won't actually make a direct claim involving the other cottages."

Melanie smiled, and he had the distinct feeling she'd done something. Something he didn't know about.

"So how did the cup end up in a shop?" She was changing the subject on him. "What happened? If it was for the cottage, why didn't it stay there? The family has owned the cottage for the duration of this cup's existence. And what about this other stuff Stewart had commissioned? The receipt lists an entire tea set and all I found is one cup. Is the rest still out there? Did he actually give it to Ada, or did something happen?"

Tristen sighed, letting her redirect his attention away from her and whatever she had up her sleeve. He sorted through the photos again, trying to pull out a thread from a fuzzy memory. "I watched a documentary on him. It said he used to do charity work up here. Left his family back in Montreal."

"Charity?" Melanie perked up even further. She had one of those dreamy looks women got when they saw a happily ever after unfolding. Which only meant any hiccups along that road would toss her all the more and make her blind to anything in the way. Such as the truth. Whatever that was.

"He was married, Melanie. Had kids."

She wasn't listening.

"Then maybe the Stewarts can answer the last of my questions," she said.

Tristen placed a hand on her arm. "Mel, hold up a sec. What if they don't know? This could not only change the way you see your family's past, but it could also alter the way Stewart's family sees their own. And even the way Canada, as a country, views the old star."

She chewed on her bottom lip, thinking it through. Finally, she sighed. "People have a right to live a happy, blissfully unaware existence, don't they? I can't make this claim without revealing secrets, can I?"

She had that defeated look again, and Tristen tried to ignore the taunting voice in his head pinning the blame squarely on himself.

"Melanie?" A man stood in the doorway, his face grim. "Can I have a moment?"

"Sure."

Melanie excused herself and Tristen took Dot her phone, weaving through the office's few cubicles to find her. The reporters, who on Sunday had been as thick as a swarm of mosquitos in Algonquin Park, had faded away, and he felt okay again with Dot working here. Although, with Melanie back in the fight, he might have to broach the topic of his daughter finding a new place to complete her work experience, since things could easily heat up once more. Not a fun prospect. At all.

A few minutes later, he spotted Melanie heading back to her office, her face pale. He caught up to her as she stuffed items in her shoulder bag. He grasped her hands, holding her still so he could figure out what was wrong. Her fingers felt small and fragile in his and the overwhelming urge to protect her took over. "What's happened?"

She pulled away and began stuffing the few personal effects she kept on her desk into her bag. "I'm being investigated for slander and my license has been temporarily suspended. Effective immediately."

It looked like it was time to let the monster out and take charge of things once and for all.

TRISTEN PACED OUTSIDE HIS daughter's room and thought about what he was going to say. He needed to kick Dot's girlfriend's father's butt. And doing that would likely undo the tentative bond he and his daughter had built over the past week. It was going to be a long haul to the end of August after this little chat. Really long.

Doubting himself, he turned to leave just as the bedroom door swung open. Dot, hand on hip, gave him an unimpressed look. "What?" she asked.

"What? Nothing." He quickly moved back.

"You've been pacing outside my room. Do you need love advice or are you grounding me?"

"What? Why?"

"What? Why?" she mocked.

"Don't do that."

"Do what?" she asked innocently.

Man, she was good. "Dot, I have to do something and you're not going to like it."

"You're marrying Melanie? Because that wouldn't be so bad. Unless you keep buying her horrible cups."

The thought of marrying Melanie with Dot's approval had, surprisingly, sent his mind off into a happy little meadow where it began frolicking and singing.

"Dot. I have to fight Rubicore."

His daughter gave a halfhearted shrug and pushed past him. "Are there any of those blueberries left?"

That was it? No Tilt-A-Whirl open for business today to give him the most terrifying ride of his life?

In the kitchen, Dot dumped the last of the blueberries into her hand and, tipping her head back, dropped them into her mouth. Trying to understand women and their moods was like trying to tag a ghost.

"You're not upset?"

"Why should I be?"

"You eat like a kid. Wipe your mouth."

"I'm a kid for another five months and six days. I've got to live it up. With the responsibilities of voting and the ability to get wed without parental permission, as well as drink alcohol in some of our provinces, I should live it up while I can. My days of being a carefree dependent are numbered."

"It might get nasty between us and Rubicore," he warned.

"Sink your teeth into them, Dad." She had her head in the fridge now and was rooting around. "Kill them for what they're doing to Melanie."

"The fudge is in the crisper."

"The crisper?" She turned, her lip curled up in the same way it used to when she was a baby and someone talked goo-goo-ga-ga at her.

Tristen patted his midriff. "Out of sight, out of mind."

She unwrapped a square of chocolate, popped it in her mouth, then another. That would be one way to put it out of mind—just let her devour it.

"What happened to you and Samantha?" he asked.

"She was *experimenting*." Dot's scowl deepened as she rolled her eyes, clearly disgusted.

"Oh."

"I know, right?" She turned, livid all of a sudden. "Who *pretends* to be a lesbian?" Her eyes grew damp. "I mean, it's hard enough. It would be like me going slumming just to see what it was like, then turning around when I had slum friends and saying, 'Nah, just kidding. I don't like your way of life, after all. Enjoy! I'm heading back to the easy path, where everyone loves me and nobody looks down at me.'" She was crying full force and Tristen froze, stunned by her revelation. He closed the space between them and squeezed her tightly, wanting to take her pain and fill the hollow spot within her with love.

He stroked her hair, surprised at how soft the shorn bit at the back was under his palm. Despite the makeup and perfume she still smelled like his daughter.

Dot pushed away. "It's *so* hard finding someone." Her bottom lip folded in pain and she crashed back against his chest.

"It is."

"You met Mom in high school—what do you know?"

"Yeah, okay." He'd give her that one. What did he know, truly?

"The odds were in your favor, too." Dot broke contact again, glowering at him, and he tried not to smile. She looked like a lost tyke with her cheeks wet and her lips pouty from the injustice of her lot in life.

"We all lead lives of quiet desperation." He buffed his knuckles on his chest and let out a loud sigh as though hard done by. "It's my lot in life to carry the burden of being so devastatingly handsome."

"The odds are in your favor because you're not *gay*."

He tipped her chin up with a finger. She'd stopped crying, but frustration still had her in its grip. "I'm always here."

"Right here in the kitchen?" She gave him a cocky scowl.

That was his girl.

"Yep." He grinned. "Right here. Just waiting for you to need your old man. I might not always be able to say the words you need to hear, but that doesn't make them any less true."

She swallowed hard. "I know."

"Good."

"Now go crush Samantha's dad so bad he has to use a catheter to take a piss."

Tristen ran a hand through his hair uncomfortably.

"*Metaphorically*, Dad. Yeesh." Dot rolled her eyes, scooped up the last of the fudge and disappeared back into her room.

He let out a long breath.

Things were probably going to be okay between him and Dot. But Melanie? That was a whole different story.

Chapter Thirteen

Tristen pulled out a stool at the granite island and poured Melanie a glass of lemonade, smiling as he recalled the nickname the bikers had given her only a week and a half ago, when she'd rescued him. He set the tall glass in front of her, wondering if she needed something stronger after the way Rubicore had proceeded to run her career and credibility off the tracks in a mere handful of days. He could probably use something stronger himself, considering he was about to reveal his hidden side to Melanie.

He was surprised how nervous he was. But he'd been plotting and organizing things behind Melanie's back for days and it was time to let her in on what he'd done.

He'd already hurt everyone he cared about once. Why not again, when this time he'd be on the right side? He needed to protect them from Rubicore, whose leaders were gearing up for a grand slam.

But the Rubicore team didn't realize that Tristen was planning to add their blood to the battle this time. And a battle it would be, because helping Melanie he finally understood that his failed marriage hadn't been entirely his fault. While he still didn't know if he could control the monster, he knew his wife could have told him sooner that she didn't want gifts. Melanie had returned the antiques money; why couldn't his wife have done the same, if it wasn't what she needed or wanted? Cindy could have asked him to take a different job, or asked for help, as Melanie had. The truth was Tristen and his ex could have done a lot of things differently. Separately and together. But he hadn't ruined her life all on his own. She'd been half of that marriage, too.

But now he had another chance. Melanie saw him, understood him and was strong enough to push back if she needed to.

Tristen Bell wasn't as broken as he'd thought.

"It's time to blow everything out of the water," he said, taking in the bags under Melanie's eyes. He held her hands in his, hoping she'd pull from him the strength she needed, and that he would be able to provide whatever it was she required in order to carry on.

He knew he'd been misguided, thinking money, power, and prestige were everything. But no, with Melanie, he could be on the right side and, for once, do some good things in this world. She was his chance to make things right.

No more hiding out. He was ready.

"I've suited up, Melanie. I'm all in. If this fight matters to you, it matters to me. I should never have chickened out and left you to do this on your own."

She laughed, sounding slightly teary, and leaned hard against his chest. Holding her, he felt as though the things he could do for this strong woman would never be enough.

But he'd do his best because she was what mattered.

"We're going to tackle Rubicore from a united front. I have your back." He placed a light kiss in her curls and she tipped her head up, bleary eyes searching for an answer he hoped she found.

"Really?"

"I'm not backing out this time. I've already called some folks in Toronto to do some investigating. It's going to get ugly, I won't deny that. But we'll be careful so they can't pin things on you. I don't want this situation with the bogus slander claim to get worse. I need you to go apply for heritage status, so you can save Trixie Hollow from the mice and the taxman. Rile up Rubicore by mentioning their place in Heritage Row, too."

She gave him a doubtful glance.

"Do it. They can't touch your license for that. Next, we'll file formal complaints against Rubicore and the municipality. The way they are pushing this resort through is not right. We'll get an unbiased, secondary party to do impact studies—I've already got the process started on that and have paid to have it expedited. As well, we need to get people stirred up people about the parking lot and the camp. I've got a few people working on that as well."

"There's no time," Melanie sighed. "Everything's already so far along."

"I've asked a friend to look into the slander claim. He says there is a good chance he could have you back in the office by next week."

"You're joking?"

"You may have a case for loss of income, as well as them tarnishing your reputation."

She gave a small laugh. "Sometimes we live in a ridiculous world, don't we?"

"We'll get Rubicore, Melanie. We will."

She sagged back onto her stool, taking a sip of her drink. "There's not enough money or time to fight them the way we need to, Tristen."

"I have so much money to pour into this it's disgusting. So much that Rubicore won't know what hit them."

"Tristen you can't."

"I can and I will. This is important."

She gave him a look and he said, "It's my money." He topped up her glass, even though she'd barely taken more than a few sips.

"And once we get these proceedings shoved through, the municipality can't approve more permits until it's resolved. We'll stall Rubicore and hit them where it hurts the most—"

"Their bottom line. How are you going to get proceedings through in time to stop anything?"

He smiled knowingly.

"They're going to be so pissed," Melanie said.

"Are you ready for me to rock your world?"

"You already have." She blushed, then stood on the lower spindles of the stool, hands on his shoulders as she gave him a light kiss, before sitting again.

Tristen blinked, his mind leaving the task at hand. He forced himself to take a seat on the other side of the island, away from Melanie and her tempting lips. He really wanted to take that kiss somewhere else right now, but he still had more to tell her, and if she kissed him again he'd have her in his bed in less than a second flat, their battle plans forgotten.

He focused once more, but found himself unable to sit. "On a more personal note, I sweet-talked a lady named Betsy into bumping up your claim for tax reassessment. Not only did she do that, she also gave consideration to making your reassessment retroactive."

"Get out of town!" Melanie launched herself around the granite island and into his arms. He held her tightly, inhaling her coconut scent. After a second, she went to pull away, but he tightened his grip, not wanting to let her go, fearing that since he'd started to allow his had-to-win-at-all-costs side out, he might not have the chance to hold her again. Cindy hadn't like that side of him; what were the chances a gentle, sweet woman like Melanie would?

She laughed and placed her hands between them. "Okay, you can let go now."

He rested his head in the crook of her neck, inhaled once more and slowly complied with her request.

A blush tinged her cheeks as she seated herself again and he could see that she was having a tough time focusing, too. "How did you manage to get Betsy to consider that? I've talked to her *three times.*"

"I need a shower after all that schmoozing." He used to put on the charm almost daily to smooth the wheels of progress, and hadn't thought twice about it. But now it made him feel dirty, manipulative, and exhausted. And yet he'd done it. And he'd do it again for a woman like Melanie. He'd seen her tax bill for that old cottage and it was horrendous. "I should probably mention," he said, moving to the open living room, "she didn't just give you consideration. She had your taxes reduced and gave you one year retroactive at the new rate."

He fell backward onto the couch as Melanie leaped at him, peppering him with kisses. Max, waking up from his spot on the cool stone apron surrounding the fireplace, jumped up, barking.

"Shush, Max," Tristen said with a laugh, trying to shove the dog's massive snout out from between him and Melanie.

"Thank you, thank you," she said between kisses. "You don't know how much this means to me!"

He held her tight, kissing her with everything he had so she'd know just how much she mattered to him. His hands ran down past her waist, giving her backside a squeeze.

"What's Max so—" Dot began, entering the room. "Oh," she said with mild disgust. "Never mind."

Melanie jumped off Tristen, leaving him feeling strangely bereft, and ran over to lift Dot in a massive hug. "Your dad is so awesome!" She dropped the teen back on her feet and raced to the front door, flinging it open wide so she could holler to the chickadees and squirrels, "So totally awesome!"

She returned to the room, grinning, her excitement pulling a smile from Dot.

"I can't wait to tell my sisters. They'll be so pumped."

"Is this about Rubicore?" Dot asked.

"He's saving me money on taxes."

"Wait, there's more," Tristen said.

"Not more ugly teacups," Dot grumbled as she slouched back to her room, likely to commiserate with her teenage friends about the instability of adults.

"I talked to the camp director and he says he'll stay on board even if we have to start fresh somewhere else," Tristen said.

"He shouldn't have to move."

"I know."

"But I guess an open camp can still help kids, no matter where it's located, right?" Melanie's smile was weak, her eyes lost in the past.

"What is it about you and this camp, anyway?" He pulled her close and tucked a curl behind her ear. He felt strongly about a few of the charities he'd supported over the years, but it was nothing personal like the camp was for Melanie. She acted as though it was a part of her.

"I went there. As a camper and as a counselor. I fund-raise for them." There was a steely glint in her eyes.

"I can't see you as a troubled kid."

"I'd experienced trauma." She sat on the couch, eyes blank. "My dad died in an accident. I took it the hardest out of all us girls. Mom sent me to Adaker because I wouldn't stop crying." Melanie gave Tristen a sheepish smile that faltered. "Puberty, you know how it is. But that camp showed me that I still had a lot, and that there were kids much worse off than I was. They help so many children. I can't bear the idea of it not being able to do that any longer."

"We can still help kids."

"If the camp closes, that's it."

"There is funding for the camp no matter where it ends up."

"But Rubicore won't pay to build a new camp somewhere else."

"I hope you don't mind, but I've taken care of that, too."

Her jaw dropped open.

"I've agreed to be a private donor."

She landed on him again, but this time he was ready. He grabbed her as her legs wrapped around his waist, and pivoted so her body was pinned between him and the wall. When her lips met his, he leaned into her, deepening the kiss until her body slowly melted.

As he kissed her, he wished he could find a way to tell her that he didn't want her to run away when this was all over.

"You're amazing," she whispered, and in that moment he felt like the hero he'd always dreamed of being by taking control of things for others. It didn't mean Melanie was any less strong, only that he could be there to remove barriers that stood in her way.

With one hand against her soft cheek, he pulled back so he could look her in the eye. "You're the most beautiful, strongest thing I've ever seen. You know that?"

Her legs loosened around his hips and her feet slid to the floor. She started to push him away, but he blocked her.

"What? You don't want me to help?" Damn. He'd been so sure he'd gotten it right this time.

"It's not that. Let's just…let's not complicate things, okay?"

"There's nothing complicated here." He kissed her again, pulling her close. She softened into his embrace, and he lost himself in the feel of her skin, her mouth, the moist warmth of her tongue.

She angled her mouth away, panting slightly. "Tristen?"

"Yeah?"

"I can't do one-nighters. I just…" She looked at him, her eyes full of pain and a deep affection that surprised him so fully he dropped his arms, stepping away.

He watched her walk back to the island, take a sip of her lemonade with a trembling hand, then say, "Let's just get back to killing Rubicore, okay?"

Without thinking, he joined her, his mind on everything but Rubicore.

"WHAT THE HELL KIND of tricks do you think you're trying to pull?" Aaron Bloomwood backed Melanie down a side street, away from the commotion of the protest she and Daphne were leading with Tristen in front of the municipal office, over the parking lot issue. One last protest and then it was nothing but hard-core business. Tristen had been up half the night, setting things in place for the upcoming battle. He'd called in favors, talking to people she'd only heard about in the news. Their net was ready and about to fall down on Rubicore.

Spittle flew from Aaron's mouth as he jabbed the air around her, making her wonder if he'd caught wind of their plans. "First that goddamn whiney-nosed camp for losers, and now this stupid museum and island that nobody cares about!"

She kept backing up, staying out of range.

"Aaron, so lovely to see you," Tristen said casually, appearing beside her and she stepped into his shadow, relieved to not be alone. "The horns never did recede, did they?" He reached out and patted Aaron's head, studying the man with a curiosity that would have made Melanie laugh if she hadn't been so worried about the reaction he was about to earn. Not only was Tristen taunting the raging bull, he was ballsy enough to touch it.

The man focused on Tristen. "Are you behind this?" Aaron pitched forward, hands squeezed into white-knuckled fists.

Tristen smiled an innocent, infuriating grin. "Oh, Aaron."

The patronizing tone hit its mark, sparking the executive's temper as though Tristen was a torero, prepping the bull for the matador with another well-timed spear. Was Melanie supposed to be the matador? She hoped not. She wanted to run far away, not escalate this battle.

"Do you have any idea what this two-bit lawyer is doing? The mess she is causing?"

"Oh, has she caused a problem?" Tristen asked casually. There was a steely glint in his eyes that Melanie hadn't seen before.

"She just got our renovations for Heritage Row shut down."

"I did?" Melanie grinned at Tristen, who gave her a small head tilt as if to say, *Keep a lid on it, woman.*

"You are never going to practice law again." Aaron was on her once more, but Tristen wedged his shoulder between them.

"No." He shoved a finger so hard into the man's chest, Melanie was surprised it didn't draw blood. "Now you listen to me, you jackass." His voice was low, a primal warning that sent chills up her spine. "This woman is off-limits. You say nothing to her. You don't touch her. Threaten her. Sabotage her or her reputation in any way. You understand? If anything bigger than a sliver happens in her life, I am holding you personally responsible. Do you understand what that means?"

Tristen was forcing Aaron to back away. The developer had a look in his eyes Melanie hadn't thought possible: fear.

"You're a nobody now," he retorted. "You carry no clout. The whole world has forgotten about you and the way you ran scared from Toronto."

"Well, then I suppose it is a good thing that a tip from a

nobody can still set up an investigation for corruption, wouldn't you say?"

The way Tristen rocked back on his heels, so cool and relaxed, made Melanie's heart pulse madly. He had their quarry right where he wanted him, and was playing it all so easily and with such confidence it made her want to jump on Tristen and kiss him so hard he forgot his name.

"You don't scare me." Aaron's voice trembled with rage.

"I know where you live, I know where all your partners live, Aaron James Bloomwood. I know how you play your games. Shall I set up a watchdog committee? Oh, wait. I already did that. Have fun answering to them."

Chills raced down Melanie's spine again. Tristen was so...this other side to him... It was hot.

"You lie," Aaron spit.

"So sorry to spoil the surprise for you. Oh, and the municipality? We're pretty sure you have someone you're paying under the table to push things through. I've got people looking into that, as well."

"You'll pay for this, Bell. You'll pay!" Aaron backed away, his finger raised in warning.

"Don't worry. I already have. Several times over."

Aaron stormed around the corner and Melanie worried he was going to come back with Mario and others carrying weapons. She shivered and tugged Tristen in the opposite direction.

He stopped her, his hands bracing her shoulders. "I'm sorry. Are you okay?" He looked worried.

"Yeah, fine." Her voice was as shaky as her legs.

"Liar." He drew her around the building and back into the crowd, where the protest against Rubicore continued.

She sagged against him in the safety of the gathering.

"I'm sorry you had to see that." Tristen kept his attention on everything but her, as though he was afraid to face her.

"I'm not."

He gave a sad sigh, shoulders drooping. "This stuff doesn't bring out the best in me, Melanie. I get lost in it. I want blood when I fight someone like Rubicore."

"Well, I've never seen a man act sexier. Thank you." She pushed her hands up his firm, wide chest and smiled, leaning into him, hoping he'd kiss her. "My hero."

He seemed stunned and took a half step back, then struggled to recover his balance. "I'm sorry, did you just say that monstrous scene was sexy?"

"Very." She drew a finger down his jaw, incredibly turned on. "I like how you stuck to your guns and stood up to him. He's a big bully. And in case you didn't notice, I'm a lawyer. We're always out for blood." Melanie pushed her chest into Tristen's, trying to get closer, hoping he'd see how much he'd aroused her. "I happen to think a man coming to my rescue is unbearably sexy and I feel safe around you, Tristen Bell."

His arms finally wrapped around her, so tight her breath left her lungs. His kiss was so deep and full of need her knees buckled, forcing his broad shoulders and strong arms to get to work and hold her up. Yet another reason to love the man.

Tristen cared about her. It wasn't just his gestures that said it, such as when he hurried ahead to get the door for her, but the bounce in his step that couldn't be faked when he came up to her. He was a man of gestures, and he'd just shown her that she was his. His. His. His.

They broke apart and Melanie simply stared into his eyes, wanting him to know that she liked him, too. That she wanted him. Just him.

No pressure for "I love you" or a big commitment. She just wanted to be with him and receive whatever he could give.

Dot materialized out of the crowd beside them, Tigger in tow. "That was so awesome, Daphne!" the teen exclaimed, when Melanie's sister appeared as well. "Did you see those Environment Canada guys totally scouting you out?"

Daphne gave her a half smile. "Yeah."

"Can I interview you for an essay I have to write for work experience?"

"Yeah, sure." Daphne still seemed distracted and Melanie tried to pull her mind off Tristen long enough to figure out what was up. He hooked her pinkie with his index finger, keeping her close as she drifted out of his arms.

"You okay?" she asked Daphne. Her sister wasn't herself at the moment and Melanie wondered if Aaron had talked to her, too.

"Yeah, fine." She gave a small smile. "Just thinking."

Tristen, standing behind Melanie, lightly touched her elbow, letting her know he was still there. Tingles ran up her arm from the contact, giving her shivers despite the early evening sun. Melanie turned to face him, hooking both hands in his, becoming lost in his gaze.

She heard Daphne say, "Okay, I have Dot, if that's okay with you, Tristen?"

He gave a chin lift that sufficed for a nod.

"Okay, then. See you later. Much later," Daphne said, giving them space.

"I have the best sister in the world."

"I agree. Unless you are plotting my murder and she's dealing with potential witnesses, in which case I may retract my agreement." There was a hint of a smile in his eyes.

Why were they still standing here? She was desperate to have him. Something carnal to prove to herself once again that his gestures, kisses, and smoldering looks were the beginning of something.

Melanie slipped her arm through his, holding her breath as she asked, "Want to do something?"

He didn't say a word for a moment, then murmured, "Yeah, let's do something." His eyes were caught on her lower lip and she ran her tongue over it. His attention was making her nervous. He drifted closer, his side pushing into hers.

"Kiss me," she said.

"Better idea." He pulled her toward the parking lot. "You drive here?"

"No, Daphne gave me a ride."

"Good."

Tristen opened the passenger door to his truck with a creak, and hurriedly helped her in. He was in a rush and that was fine by her. She needed to find out if what she felt and saw between them was as real as she believed.

Tristen, in a move that surprised her, leaped into the passenger's side, clutching the door frame with his left hand as he swung his lips to hers. His warm fingers clutched the back of her neck and her arms flowed around him, pulling him closer. He kissed her long and deep, his tongue probing.

Hurry, they needed to hurry.

His eyes were hooded with passion and longing when he leaned back, his broad shoulders blocking her view of the outside world. "Can I take you home, Melanie Summer?"

"Please do. And ignore the speed limit."

MELANIE COULDN'T STOP SMILING. She snuggled closer to Tristen's warm, naked body, her cheek resting on his firm pectorals. He was even more ripped than she'd remembered. All that working with rock had done amazing things to his body. And in turn, his amazing body had done mind-blowing things to hers.

She never wanted to leave his bed. If he trapped her here forever, not letting her go, she'd be more than okay with it.

His fingers lazily drifted up and down her bare back, pausing to lift a handful of curls off her neck. She felt as though she could melt into him.

"I love it here," she whispered.

"My house?"

"In your arms."

He pulled her tighter, kissing the top of her head. "Yeah."

It was difficult not to say the words that wanted to trip off her tongue. That she loved him. That things felt right when he was around. That, finally, she felt as though someone understood her and shared the same wavelength. That someone was there. Yet it wasn't about loneliness. She'd come to terms with that long ago. This was about being *alone*. When he was around she didn't feel as though she had to do it all herself. There was someone else there to lean on. To be her rock. A teammate.

She was falling hard. And she didn't know if he was, but it felt as though he might be. She didn't believe she was someone who needed to hear the words, but she still wanted to. To ensure that the gestures meant what she thought they did. He was a gentleman, but he took extra care with her. She could see that. The way he was always there, watching, ready to catch her.

Would he say those words she needed to hear?

Did it matter if she was happier now than she could ever remember?

She wanted to tell herself it didn't, but she knew that it would be lying.

IT WAS CINDY. GREAT. He'd just made early morning love to Melanie, making that slight worried, questioning look in her eyes disappear almost completely, and now his ex had to show up, ready to ruin everything.

A large ring that hadn't been purchased by him flashed on Cindy's finger. Its significance both bothered and relieved him. Bothered him because she hadn't told him she'd found someone new. Relieved him because she *had*.

"Hey," he said, walking to her car, cup of coffee in hand. He was still in his pajama pants and an old T-shirt, and it made him wonder just how early his ex had gotten up to drive all the way here for her latest mission.

He blocked her from moving forward. He didn't want her in his home. Didn't want her acting as though she owned the place.

A man he presumed to be Cindy's new husband got out of the passenger side and Tristen shook the short man's hand, offering them both congratulations.

"Does Dot know?"

Cindy shared a guilty glance with her new man. She gave a small nod. "Yeah. She didn't want to go with us for the elopement."

"So you dumped her on me?"

That sounded wrong. His daughter could never be dumped on him because she was always welcome.

"Yeah. I figured it was your turn to deal with all of that." Cindy gave him a smirk.

"Thanks."

Another smirk. She obviously thought he was being sarcastic.

He took a sip of his coffee, wondering how he hadn't been able to see how jaded and bitchy Cindy had become. She used to be... well, she'd always sort of had that side to her, but it seemed as though his presence amplified it these days. "For what do I owe the pleasure of your visit?"

"Dot texted me a few days ago. She said she wanted to come home," Cindy replied.

"And so you're just coming now? Unannounced, I might add." Tristen widened his stance, knowing his attitude would intimidate the new husband, who was likely here for one reason only—to intimidate Tristen into doing whatever Cindy wanted.

Get a real job, buddy.

This was his turf, his kid. Dot may have wanted to go home, but he was certain she'd prefer to stay now that the Rubicore thing was heating up. She'd want to see it through as far as she could.

"She still has fifteen hours of work experience to complete," he said, arms crossed. "I think she'll want to stay."

"I'd like to hear it from her."

"By all means."

His ex began moving to the front door.

"I'll have her come out." His voice was firm, a warning, and Cindy halted and muttered something under her breath. He turned. "What?" he demanded.

"I know that look, Tristen." Cindy's voice had an angry tremble. "Like you own the whole friggin' world. Well, you don't, okay? You don't. I liked the new Tristen better."

The new Tristen was a scared pansy hiding out from the world. The old Tristen had been powered by greed and a need to prove himself to Cindy, so she'd finally show him some love. How wrong he'd been. The two of them had never truly understood each other.

There had never been anything wrong with him. He'd simply been with the wrong woman. But now he wasn't, and life was about to get good.

"This is who I am," he said, spreading out his arms. "Take it or leave it."

"I think I already did."

He smiled. It was time to set the record straight on how things were going to be from here on out.

"If you need help with your business, let me know. Dot said it's struggling."

"It's fine," Cindy said, her voice tight.

"What do you need?"

"From you? Nothing." Her eyes snapped and flashed. "You sold it, remember? Ran away from it all."

"As a wise woman once told me, we're all still connected. I'd like to help if I can. Not a lot, but somehow."

"Get over yourself. I'm here for Dot."

"She's come into her own, you know. And I'd like to see her more. Maybe every summer. Holidays. Every other weekend. I'll make the drive."

"Oh?" His wife gave him a saucy look. "In the less than two weeks you've had her you've turned her around and think you're going to make daddy of the year? Bring her out."

"*You've* done a good job with her." His voice was just above a whisper, and Cindy froze, caught, hanging on his every word. "She's an amazing young woman."

His ex blinked back tears, chin raised. "Yeah, on my own."

"I'm sorry I didn't realize what you needed. It didn't occur to me that what I was giving you and Dot meant nothing to you."

Cindy was blinking rapidly now. Her new husband moved closer to try and save the day. *Too late for that, man.* His old life with Cindy had crashed and burned. It was time to listen to the relationship's black box and bury the dead.

"She values spending time together more than gifts," he said to the man.

"Yeah, I *know*."

Tristen smiled. He'd had her first and it was killing the other man. Good. These two might actually make it together.

"I'll get Dot for you."

Their daughter was already at the door, listening, her eyes puffy from sleep. And he hoped nothing else. She crossed her arms, Max growling at her side. "I'm not going back to Toronto."

Cindy's plucked brows lifted.

"I have a work experience job here. And I need to help with Rubicore."

"Rubicore?" Cindy's eyes widened and she turned to Tristen. "Rubicore?" she repeated. "Do you not listen to me, ever?"

"Pretty much...nope." He slung an easy arm around his daughter, as Max kept an eye on the strangers. "We're showing them a thing or two about how to treat the environment. Aren't we, kid?"

Dot smiled. "Damn straight, Dad."

"Language," both parents warned at the same time.

Cindy drew herself up, uncertain.

"Can I keep her until the end of summer?" Tristen asked. "We have some lost time to make up for."

TRISTEN STOOD IN HIS kitchen, his ex gone, his daughter tossing a stick for Max out on the small grassy slope beside the house. Being with Melanie, he felt as though he could slip into infinity. His world was already losing its edges, bleeding into hers.

He understood it now. The puppy dog men who seemed content to lead the life of the completely whipped. The husbands who followed their wives through the mall, carrying their shopping, holding their purses, waiting outside stores and doing the "man stand" outside change rooms. It wasn't being whipped, it was about contentment. About being close to the woman you loved, and receiving comfort by being in her presence.

It was about being with her. When you were apart, you no longer felt whole. Now he understood why Cindy had felt neglected. It wasn't just about him not saying "I love you" enough.

He poured a fresh cup of coffee, mixed in cream and sugar, and brought it to his bedroom, where Melanie was dead to the world, stretched out under the sheets like a Renaissance painting. His.

Or he'd like her to be.

They needed to talk, and putting his feelings into words would be hard. He'd failed Cindy, but he wouldn't make the same mistakes with Melanie. He could show her his love, but he needed to find a way to say the words.

He waved the coffee under her nose, careful not to spill it on the robin's-egg-blue sheets. She smiled and stirred.

"I had a dream your ex was here to take Dot away from you," she mumbled, her voice endearingly thick with sleep.

He leaned down to kiss her lips. "It wasn't a dream, my fair maiden. But I vanquished and triumphed."

She rolled onto her back, careful to keep the sheet covering her breasts. Her pale skin was so plush and beautiful he wanted to pull her against him and make love to her again and again.

"Vanquished?" she asked.

"Cindy was here. But Dot is staying."

Melanie propped herself up, exposing more pearly skin as she sipped the warm drink. Her eyes closed and she inhaled happily. "This is perfect. Thank you, Tristen."

He smiled and massaged her foot. He loved the fact that she'd thanked him and relished this quiet moment between them, in no hurry to run off anywhere. It was a privilege being the first person she saw when she woke in the morning, and he hoped it was one he would have again and again.

"I really like having you here, Melanie."

She flashed a hint of a smile.

He felt bashful, like a ten-year-old boy revealing his crush to the object of his affections. "I like *you*."

"Good." She gave a small nod and got out of bed, the sheet trailing behind.

That was all? No *Where is the 'I love you'?*

"We're okay?" he asked tentatively.

"Is there a reason we shouldn't be?" Her expression turned wary, her shoulders tight.

"Not at all. But what about you?"

"Me?"

"Do you like me, too?"

"Well, I *do* hop into bed with just about anyone." She shot him a sassy wink. "So I can see how you might get confused." Smiling, she came close and stroked the stubble on his jaw.

"Okay, so we like each other. Do you trust me?"

"Yeah," she said thoughtfully. "I do."

"Even though I am not always so great with words?"

She laughed, her chest bouncing. "You're kidding me, right?"

"Er, no."

"Tristen Bell, you are the complete package. You know that?" She slipped her fingers over his shoulders, plucking at the fabric of his old T-shirt. "You show me you care in so many ways. All the little things you do for me, making sure I'm okay. Those mean more to me than silly words." She turned shy, her cheeks pink. "It's how I know."

Feeling lighter than he had in years, he cornered her by the dresser, pulling her tight against him. He gave her a kiss that should resolve any lingering doubts as to his intentions. "You look like a goddess with your hair all disheveled, the sheet draped in front of you like that. Very Renaissance."

"Okay, now you're just trying to get me back into bed with you."

"Is it working?"

She laughed and pushed him away. Then tipped her head in the direction of Dot's room, eyebrows raised.

Tristen eased closer, placing his hips against hers. "She's outside playing with the dog." He kissed Melanie again, the sheet dropping from her body as they wrapped their arms around each other and fell onto the bed.

An incredible way to start the day.

Chapter Fourteen

Before Melanie could figure out what had gone wrong at the picnic, Tristen was flying around her, his fist connecting with another man's face.

"Not on my watch!" Tristen shouted as bones crunched.

Tigger, who had been talking to the knuckle-sandwich eater, raced to her mother's side, eyes wide with fright. Melanie, still not comprehending what was happening, pulled Tristen away from the man.

Mistral.

Oh, of all the rotten luck. Daphne's ex-boyfriend had blood pouring everywhere. He'd press charges for certain.

Melanie tried to hand Tigger's father a wad of napkins from the picnic basket, but Tristen blocked her, grabbing them and tossing them at the man, who tried to snag the fluttering objects, one hand to his gushing nose.

They'd been having a picnic with Daphne and Tigger by the docks in Port Carling as they planned their next move against Rubicore.

"What's going on?" Melanie asked in a calm, even voice.

"He was taking Tigger," Tristen said, his left hand clenched around his right fist.

"Whoa." Dot, who had gone to grab ice cream, came to a

sudden halt as she took in the scene, the cones in their cardboard holder tipping precariously.

"He was taking Tigger," Tristen repeated, jaw clenched.

"I was introducing myself!" the man shouted, his own hands clamped over his nose, which made his voice sound nasal. "I'm her father!"

"What?" Tristen's eyes were fire and ice. "Why were you trying to lure her away? Answer that!"

"We were going to play Frisbee."

Daphne was strangely quiet, but her hands trembled as she held her daughter close.

"You don't lure a girl away from her mother." Tristen's face was red, the vein in his forehead bulging. Judging from how fast it was pulsing, he was in danger of a heart attack.

Melanie placed a hand on his shoulder, hoping to settle him before he could attack the man again.

"A father has rights." Mistral's nose was still flowing, the napkins so red it made her head spin.

"From what I've heard, you don't," Tristen snapped. "You're lucky I didn't knee you in the sack and push your deadbeat ass into the lake."

"I, um, I said he could come," Daphne said meekly, idly swiping Tigger's tears away with a thumb. "I'm sorry." She moved around Tristen, who staggered in surprise, while Melanie gaped at her sister.

"You *what*?" Melanie asked.

"He was supposed to be here before everyone else, so I could introduce him."

"But he's...he's the *enemy*," Melanie sputtered. What was her sister thinking, inviting Mistral Johnson, who was not only one of the owning partners of Rubicore, but was trying to steal her daughter away? She'd definitely lost her marbles.

"He's not the enemy," Daphne said hotly. "You're taking things too far, saying that, Melanie."

"Too far?" Okay, she was booking her sister into the psychiatric ward to have her brain checked. "He was trying to kidnap your daughter."

"I was not," the man retorted.

"Just leave it alone, Melanie," Daphne said. "You don't know everything."

Melanie stepped back, shaking her head. That was it, wasn't it? She didn't have a clue who her sister was any longer.

BACK AT THE HOUSE, Melanie waited as Dot took Tigger to the backyard to play, probably sensing things were about to get crazy.

"Why would you let him come around you?" Melanie asked Daphne, setting the picnic basket on the front steps.

"He's receptive to working together and he wants Tigger to be part of his life."

"Think about the timing on that," Tristen snapped. His jaw was so tight Melanie thought his teeth were going to crack. "He is using you, Daphne. Never speak to him until this is over, you understand? Don't let him be around Tigger alone. And if you do have to talk to him, make sure I'm present. And a lawyer. You got that?"

Daphne glared at Tristen with an expression so vehement Melanie had to look away. How did a fine picnic turn so ugly so quickly?

"I don't appreciate the way the two of you are ganging up on me," Daphne said. "I'm an adult and this is my life."

"Tristen is right, Daphne. Mistral is playing both sides. He's taking advantage of your loving, forgiving and trusting nature."

"He wants to be a part of Tigger's life. It's not my right to deny that."

"His timing is rather convenient, as well as suspicious," Tristen said gently. "I think a bodyguard would be a good idea."

Daphne unlocked the front door, calling Tigger to come around the house, effectively dismissing them.

"I agree with Tristen," Melanie said softly. "That was scary."

"You two can take off now," Daphne said. "I don't need this toxicity around me at the moment."

"I live here," Melanie said.

"I need some space to think, or I'm going to say something I'll regret."

Melanie watched as her sister hurried her daughter into the house, the sound of the dead bolt snapping into place behind them.

Kicked out? By Daphne? What alternative reality had Melanie landed in?

"You can stay with us," Tristen said, giving Melanie's shoulder a squeeze. "She just needs time. She's confused."

The three of them began walking the way they'd come, backtracking to get Tristen's truck.

"Do you think she'd mind if I had her tailed?" he asked eventually, taking Melanie's hand. "That Evander fellow Connor's mentioned could keep an eye on her."

"If she found out she'd be livid."

"I can handle her."

"I kind of want my family to like you, Tristen."

He cupped her chin, his expression serious. "And I kind of want your family to stay safe."

Warm and cozy. That's how Melanie felt when she looked into his eyes. "Yeah. Me, too."

"Ew. I'm walking ahead if you guys are going to be all yucky."

Dot positioned herself up front so she didn't have to see them smooch.

Melanie smiled and kissed Tristen lightly, careful not to lose herself in the process, which was so easy to do with him. Breaking away, she threaded her arm through his and began the process of catching up with his daughter.

The tension that had gripped Tristen only moments ago wafted away.

"How's your hand?" Melanie asked, holding it up to take a look.

"Sore. But worth it. That man..." Tristen's face clouded over and his neck reddened, the tension returning.

"I know." Melanie swallowed hard. "There's something happening that I don't understand, and it freaks me out." She sighed. So much to say, so few words to encompass it all.

Tristen wrapped his arm around her shoulders, giving her a squeeze. "The worst part is he's playing to her heart. She wants this. She wants a happy family."

"I just hope she doesn't do something she regrets. She's stopped listening, and I don't trust Mistral one tiny little bit."

It was as if Daphne wanted Mistral back, when all he'd ever done was cause her pain. How many times had Melanie's sister claimed that she didn't need a man to help her raise Tigger, and that it was a blessing Mistral wasn't involved? Had they just been words to cover up her true desire?

Chills raced up Melanie's spine and she snuggled closer to Tristen. When it came right down to it, she didn't feel as though she knew her sister very well.

"Can you give me a ride to my boat?" Melanie asked, as Tristen moved a few steps ahead to unlock the truck for Dot. "I want to go to Nymph Island."

"Alone?" Tristen was back at her side in an instant.

"Unless you two wanted to come keep me company?"

"You're not going anywhere without us. Dot! We're going to Melanie's island."

While Melanie's world might be turning upside down, at least she had Tristen by her side.

"THIS IS GETTING SCARY." Melanie stood beside Tristen on Nymph Island's dock, staring at the charred hole in the trees where another cottage of Muskoka's Heritage Row was missing. "What do you want to bet they burned it down themselves?"

Tristen didn't say a word, just clenched his jaw and kept an arm around her, squeezing a tad too tight.

Rubicore wasn't playing fair. Two of four heritage cottages gone. Just like that.

"Looks like it's time to fight fire with fire." Dot laughed, plunking herself on the edge of the dock, feet in the water. "Can you believe the gall? Of course we're going to investigate that." She looked over her shoulder at her father. "Right, Dad?"

"Definitely. I'll call in some favors and get investigators in here before any evidence is gone."

Tristen began dialing someone and Melanie sat in a Muskoka chair, fingers against her lips, thinking. She inhaled the scents of warm wood, lake, pines, and a hint of wrongdoing that smelled a lot like the evil side of progress and the slaughter of what was real and meaningful.

She pulled out her cell phone, checked for a signal, then called her big sister Hailey. "Hails? You back in town? You're going to need to come photograph something for me." She dialed another number. "Mrs. Star? Can you get on the phone—call everyone you know? Another cottage on Heritage Row was just destroyed. Fire this time. Owned by Rubicore, too."

Tristen, who was done with his call, gave her a warning look. Slander, yeah, yeah, yeah. She wasn't saying anything, just providing information that could be put together however Mrs. Star felt inclined.

Melanie made another call. "Austin? Yeah, Melanie here. I need you to stir up shit about Mistral Johnson, Aaron Bloomwood, his partner Mario, and any other Rubicore bigwigs you can find."

"Jim Hanna!" Dot interjected.

"Jim Hanna. Yes. Anything. Photos would be good."

Another call. "Connor? Does that Evander guy do any bugging? Think he could bug Mr. Valos's office? Perfect. Thanks."

Melanie punched in another call. "Rick? I don't care who Rubicore is to the paper, I need you to find a way to get something into the press in Toronto—use a pseudonym if you need to—and reveal how the company owns Adaker as their own personal charity, but have been lying to their board members about the camp's solvency. If you get in trouble, I'll be your lawyer. By the way town council tomorrow—I think things might get interesting. You might want to be there."

She glanced at Tristen, who was still watching, arms crossed, eyebrows raised. "One more call," she told him. She dialed the last number. "Christophe? I have a mystery for you. Can you find out what charity my great-grandmother Ada and Stewart Baker started together and why? I have a feeling it is local." She hung up the phone, staring across the water at Baby Horseshoe Island.

"What was that last call about?" Tristen asked.

Melanie turned to him, her mind still elsewhere. "Adaker. Sound like any names we know, fitted together?"

A slow grin lit like fire and he pulled her close. "You are brilliant, Melanie. Absolutely brilliant."

She could see it all clearly now. The path she was supposed to —no, was *destined* to—take. She was finally where she was supposed to be. She'd never felt that connection to the world and her place in it before, but now she finally could.

And it felt good. Powerful.

Everything was unfolding as it should, even if Rubicore was still winning. It wouldn't be long, though, until she had them where she wanted them.

She just hoped she had enough time to make it happen before it all came crumbling down around her and her sisters. It was like the parachute game they used to play at Adaker, and she'd just lifted the round chute into the air, dived under and tucked it all around her. It would stay inflated before collapsing and protecting her inside. But would there be enough time before it sank, trapping her?

Tristen weaved his fingers through hers as Dot wandered up to the cottage to see if there were any good snacks there. His chest expanded as he drew in a deep breath, and Melanie placed her free hand against it.

"I love you, Melanie." He looked so solemn and so much like a small boy afraid of being rejected that she gently took his chin in her grasp, wanting to see every emotion running through his eyes.

"Thank you for telling me. I know it isn't your style to express yourself in words."

"I'm sorry I'm not very good at this. And while I know you like me, too, I hope you feel the same. The same depth. Maybe not today, but someday."

Melanie laughed, tipping her forehead to touch his. "Tristen Bell, you silly man."

"What?"

"I love you, too, and have for some time." Tears filled her eyes suddenly and trailed down her cheeks. With his thumbs he brushed them dry.

"I am very glad to hear that." His shoulders relaxed and he let out a long, slow breath.

"I feel less alone when you are around," Melanie sniffed. "It sounds corny, because of course I am less alone, but I mean in my heart."

It was as though Tristen saw that broken part inside that she'd been trying to heal for years. That dark corner she wanted to finally squash so she could fill it with light. But Tristen was already there, doing it for her.

"I feel connected when you are around," she said. "Like there is someone with me and that it will all be okay. It's not like that when I'm with others. I still felt lost and like the odd one out. With you, I feel…love. Trust. Beautiful, even. Everything good."

She leaned against him, loving the way he enveloped her in his arms, pressing his lips firmly to her temple. He was protecting her from the world, telling her in his own way that it would all be okay.

Chapter Fifteen

Melanie was red in the face, pounding her fist on the table in the council meeting, and Tristen couldn't help but feel turned on.

Last night they'd spent the night on Nymph Island, Dot tucked away in the cottage's loft, as he and Melanie had wrapped each other in love.

It made it difficult to pay attention to anything but her now. The way Melanie was revved up, her butt wiggling in her dress pants as she laid into the council for not following protocol and posting permit applications in a public place. For failing to have an official open house regarding the proposed resort, and other such business. This was on top of her presentation against Rubicore—which was very thorough and convincing. The council was getting a dressing down from his gal, Mel. Nothing could be sexier to witness, and Tristen had the best seat in the house.

She glanced at him over her shoulder with a wink, then beckoned a man wearing a snazzy suit to hand out sheets of paper to the row of men seated before her.

"Consider yourselves subpoenaed for breach of regulations," the man said coolly.

Tristen sat up. Whoa. That was *not* part of the plan. Is this what she had been doing at the crack of dawn when he'd gone looking for her after finding her side of the bed vacant?

The subpoenas were being delivered to the council, as well as several Rubicore administrators who were seated in the audience.

Hadn't Melanie agreed they were going to let agencies take care of Rubicore and the municipality? As a first-year lawyer one didn't take on the big guns, who had a herd of lawyers bred for going in for the kill.

The men at the table stared, faces aghast and open with fear. Members of the press, who had been lounging against the wall, stood straight, alert, cameras clicking.

She had them.

Was this all a ploy? A tactic to get them to comply? But no, then she would have only threatened. Did she not understand what she was up against? She'd just sent a very large boulder in motion and down a very steep hill. He only hoped she wouldn't be the one to get crushed.

Tristen moved to the back of the room so he could secretly use his cell phone, which wasn't technically allowed in chambers. He needed Connor to get that Evander guy on both women. Now. No more thinking about it. It was go time. Especially since Daphne still wasn't talking to Melanie, who had just pitched a flaming barrel of oil over Rubicore's fence.

If Evander was half as good as a bodyguard as Connor said, then the man could at least tail Daphne while keeping her safe. And if the man had a brother, Tristen would hire him to sit on Melanie's tail. She wouldn't like it, but there was no way she was arguing with him on this one. Nothing was going to happen to his gal, and her risk factor had just multiplied like fruit flies near overripe bananas.

Tristen blinked, focusing on the men lining the back of the room. He took in their black leathers. Their headbands and gnarly beards. Arms crossed over their barrel chests. Scars and tattoos.

Holy hell. What were the Hells Angels doing here? Were they on Melanie's side? He watched as they gave brief, approving smiles when she sass-talked a Rubicore man. Maybe she wasn't as vulnerable as Tristen had thought. Maybe she really did have this all tied up. But why hadn't she told him she was going to drop-kick Rubicore's baby?

Because he would have tied her up at home until she saw sense. That's why. Smart woman. She'd warned him she'd do it his way, and if she had time, also do it her way. Looked as though he needed to keep her busier.

He sat beside Gnarly Beard, hoping he hadn't come off as too big of a prissy prick during their prior meetings, and that the biker would agree to a favor in Melanie's honor. Tristen needed as many people as he could round up to cover her sweetly shaped butt.

"Can you keep her safe?" he asked Ezra.

The biker narrowed his eyes as if trying to read him.

"Can you?" Tristen repeated. He knew he looked scared, but he didn't care. "She can't do this alone. I'm helping her, and I'll do whatever I have to do. But I only know the business side. I need to have someone keep her physically safe. Can you help?"

Without a word, the man gave a tiny nod, then turned back to listen to Melanie give the corporate scum dogs hell.

"I THINK YOU DEFINITELY found your place, Melanie." Tristen shook his head and pressed a kiss against her temple, leaning against his old truck. "This has certainly cranked the heat under Rubicore."

They were so screwed, but he'd promised to back her and he would. This time he wasn't going anywhere. He would use every last resource at his disposal to help keep her safe—to ensure she was the one who came out on top in this battle.

He'd beaten Rubicore before and together they'd do it again.

Several men in black leather loitered nearby, chatting as they leaned against the parking lot's brick wall. Watching. Waiting. Listening. They has his woman's back.

Melanie was vibrating from taking on chambers, and he ran his hands up and down her arms. There was no way he was letting her get back on her motorbike in the state she was in. She'd drive right off the road and into the towering pines surrounding this part of town before she got more than a block or two away.

"You know what Valos means in Finnish?" she asked.

"You know Finnish?"

"It means cast. He's empty. That man could be filled with anything and right now he's filled with deceit and lies and everything that is wrong with this world."

She was punctuating her sentences with pokes to Tristen's chest. He wrapped a hand around hers, stilling the jabbing finger.

"It's going to be okay. You'll get him. You just turned it all upside down and gave it a shake. I'd be surprised if any of those goofs are still in politics six months from today, or that Rubicore is still in business. You're making a name for yourself and standing up for what you feel is right, despite the odds. I admire that. Not everyone can do it."

She let out a shaky laugh and he gave her a hug, feeling incredibly proud.

"It's called being insecure," she said. "You think about others and what they are thinking and needing so you don't have to think about yourself."

"I don't believe that's the reason. Besides, you seem pretty confident and secure to me."

"It's an act." Her voice was shaky, her cheeks flushed.

"Well, there's no reason to act that way, Little Miss Dynamo. Not that you need taking care of, but I'll spend the rest of my days doing so, if you'll let me. And I'll show you in every way I can that you are important to me. Do you understand that? No matter what happens with Rubicore, the council, and the press. Okay?"

She snuggled her head against his chest. "I know you care. I care about you, too."

"I know your mind is still in chambers, but I need you to hear this, Mel. Sometimes I have trouble expressing myself, and I need you to talk to me, even when things get hairy and I go a little berserk after attackers."

She glanced up, her eyes worried. "What do you mean?"

"I need you..." He had to pause to collect himself, since his heart was racing. "...to not run away or kick me out. If you don't feel loved, then tell me, okay? And I'll try to do better."

"I don't think you would ever fail at showing me your love, Tristen." She took a step back, clenching his hands so tightly it made the one that had punched Mistral Johnson ache. Had that been only yesterday?

"Trust me, I could fail. I have before."

"You won't. I trust you, Tristen. You have already shown me in so many ways."

He swept her curls from her shoulders. He'd pulled her back into bed that morning and she hadn't had the time to do it up. "Do you really trust me?"

"With my life."

"Then trust me when I tell you you're beautiful."

Her eyes glimmered with tears and her throat bobbed as she swallowed hard.

"Trust the fact—even if I never say it again—that you are the most beautiful thing I've ever seen and that you always will be."

She let out a self-conscious laugh and bit her bottom lip. He ran his thumb over the pinched flesh, tugging it out from her teeth's grip. "Trust me?"

Finally she nodded, a blush spreading across her pale cheeks.

"I love you, Mel."

This time he would do it right.

MELANIE FELT AS THOUGH her heart was going to explode into flowers and rainbows from all the love she felt inside. She'd just totally busted some balls in chambers and Tristen was all over her like she was the sexiest thing in the world.

His world.

And his world was a world she wanted to live in for the rest of her life.

Nothing could feel better. He'd called her beautiful and meant it. But most importantly, she believed it. He didn't think she was a Sasquatch and he was man enough to handle her splendor and size.

When he told her she had a place, was important, beautiful, and loved, she felt it. Believed it. Trusted it.

He was one-of-a-kind. And hers. All hers.

She felt a rush of adrenaline as a crazy idea flipped through her mind. She could propose. Right here in the parking lot where people were walking to their cars, murmuring to each other about her little showdown. It felt as though she'd just kicked a hornets' nest and her life was finally going to go on that big ride she'd always wanted to take. So why not have her love life take off on that ride, too? She didn't want anyone else by her side as she took on Rubicore and the municipality. At night. In the morning.

Him. Only him.

Tristen was the man who could be by her side through it all, helping her. Not taking over, but trusting her to make her own moves, and clearing obstacles when she needed help. Because of him she knew what path she needed to take in order to save Muskoka. Plus with the tax break he had assisted in wrangling, her sisters had decided that would count toward Melanie's portion of the debt.

She'd done it. She'd finally contributed to the cottage. And it was all due to the wonderful man in her arms.

"I love you, Tristen." She squinted against the gorgeous August sun. She loved the way the light picked up the highlights in his short hair. He was handsome. Strong. Supportive. Everything she never believed she could ever have.

He bent his head to meet hers, kissing her in a way that had her arms wrapping around him and her legs wishing they could do the same.

"You don't know who you are messing with!" shouted an angry voice.

A breeze picked up and Melanie kept kissing Tristen, not wanting to break the moment, not wanting to be distracted or to find a way to chicken out on asking him to be hers forever.

The shouter repeated himself, closer this time. The clinking of chains and the sound of heeled boots crunched on the gravel. Tristen had her out of his arms and pinned behind him in an instant.

From there, she couldn't see the man yelling at them. Ezra and Kane eased up beside her, their friends flanking them. She scooted to Tristen's side, frustrated by how he kept trying to hold her back.

If they were calling her out, it was her battle, and she wanted to see who she was dealing with.

"You don't know who you have messed with, Melanie Summer."

It was Mistral Johnson, his face black-and-blue from Tristen's punch. His cronies were lined up in their spiffy suits and pointed, polished shoes, ready to do his dirty work.

"And vice versa!" she cried. Tristen hushed her with a low voice, as though trying to calm a spooked animal, but she added, "You can't just walk over people and the planet because you have more money."

"You're on the wrong side and your sister is going to pay."

Melanie's heart seized painfully. "Which one?" she called, her voice stronger than she felt. Inside, she wanted to hide her face in Tristen's shirt and let him take care of it all.

"Daphne is going to pay."

"Hey, now," Tristen called, stepping forward, away from the row of cars behind them. "This is nothing personal, boys. Just business."

The bikers took Tristen's cue, stepping into a line, with Melanie blocked behind them, a united front against Toronto's business sector.

"I think it *is* personal," Mistral replied. "You've embarrassed us and shamed us with that stupid charity case of a camp. Slamming us in the papers. This is my chance to shine and prove that the company's worth something and you're over here insinuating that we burned down that crappy old cottage on Heritage Row. You've got all of Muskoka pissed at us for trying to bring prosperity and tourists to the area. And now this crap-case legal thing? We're going to bury you." He took a step nearer, body angled so he could escape Tristen's wrath if he got too close. "You won't think you're so great when you go down in flames."

"This has nothing to do with you and everything to do with fairness and proper proceedings. Laws. Bylaws." She squeezed between Tristen and Ezra, feeling safe.

"Daphne knew I was part of Rubicore. She encouraged this, and now she's going to pay."

Melanie watched them take off, her breathing coming hard, as though she'd sprinted to get here. "Daphne. We have to get to Daphne before they do."

Tristen, expression grim, shared a silent look with the surrounding bikers, and Melanie wondered what she'd gotten her family into. And whether they were going to survive it.

Book Club Discussion Starters

1) How is Tristan's 'monster in the closet' symbolic of his old life and the life he is trying to lead now? Do you feel it is normal reaction for him to try and hide that side of himself?

2) Do you believe that billionaires have more trouble remaining in a stable marriage compared to non-billionaires? Why do you believe it would be harder or easier?

3) Why do you believe Melanie Summer is drawn to antiques and old stories? How are they symbolic of her life and how she views herself at the start of the book?

4) Why do you believe it is so difficult for Tristen Bell to express his emotions? How did bonding with his daughter Dot and being with Melanie help him overcome this issue? Without them, do you think he would have moved past this issue? Why or why not?

5) Melanie connected with some unlikely people in Love and Trust. What do you think it was about Melanie that led to her connection with the bikers?

6) Do you believe it was difficult for Tristen to dress in drag in order to help keep Melanie safe? Did this feel in character for him?

7) In Gary Chapman's book "The Five Love Languages" he puts forth the idea that people interpret actions of love in five different ways. (Love expressed through: kind words/words of affirmation, receiving gifts, quality time spent together, doing little things for each other/acts of service, and/or physical affection/touch.) In which way do you believe Tristen expresses his love for others? Which way do you believe Melanie interprets feelings of affection? How about Tristen's ex-wife Cindy? Do you believe these different ways of interpreting love was the root of Tristen and Cindys' marriage issue, or do you believe it was something else?

8) The theme of overcoming one's obstacles in order to grow and become the person we dream of is threaded throughout the series. What obstacles does Melanie overcome? What about Tristen?

9) The Summer's friend Polly Pollard married for money instead of love. Do you think she made a mistake? Do you believe the author is making a statement? Why or why not?

Did your book club enjoy this book? Consider leaving a review online.

<u>The Summer Sisters Tame the Billionaires</u>

One cottage. Four sisters. And four billionaires who will sweep them off their feet.

Love and Rumors ~ Love and Dreams
Love and Trust ~ Love and Danger

The Blueberry Springs Collection

Book 1: Champagne and Lemon Drops—ALSO AVAILABLE IN
AUDIO
Book 2: Whiskey and Gumdrops
Book 3: Rum and Raindrops
Book 4: Eggnog and Candy Canes
Book 5: Sweet Treats
Book 6: Vodka and Chocolate Drops (Coming Summer 2015)
Book 7: Tequila and Candy Drops (Coming Winter 2015)

Do you have questions, feedback, or just want to say hi? Connect with me! I love chatting with readers.

Youtube: www.youtube.com/user/AuthorJeanOram
Facebook: www.facebook.com/JeanOramAuthor
Twitter: www.twitter.com/jeanoram
Website & Lovebug Blog: www.jeanoram.com
Email: jeanorambooks@gmail.com (I personally reply to all emails!)
Full book list—I'm always adding to it: www.jeanoram.com

I'd love to hear from you.

Thanks for reading,

Jean

Jean Oram grew up in an old schoolhouse on the Canadian prairie, and spent many summers visiting family in her grandmother's 110-year-old cottage in Ontario's Muskoka region. She still loves to swim, walk to the store, and go tubing—just like she did as a kid—and hopes her own kids will love Muskoka just as she did when she was young(er).

You can discover more about Jean and her hobbies—besides writing, reading, hiking, camping, and chasing her two kids and several pets around the house and the great outdoors—on her website: www.jeanoram.com.

Made in the USA
Charleston, SC
15 May 2015